Make Me Whole

COAL HAVEN, BOOK 1

MARIE JOHNSTON

LE PUBLISHING

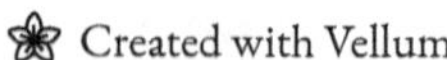 Created with Vellum

I had a perfect life. Schoolteacher. Married to my high school sweetheart. Little starter house that we called charming but was really just old. All I needed was the two-point-five kids and I'd be living my perfect dream. Then my husband died.

After the funeral, I had a breakdown that lasted for a month...or twelve. But now I'm reemerging, healing, finding my way. It's time to learn who I am now, and whether or not I can fix a leaky sink. And by my side, the entire time, is my husband's best friend, Liam. The single dad knows a thing or two about personal struggles, and about how to replace faucets.

With Liam, I feel alive again. Confident. Capable. Liam has become my best friend too. Except if my parents, my in-laws, and the rest of the town had any say, I'd stay far away from him and his bad boy reputation.

How do I admit to them what's so hard to admit to myself? That I'm starting to look at him like he's more than a friend. That the heat in his eyes when he looks at me is far beyond friendly. That like it or not, Liam makes me feel whole again.

One

KENNEDY

"Did you shower today?"

I scrunched the phone between my shoulder and my ear as warmth spread through me. As long as Liam Barron kept asking me that question, I knew someone cared about me.

A lot of people cared, but it was the mischievous way he asked that meant he not only cared, he was comfortable enough with me to joke about it. "Yes, Liam. I showered. You don't have to ask me that anymore."

"Mmm." His dubious low rumble went right through the phone into my ear. I suppressed a shiver. Liam had a nice voice. I'd always known it. It was just more noticeable today because I had the phone squished against my ear, so his voice was like an injection to the brain. I'd set it down, but then he'd know I was up to something.

I pulled another flannel shirt off a hanger. Hints of cedar and the fabric softener I used surrounded me. My eyelids drifted shut and I inhaled. Longing tugged at my heart, but the feeling didn't topple me over like it used to. Didn't mean today was easy, just that I could keep moving forward without succumbing to grief.

"Kenny." Liam was the only one who got away with calling me Kenny instead of Kennedy. Not even my husband had given me a nickname, but as Derek's cousin and best friend, Liam felt the need to set himself apart from everyone else in my life. As if he had to work hard to do that.

"I'm fine." I'd been saying that to keep my mother and my in-laws from worrying for the last few months, but this time I meant it. Today was hard, but it was something I had to do. It was something I couldn't mess up. "I really am."

"You slept okay?"

"You don't have to do this anymore." I hated that he was compelled to check on me in the first place, yet I was terrified that he'd quit. And I wouldn't tell him that he'd called at the perfect time. Liam knew how to not only stick with me in a dark place but to also see me through to the other side.

"How's work?" he asked, undaunted.

I slipped another navy-blue polo shirt off a hanger. I discreetly sniffed the shirt. Funny how smells could unbury memories faster than a blink. I could almost feel Derek's body heat when he'd hug me tight after he got home from work. I missed it. So damn much. Tears seared the backs of my eyes, but I blinked them away. Carefully, I set the hanger down.

If Liam had one inkling of what I was doing, he'd rush over. If anyone else knew what I was doing, they'd try to talk me out of it. My mom would fret and think I was overtaxing myself. My in-laws would tell me it was fine to keep the house the way it was for eternity.

Maybe it was, but I needed to do something different with this place. I needed to feel like it was mine and not a monument to what once was and would never be again. And I needed to do it now. Emptying my husband's side of the closet a year and a half after I watched his casket be lowered into the ground was something I had to do when I was motivated. I couldn't wait. I couldn't let the dread build.

"Work is fine."

"Mmm." That rumble.

I slowly folded the polo and put it on the giveaway pile. I'd save whatever I wanted to save. When I'd first started this, I thought I'd pack Derek's side of the closet and end up unpacking everything right back onto hangers. Maybe I still would. "What? It's fine."

"Kenny, it was Derek that told me that when a woman says fine, I'd better turn into a private investigator and find out what I'd done wrong."

My lips quirked. Liam didn't listen to anyone. Derek had been different. Liam's grandma, Gin, was the only other exception. The town held Liam's attitude against him, but I understood. As the illegitimate son of one of Coal Haven's most affluent and powerful men, Liam had had a rough start. He'd tragically lost his mother when he was a baby and was raised by her parents while the rest of his family resented his presence in the world. Everyone but Derek. "Work is good. Really. I vibe really well with Marion, and she respects my experience." Most of the time.

"But you're still just *helping* the teacher and not *the* teacher."

I sighed. For striking out so bad when it came to women, Liam was an incredibly perceptive friend. Just after Christmas break was over, I'd gotten a job as a paraprofessional at the school where I used to teach. Being an aide for the third-grade teacher for the last three months had been nice. She was a good teacher—proficient and competent.

But helping wasn't what I'd done before. I'd been the teacher, not the aide.

"I messed up. I have to do my time and climb back up the ladder. Wait for an opening and hope my withdrawal from life for over a year won't be held against me."

"You didn't mess up; you're too good for that. You were in mourning, and they'll understand."

Only time would tell how understanding my boss would be. He'd been the one who'd had to figure out what to do with an entire classroom of kids when I couldn't stop sobbing in the bathroom and then had just walked out.

Would I land a full-time teaching gig before my bills said *time to move*? I didn't want to think about it today. "How are the boys?"

"I'm not home yet, but Grandma Gin said they've been pure hell."

My laughter made the task of slipping another shirt off a hanger a little less painful. Two five-year-old kids against an ornery grandma? "I feel like they'd be more likely to say Grandma Gin has been pure hell."

He laughed, then his tone turned serious. "She wants to put the place up for sale soon. Like in the next couple of months."

Liam's grandpa had died a few years ago, and Grandma Gin had floundered. Liam had helped her liquidate the cattle to pay off lingering debts. Then, he'd moved home to Coal Haven but commuted to his job on an oil field outside of Williston almost three hours away.

Each month, Liam worked a twenty-day stretch, followed by ten days off. During those ten-day periods, he'd helped Grandma Gin move to a senior living apartment and made improvements to her house. Selling it at top dollar would help keep a roof over Grandma Gin's head. In return, she'd insisted on staying with the boys at the house while Liam worked.

"So soon?" A spark of panic flared in my chest. Those ten days Liam was home, I had a friend around. He not only called, but he stopped in. I sucked in a calming breath. I'd always have Liam and the boys, no matter where he lived.

I'd miss his regular visits though.

His deep chuckle wound through the phone and eased my anxiety. "It's been over three years since I moved back, Kenny."

"I know, it's just... It's been nice having you around." If for only ten days at a time. "Look at what you've done with the place." The old ranch house on his grandparents' land hadn't been maintained as well as it could've been, as Liam's grandparents had worked to raise him and run a ranch in their golden years. Then Grandpa Bob had gotten sick and things had fallen apart. "It will be so nice when you can be with Eli and Owen more, though."

"I know. I haven't even touched the whole before- and after-school issue yet. It was hard enough to find day care after I won full custody from Payton. That's why moving home worked so well. Grandma Gin saved me as much as I helped her. But I don't want them to start kindergarten in Coal Haven. They don't need to deal with the bullshit I did."

The bullshit had stemmed from one man. Cameron Barron liked flexing his power and showing his illegitimate son how he wished Liam hadn't been born—never mind that Cameron had been the one to have the affair that resulted in Liam's birth.

Cameron wanted nothing to do with him, and he expected everyone in his circle of friends, family, and acquaintances to behave the same. Derek was the only one who'd defied Cameron.

"Well, I'll miss all of you." I loved being with him and the boys. To them, I wasn't Kennedy the Widow. I was Kenny, their dad's friend, who coerced them to eat green beans once in a while but also let them destroy the bathroom during bath time.

Liam had shamelessly used them to help bring me back into the land of People Who Got Off the Couch and Showered.

"What are you up to today?" He asked the same question every weekend he was home. Today was Saturday, and since he worried when I didn't have my Monday-through-Friday job to motivate me, he wouldn't be satisfied until he knew I was doing okay.

I hadn't showered yet, but only because I planned to work around the house all day.

And maybe because I was packing up Derek's clothing.

"I have some cleaning to catch up on. You raked for me last fall, but I was going to see if the lawn needed some attention before Bruce came over and did it." I'd told Derek's dad, Bruce, that I could take over lawn care now that all the snow had melted, but I wouldn't be surprised if I got home from work one day to find my lawn had been neatly tended to.

Bruce Barron had been second to Liam in taking care of me. Derek's mom, Willow, and Bruce checked on me each week and took care of any repairs, like a clogged garbage disposal. They did what needed to be done. Especially when my neglect of myself and my house had gotten too bad.

After being sick through so many of my high school years, I had thought I'd gotten stronger. Until I had found myself alone and unable to keep a one-person household going. Those days were done. They had to be. That was what this closet cleaning was about. No one was going to do it for me, so I hadn't told anyone my plans.

"What else are you doing?" Liam asked.

I scowled. When did Liam's bullshit meter get so sensitive? "I'm...sweeping."

There was a knock at the door. I jumped, dropping the maroon polo I was in the middle of folding. It wouldn't bother me to give that one away. Derek had complained the tag itched but he'd refused to cut it off, and, in turn, had never worn it.

"Can I call you back?" I didn't want to get off the phone with Liam. I wanted him to talk to me through this whole closet-cleaning process. "Someone's here."

"I'll wait."

"Liam. I'm fine." I scrambled off the floor, holding the phone with one hand and tugging my shirt down with the other. It used to be roomy, but my venture back into the workplace had come with an increased appetite. I'd gone from unintentional calorie restriction to tasty overload thanks to the teachers' lounge and its constant parade of goodies.

I didn't bother to check who was at the door. It was Coal Haven, North Dakota, population 2200. There weren't any surprises when it came to who might be at the door. Could be the mail. Another delivery from Mom, who thought I was still too withdrawn to go to the grocery store. For the last year, I'd received deliveries of dried goods. I had more rice than I could eat in a lifetime. But it was probably Bruce. He hadn't stopped by for the weekend yet.

I whipped the door open, my mind whirling about what to tell Bruce. I didn't know how he'd handle it if he knew I was packing Derek's things. He never called first, and maybe I should've thought of that when I'd started. Or maybe I hoped that Bruce would notice how much better I was and he'd start calling or messaging before he popped in.

The man on my doorstep was not Bruce.

Where Bruce was six feet tall, this man was a couple of inches taller, with wider shoulders and a chest hard enough to bounce a quarter off. His unrepentant grin was all Liam.

I slammed my hand onto my hip as delight almost had me jumping into his strong arms; I wasn't normally a girl who did that. But he'd catch me. Liam wouldn't let me fall. "I can't believe you!"

Liam spoke into his phone but grinned at me. "Believe it."

I mock glared at him and hung up. I shoved the phone into the pocket of my sweats. Ugh. Of all days not to shower.

I wasn't usually self-conscious around Liam. He'd seen me at my worst. I was no longer there, but my hair was up in a messy bun, and not the trendy kind. Strands hung over my eyes and down my neck, looking as spindly as the dried flowers I hadn't had the energy to throw out for weeks after Derek's funeral. I was wearing an old sports bra that didn't hide as much as it should under the snug T-shirt. And my sweats needed a trip through the washing machine, like, yesterday.

I looked exactly like I'd lied to him about taking a shower, while Liam was dressed in worn jeans that hugged his muscular thighs and an olive-green, long-sleeved, waffle-patterned shirt that his biceps managed to flex through. He definitely looked showered.

He stepped inside and took off his navy-blue Coal Haven Drillers ball cap and hung it on the welded "The Barrons" sign that he'd made for Derek and me as a wedding gift.

"Gonna tell me what you're really doing?"

I huffed a hunk of hair out of my face. It barely moved. "How did you—? Never mind. *Fine*," I stressed the word around a playful scowl.

I considered making up something, telling him I was finally working in the basement after it had needed to be gutted last year, and staying away from my bedroom, but this was Liam. He didn't plow into my life and take over. I trusted him.

Before I lost my nerve, I spun and went to the bedroom. He stayed on my heels through the small living room and the narrow hallway. The house was over fifty years old, built by a couple who'd moved in after decades on their farm. The style reflected it. Small rooms crammed into minimal square footage. The master bedroom was master only in that it had a few more square feet than the other one on the main level.

I entered my bedroom and stood by the bed. I went to cross my arms but ended up hugging myself. "I thought it was time."

Liam's chiseled jaw flexed. He ran a hand through his hat hair and ruffled it enough to give his hard edges a boyish softness. He took a moment to inhale and slowly let it out. Moments like these reminded me that he was mourning the loss of his best friend, not just helping me cope with the loss of my husband. "Are you sure?"

"A few tips I learned from my online support group were to give myself permission to keep whatever I want. I have a tote bin." I nodded toward the blue Rubbermaid on the bed. "I also gave myself permission to quit if it was too much."

"What else did... What is your group's name again?"

"Sexy, Young, and Widowed." I was young and widowed. Didn't exactly feel the sexy part, but reading experiences from others my age was critical. "But I also talked to my therapist during our last session. Both really just say that nothing's abnormal and I can't do it wrong." Which meant I had to do something, and after way too long of doing nothing, I was ready to prove myself, mostly to myself.

Liam and I stared at the pile of shirts and pants on the floor. I'd opened the folding doors, taken a huge armful, and dumped it on the floor. It was easier than undoing the meticulous job Derek had done when he'd hung one article at a time.

I bit my lip. Should I have asked Liam if he wanted to help? Should I ask if he wanted to keep anything? He and Derek had been like brothers.

Liam planted his hands on his lean hips. The stance made his shoulders appear even wider. "I told Grandma Gin I'd get there by four, so I got a couple of hours. What can I do to help?"

* * *

Liam

I pushed the lid down on the blue tote. It wasn't half full. Kennedy had kept a pair of Derek's cargo shorts. They were the ones he'd proposed in when they were walking along the Missouri River after a romantic date. Same with the white-collared shirt that sported the logo for the pesticide supplier he'd worked for as a salesman. She'd also kept a pair of his boxers that they'd bought during their honeymoon in the Black Hills—I didn't want to know what those had signified, a Drillers ball cap he favored, his unused cologne, and a pocket watch that he'd gotten from one of his great-grandfathers. It was probably the Grandpa Barron that had started the town—also my grandpa, but I didn't care. I considered Bob Pewter my only grandfather.

I hefted the tote. "Want this downstairs?"

She was staring into the empty half of the closet. With my help, she'd been efficient, almost ruthless. I didn't want to rush her, and if she wanted everything hung back up and put in its spot, I'd do it in a heartbeat.

She worried her plump lower lip with her thumb and forefinger. "I should move my stuff over."

"There's no rush." There was a time I hadn't thought she'd make it this far in her grief. She'd been lost to all of us. Me. Her mom and sister. Her in-laws. I hadn't been able to talk to anyone but Grandma Gin about how worried I was. My uncle Bruce liked me less than he had when Derek was alive. He probably hated that he couldn't blame Derek's death on me. At first, we'd all thought Derek had had a car accident. He did—after he'd had an aneurysm on some country road where he was going to meet a farmer to talk about pesticide.

All the trouble Derek and I used to get into, and he'd been taken out by a tiny broken blood vessel in his brain while he was working a job we would've laughed at as kids. But when two twelve-year-old boys were riding horses through a river that could have and should have swallowed us alive, it wasn't like we'd thought he'd be a salesman and I'd be a single dad by the time we were each twenty-two. Or that he'd be dead by the time he was twenty-five and I'd be making sure his widow took care of herself so I didn't have to bury another friend.

I drank in the sight of Kenny. She had always been attractive. When she'd shown up as a new junior on the first day of my senior year, I'd plotted my approach. But Derek had swooped in, and I'd been friend-zoned ever since.

Her creamy skin was regaining a healthy glow. Her face could summon a blush now instead of remaining perma-pale. And her hips—those were good to see again. For months, she had wasted away. Short of sitting on her and forcing donuts past her lips, I hadn't known what to do. She had barely talked, but I was grateful she'd at least answered the door.

Today was a big deal. She knew it. I knew it. And when I had called home, Grandma Gin had known it. She'd told me to come home when I thought Kenny was okay. The boys had earned a movie for picking up their room and sweeping the kitchen. I missed them. I wanted to get home to them. But for Kenny, I'd wait a little longer.

"Yeah," Kenny finally said. "I think I did enough for the day."

"I think you earned dinner out. With me. You're a lucky lady."

She laughed, her head dipping back and baring her slender throat. "I would be the envy of all the single women in the county, but I don't feel like peopling right now."

I wasn't interested in any single women in the county. Those who knew about my past and that I was the mighty Cameron Barron's greatest shame either wanted to fuck me because of it or wanted to fuck me and ditch me. I didn't come with the Cameron Barron bank accounts. None of the oil money he'd inherited from his parents or that he had accumulated as the CEO of the refinery would come to me, nor would any of the profits from the large ranches he and his siblings ran. And that was okay. I wanted nothing to do with Cameron Barron or any of the rest of the family.

Derek had been the only one worth my time, and he was gone. "I can pick up some pizza."

She slanted her gaze to me, her warm brown eyes questioning. "You need to get home."

"I already talked to Grandma Gin. They're watching a movie."

She shook her head. The move was enough to knock her bun halfway down her head. The knot of her rich brown hair had loosened throughout the day, and I'd gotten way too much joy watching it fall.

She crossed her arms and kicked a hip out. I yanked my eyes off the way her boobs hitched over her arms. Kenny had been off-limits for eternity. Nothing had changed—except my schedule and two little boys who kept me from dating, getting laid, and enduring all the trouble the two former activities caused. Kenny was my safe zone.

"I'll shower. You grab the pizza, and I'll meet you at your place." Her brows crinkled.

There was something she wasn't saying. "What do you need me to do?"

She worried her lower lip. "Nothing. I was thinking maybe I'd stop by the cemetery before I went to your house."

She'd cleaned out Derek's clothes and now she needed to let him know that she hadn't forgotten him. Her intentions were written in the depths of her chocolate-brown eyes. The first time she'd told me that she talked to Derek regularly, she'd whispered it like she was confessing state secrets. She continued to trust me with that information, and I had a feeling she didn't tell her family or her in-laws.

"Take your time. The boys will be thrilled no matter when you show up." But I'd keep an eye on the time. Three months after Derek died, I'd had to carry her from his cold resting place. She hadn't answered her phone, and she hadn't been at home. I'd found her there. She'd gone there and cried for hours after she'd quit her job. Eventually, she'd been too cold to think clearly. Today she seemed fine, but when it came to Kenny, I didn't take chances.

"Thank you." She breezed past me, smelling faintly of Derek's cologne, fabric softener, and herself: roses and vanilla.

I had no business inhaling, but I rented a bedroom in a

welding buddy's place in Williston. By the end of our shifts, we smelled like singed cloth, hot metal, and sweat.

"Canadian bacon pizza?" she asked over her shoulder.

"With pineapple."

She spun, her eyes narrowed. "Don't. You. Dare."

I grinned, letting her know I would indeed dare.

With one last determined glare, she disappeared into the bathroom.

I waited for a few moments. The shower curtain rings clattered. The water kicked on. The cabinet under the sink where she stored the towels creaked open. She wasn't breaking down where I couldn't see her. Which was her right, but it'd only been four months since she'd announced there was a paraprofessional opening at the school. Three months since she'd gone to her first day of work. Derek died over a year and a half ago, but Kenny had only started resembling her former self since she'd mentioned the job opening.

I wasn't leaving until I was confident she wasn't breaking down in the shower. If she made it through the shower, then she might withstand the graveside visit.

Leaning against the wall, I closed my eyes. Sometimes I forgot that I needed a moment too. Derek and I had grown up next to each other. My grandparents, Bob and Ginny Pewter, had raised me on a ranch next to Bruce and Willow Barron. Keeping two boys the same age from hanging out was a futile effort, no matter how hard Bruce and Willow had tried.

My family ranch was defunct. Grandma Gin owned the land, but she'd leased it out just before I'd moved home to help her. She'd made the deal with Bruce and Willow, thinking Derek would be the one to carry on the ranch after his parents retired.

Bruce hated me because Cameron had ordered him to. Same with their sister, my aunt, Kira. Their children had picked up on that and instead of cousins, I had enemies. Other than Derek, only one other cousin talked to me, and I suspected he did it to piss my father off. Derek hadn't. His conviction that I was his best friend had been stronger than any of his family's hate.

I'd have done anything for Derek, and that included making sure his widow survived his death.

* * *

I entered the one bar and grill Coal Haven had to its name, The Rattler Brewhaus. Half family restaurant, half rowdy bar and future brewery if the rumors were true. Coal Haven was home to hole-in-the-wall bars that had little more than a pizza oven, but nowhere to get alcohol and food together. The key to Rattler's long-term survival would be the hungry shift workers coming, going, and passing through on their way to the coal mine, the coal gasification plant, and the oil refinery. The rest of the town took advantage of not having to travel an hour to a bigger town for a perfectly seasoned steak that they didn't have to grill.

"Look what the oil fields puked up!" The shout came just as I crossed the door and started past the hostess station. I recognized the voice. Holden Barron. The only other cousin who talked to me. He was friendly enough, but I didn't know his motivation and remained cautious. He was still one of *those* Barrons.

The rancher swaggered toward me. His jeans were still dusty from planting. He ran a cow/calf operation and farmed small grains like wheat and barley on the side. Like the rest of my estranged family, whatever he touched was golden. Holden's pastures were full of cows that earned him three and a half grand a head. His grain bins were full, and when he needed some cash, he'd check the market and take a load to the elevator.

If I'd been able to stay in town, maybe I could've helped my grandparents' ranch. Kept our family operation from folding. But between Grandpa Bob's illness and his poor retirement planning, there hadn't been much of a choice. By then, I'd had two young kids and had needed the job and the benefits I got from welding at one of King Oil's sites outside of Williston. Splitting my time between here and Williston was all I could offer since my father had made it impossible for me to find work anywhere around Coal Haven. Besides, I wanted my kids to grow up in a place where they weren't starting from behind just because some arrogant asshole said so.

Holden clapped me on the back. He was here with a couple of other guys. My half brother, Stetson, glowered at me from a table deep in the bar. He was barely three years older than me. Which had made my birth much harder for Cameron to explain to his wife.

The third guy at the table was an employee of Holden's. Technically, my aunt Kira still ran the ranch, but she couldn't do it without Holden, and they couldn't do it without Colt. The man was older than Holden, gruffer, and not that friendly. Catnip for women with his short dark beard and intense gaze. He looked like my aunt could hire him to assassinate me as a favor to my father, but the only impression I'd gotten from Colt was that he wanted to be left alone, much like me.

I smirked at Holden before he caught wind I was in anything less than a jovial mood. He wouldn't be making a spectacle out of greeting me the way he had if Stetson weren't here. Holden and Stetson were close, but that didn't stop Holden from pissing the guy off.

Holden and Stetson were friends and cousins, like Derek

and I had been. A harsh pang of longing dimmed my smile. "How are ya?"

He adjusted a white and navy ball cap that was dustier than his jeans. "Good. Haven't seen you for a while."

"Back for my ten days. How's...?" My aunt that pretended I didn't exist? His sister that I would barely recognize if I passed her on the street? His dad, who had never been in the picture as far as I could remember? He and his sister had different dads, and neither one had stuck around. I shared the same last name with Holden and little else. Unsure who to ask after, I stuck with, "How's work?"

"Got in the fields today." He lifted a shoulder. "Planting by mid-April. It's a good year so far."

"Only cuz it just began," I pointed out.

"Are we talking old farmer already?"

"Is there any other way?" This was our usual banter. Quick and superficial.

Holden laughed until he glanced at the table he'd come from. He stiffened as Stetson's gaze turned into a laser and burned a swath to us. "Well, it was nice seeing you. Don't be a stranger."

I lifted a brow but nodded. "See you around."

Don't be a stranger. I almost snorted as I wove my way to the bar where I had to pick up the pizzas. Thankfully, it was on the opposite side from Holden and Stetson. The middle-aged bartender lifted her chin when she spotted me and scurried away. She wasn't originally from Coal Haven, but I ordered pizza often enough for her to know who I was.

I was pulling my wallet out when a sultry voice drawled, "Ho-ly shiit."

Only trouble had come from meeting women at the bar. It might work for some couples, and while Eli and Owen were the best thing to have happened to me, they'd resulted from a tumultuous—and brief—relationship that had started just like this.

I turned, preparing a quick brush-off. It died on my tongue.

This was a face I hadn't seen since graduation, when she'd lit out of town. "Laney? When did you—?" I stopped the question, but not late enough to be awkward. I'd heard what had happened to her brother. The whole town knew when and why Delaney Granger had returned to Coal Haven. "How long are you back for?"

Her crystal-blue eyes darkened, but she flipped her flaxen hair. "Here to stay. What are you up to?" She patted the empty stool next to her.

I shook my head. "Sorry, I'm just grabbing some pizzas."

"You can stay for one drink." She tipped her head in a way that came off as practiced. She'd left Coal Haven a caustic cowgirl and come back a sophisticated woman. Her bronzed shoulders were bared by a billowy top, and while it might be spring out, she was showing off enough toned leg to make me think it was eighty degrees without a cloud in the sky.

For a while, she'd been as off-limits as Kenny. Laney Granger had been almost as forbidden to Derek as me, but that hadn't stopped him from dating her. Until he broke up with Laney to ask Kenny out our senior year. The entire time Laney and Derek had dated, she'd acted like she barely tolerated me. I had taken her boyfriend's time.

Tonight, her eyes brightened like she was happy to see me, but I didn't get the impression she was hitting on me. Laney used to be an open book. Tonight, she was guarded.

"I can't. My kids are waiting for me."

Some women got panicked looks in their eyes when I mentioned I had kids. A guy my age with kids meant baggage. I had that. Other women grew hearts in their eyes and I got the sick feeling they thought my kids were the way to my heart. They were, but not in the way most girls thought. The only woman I'd brought around them was Kenny, and that was the way it would stay. Eli and Owen would have enough feelings to figure out about their mother, they didn't need other women streaming through their life.

Laney studied me, mild curiosity in her eyes. "Did not picture you the family type."

"It's just me and them, but yeah." I wouldn't be displaying a Dad of the Year award anytime soon. Pretty sure a guy had to be home at least half the month for that.

I was working on it.

People could judge my situation, but it was better than what Eli and Owen had been born into. For the first year of their lives, their mom, Payton, had used them to try to control me. We weren't together by then, and I refused to be her puppet. The next year, she'd left them with me for days until I had to track her down so I could work before I got fired. Or she'd leave them with friends until I had to track her down to find out where the fuck my kids were.

Before their second birthdays, I'd had a long talk with Grandma Gin. The next time I had seen Payton, I had papers for her to relinquish her rights, along with the contact information for my lawyer if she wanted to fight me. Payton hated having to put effort into anything that wasn't self-gratifying. She'd signed the papers and I hadn't heard from her since.

"No wife?" Laney asked.

"No time."

"There's nothing but time in Coal Haven." Her bitterness was swallowed as she took a swig from her White Claw.

The bartender appeared with my pizzas. "I'll get you a total, hon."

As she rang up my order, awkward silence descended. I asked Laney, "How are your parents doing?"

She smacked her lips against her teeth. "Peachy." Another swig.

I should ask about her brother, but her rigid posture after I'd asked about her parents was enough to make me rethink that line of conversation.

I handed a couple of twenties over the counter and waved off the change. "Well, it was nice talking to you."

"We'll have to catch up sometime."

I didn't immediately reject the idea. Laney hadn't been my number one fan, but it'd had nothing to do with my father. It had been refreshingly not personal, a product of being young and selfish, but I wasn't in a place to be social. "I'm only in town ten days at a time."

She leaned a little closer, and her soft floral scent flowed over me. After high school, when she smelled like she'd dunked herself into a vat of Bath & Body Works lotion, I had expected a cloud of smothering perfume. "I doubt it'll take long to catch up."

Was she flirting with me? Loud, obnoxious, teenaged Laney had scared off everyone but Derek, but he'd grown up next to her, as had I. The Grangers' land bordered mine and his. I'd joked with Derek about how he'd been afraid to break up with her. He'd find his tires slashed and his dog Bruster responding to a name like Petunia or something.

This Laney oozed confidence and enough aloofness to tell me she wasn't looking for anything permanent, if she were interested in anything at all. She reminded me of...me. A familiar and possibly friendly face when we were surrounded by Barrons.

I wouldn't mind catching up. Another time. I wanted to get home before the pizzas cooled off. Eli loved stringing cheese as far as he could, and I didn't want to miss the way the kids practically tackled Kenny.

"Your number still the same?" she asked as I turned away. The tinge of hesitance was new. Laney had been a bull surrounded by bullfighters. She'd pushed and challenged until she'd made her point or the other side had given up.

"It's different." I'd had to change it after I got Payton out of my life and away from the boys. She'd had the random men in her life call me and pretend to be lawyers. Or just be a pain in the ass until I lost sleep or it affected work. I rattled it off.

Laney punched it in and gave me a smile that fell just shy of real. I might answer the phone just to find out what adult Laney was really like. Losing Derek had exposed the gaping hole in my life that was supposed to be filled with meaningful relationships. I wasn't interested in dating anyone right now, but I couldn't exactly do what my kids did on the playground—walk up to someone and say, "Do you want to be my friend?"

I made my way through the bar, using the pizzas as the plow to open a path, and calculated how fast I could get home to my kids and Kenny. I hoped Laney wasn't looking for a hookup. I could use another friend. What I didn't need was more drama in my life.

Two

KENNEDY

Liam's ten-day stretch was over, and he was leaving for Williston tonight. Since it was a four-day weekend, I told him I'd get the boys into bed and then Grandma Gin could take over. A little something to give her a break. Liam had invited me over for the afternoon.

I pulled off the gravel road onto the meandering driveway that cut through two pastures into his yard. Years ago, I wouldn't have turned. I would've kept going until I hit the next ranch. Bruce and Willow's place. Cool relief that I didn't have to go there sifted through me. There, I would be Kennedy the Widow. The more I was with Liam, the more I treasured being Kenny.

Eli darted out of the big open door in the large shop and climbed the corral gates that stuck up from where they used to butt against the barn. The barn had burned down before I'd moved to town, and from what Derek had said, it was a big reason why the ranch had eventually failed.

Owen tore out of the shop and copied Eli. It was impossible to hear the engine of my little red Hyundai from inside the metal shop. They must've been watching for me.

Eli waved. When they wore little ball caps, they looked like identical twins. They weren't. Eli's hair was a shade lighter than Liam's chestnut brown, and Owen was a dirty blond, probably what his mom's natural hair color was. When Liam had dated her, Payton's hair had been bleached and touched with purple. I had liked her hair. The rest of her couldn't be improved with a bottle of dye.

I parked by the two-story farmhouse that had been majestic in its day. Now, its peeling and frayed wooden siding needed to be replaced with vinyl or steel. Liam had been debating on whether he should slap on fresh paint or foot the bill for cheap siding. The porch stairs creaked like they were going to collapse, but Liam had reinforced them. He'd kept the kids from playing on the rest of the porch until he could tear down and rebuild the whole thing. The windows were original and let in as much grit as they kept out. When the winds picked up during a dry year, little piles of dirt ended up on his windowsills inside. Liam had also mentioned replacing those.

A lot of projects and, suddenly, so little time. Part of me wanted to encourage Liam to paint and replace the windows, rebuild the deck, and maybe throw on some landscaping, open the old flower beds back up, and fix the shed in the back, all to keep him here longer. But I couldn't be selfish. He was limited on time and money, and he had good reasons to move his kids out of Coal Haven. Logically, I understood he had more career options out of his father's shadow and his kids could start school away from the scandal Liam's mother had left behind. But I wanted him to stay.

"Kenny!" Eli jumped down from the top rung, stumbled enough to make me gasp, then recovered and raced across the driveway. "Guess what?" He rambled on about a new toy truck Liam had bought him, but it was hard to follow with his lisp. Rs were challenging for him too. And Ls.

Owen sidled in between us, refusing to be left out. His speech was as clear as a lecture hall professor. "And I got a monster truck. It's called GhostStorm, and it can jump twelve feet high."

They each took one of my hands and dragged me toward the shop. My tote bag would have to wait in the car. "Does it jump dirt piles twelve feet high?"

"No. The truck jumps." He threw his free hand up and mimicked watching an invisible object fall.

Ah. The toy could do those jumps because Owen threw it. "What's your dad up to?"

"Welding," Eli answered.

"Uh-oh. What broke?"

"Nuttin'."

Liam welded ten hours a day for twenty days straight. Why would he be welding if something wasn't broken?

I was towed into the shop. Blinking to adjust to the dimmer light, it wasn't hard to find Liam. Sparks flew from the far corner, where the light from the open door had the hardest time penetrating.

The torch Liam held went dark. He flipped his face shield up so it rested on top of his head. "Hey. That time already? The afternoon got away from me."

He set his equipment on the work bench by the hunk of metal he'd been working on. He slapped his thick gloves down and took the face shield off. Then he shrugged out of his well-worn leather apron.

I blinked again, but it had nothing to do with lighting. His long-sleeved blue T-shirt with the logo of a bar and grill in Williston was plastered to his chest and back. A smattering of singe holes gathered around the collar and a few tiny ones on the sleeves where the apron didn't reach. Liam adjusted his shoulders like he was trying to dislodge the fabric from his skin, but all the move did was make his muscles ripple.

I'd known Liam wasn't the same lanky kid from high school, but I'd never had proof like this.

He ran a hand through his hair—same effect. Biceps bulging and rippling muscle.

My brain snapped a picture, like someday I might need to reference the type of man that could get my libido going again.

Which I wasn't looking for. Dating wasn't on my radar, much less...activities beyond that.

Although recently I'd been thinking... I gave myself a mental shake. My therapist said there was nothing wrong with thinking about dating someday. Nothing wrong with dating itself. Nothing wrong with not being ready. Nothing wrong with dating while still not feeling ready. I hadn't reached that point yet.

But I didn't have to think about it at Liam's. "I can play with the boys if you're working."

"No. I need to shower and finish packing." Eli straddled a metal chair and Liam shooed him off. "That's not for you."

"But it's a chair!" Eli held his arms out like he was on a movie set and had to act like he was dying.

"Not for us."

"You made this?" I wandered closer. There were three metal chairs. The hunk of metal on the workbench was starting to resemble the three pieces that made up the back.

Liam crossed his arms. Had his chest always been that wide? "It's just a hobby."

I kept my eyes on his work. It was easier than seeing his sweaty, cut body. "I knew you did a few things here and there, like our wedding gift, but these chairs aren't quick projects."

"I've been playing around for a while, when I need a break from home repairs, or when I don't have time to start another project before I leave again. Then the buddy I rent the room from in Williston was tossing these out last year. I told him he should do some shabby chic weld-over bullshit. So he loaded them in the box of my pickup without telling me."

The corner of my mouth kicked up. A makeover, but with welding. "And you thought, 'What the heck? I can do a shabby chic weld-over.'"

He grinned, and it brightened the entire shed. He'd been looking at me with eyes full of concern for so long, it was nice to see it absent from his smile. "I've done a few projects. Want to see?"

"Can I show her, Dad?" Owen sprinted to the other corner of the shop and tugged on a heavy canvas drape. Liam stopped beside him and helped take the cover off.

Watching him with his kids never failed to cheer me up. There was the ever-present tug at my heart. Derek and I had wanted kids. Someday.

I tensed, waiting for the tsunami of emotions to double me over. But it didn't. Being with Liam and the boys made me feel like I hadn't missed as much as I feared. That maybe, someday, I could have something like this again.

The cache was revealed, and I put my hopes aside. Intricately welded lamp bases. Custom coatracks to hang on the wall. A sign that said Live, Laugh, Love.

"You did all this?" They weren't rudimentary, nor were they simple designs like the sign. They were intricate work that had required a skilled hand.

"Yeah." He shoved a hand through his hair until sections were sticking straight up. Unlike when I went without a shower for too long and my hair hung limp and lifeless, he got sexier the more rumpled his hair was.

Did I just describe Liam as sexy?

Heat tickled through my body, moving to forgotten places. It was a mere observation, nothing more. And it was hot in the shed.

"I'm just playing around," he said sheepishly.

I squatted by the lamp. Metal curved like it was as malleable as taffy and wove together into a solid base. The metal had been brushed to give it an antique look. "William Robert Barron, this is not playing around. This is art."

"It's a lamp, Kenny."

Eli bent over the sign. "Wiv, waff, wuv."

He couldn't read. Liam must've told him what it said. "Yes. Live, laugh, love." I didn't stress the Ls, but the teacher in me had to gently correct him. He gave me a look like he was concerned I hadn't heard him the first time when he was standing right next to me. "Are you going to sell these?"

"Nah. Might just give 'em away as wedding gifts or something. A lot of my buddies in Williston are settling down." His brows drew together a moment before they smoothed out. Had he thought of selling them? Was he lacking confidence about his work? Worried that he could do work like this and hold down the same demanding job in Williston through having twins and moving home and commuting, but that people would still scoff that a guy like him was worth anything more than their gossip?

"The farmers market would be a perfect place to try," I prompted.

"The Coal Haven one is just a few booths."

I shook my head. "It's been really growing." I obviously

hadn't gone last year. "Marion talks about it all the time. She buys both produce and crafts. Even Mrs. Z gushes about it."

"She's still teaching?"

"She'll never retire, but she needs to. Anyway, Marion's already saying she can't wait to go, and I don't think the first market is until the beginning of June."

His brow furrowed and he shook his head. "That's less than a couple of months away."

"You have enough to do a one-day market. I'm sure Williston has them, but if you do one here, I could help." Ideas whirled in my head, but I had to be careful. This would be his thing, not something for me to do to pass the time.

"No one's gonna buy this crap."

"It's not crap, Daddy," Owen chirped. "It's art."

"You've made it into something beautiful." I rose out of my squat, tempted to run my hand over the back of the chair. How'd he get metal to look so fluid? He wasn't a rookie welder, but these were his first pieces, meant to be as visually appealing as they were functional. "This is really good."

"Nah, I know. I mean, thanks. It's just... It's Coal Haven." He shrugged, but his concentration was on his collection of pieces. "I could use the extra cash for some of the repairs I need to do before we list the house."

"Just something to think about. These are too good not to share."

He was guarded about the town and how he was received, but not everyone in Coal Haven was a Barron, nor did everyone view him as the touch-on-the-wild-side high schooler. I had to believe that my friends and neighbors would not only see how high quality these pieces were but also how amazing the man behind them was. Like I did.

* * *

Liam

My boys were piled in my arms for our goodbye hug by the front door when the purr of an engine caught my attention. Had Grandma Gin decided to arrive early?

A chunk of me hated leaving for good. I'd still come back for Grandma Gin—and Kenny, of course. I'd thought of moving back, but money was an issue. I made twenty grand more a year than I would working around Coal Haven, a fact that made having to seek employment away from Cameron's influence easier to tolerate.

The house was draining much of those extra funds that the commute and my extra rent didn't burn. I needed to sell the place to afford Grandma Gin's senior living condo. I'd told her I'd make payments in return for her watching the kids when I was gone. She was sorely underpaid, but her pride wouldn't let me compensate her more. So I paid her mortgage and utilities too, and the land rent paid for her groceries. Grandpa Bob hadn't left her with anything but a run-down house and a giant shop she didn't need.

Kenny was in the kitchen making homemade macaroni and cheese even though I'd stocked up on enough Kraft boxes to build a replica of the barn that had once stood next to the shop.

I fucking loved Kenny's homemade version.

Eli heard the car first and tore himself away from me to dart to the door.

Owen followed. "Who's here?"

I straightened and looked out the window. A familiar red and white F250 lumbered to a stop in front of the house. Aw, hell.

"It's the neighbors," Eli lisped.

"Wait here." I stepped outside and shut the door behind me. Bruce didn't stop by to chat. He was always nitpicking on something. When Grandpa Bob had been alive, it'd been the cattle getting into the pasture or, worse, nibbling on his hay bales. Bruce had been critical of everything Grandpa Bob had done—from when he hayed to how long he kept the cattle in the pastures.

I didn't want it to spill over on my kids. Now that Bruce leased the land, he found reasons to pester Grandma Gin, dragging Willow along as a pretense. Bruce already acted as if he was the only one who gave the boys a stern talking-to when they acted like the five-year-old kids they were. He probably assumed I was a crap dad, just like I assumed that he was only interested in when Grandma Gin was going to sell.

Bruce slid out of his pickup, his hard gaze on Kenny's car.

"Is Kennedy here?" he growled, his dark brows heavy over his eyes.

"She's watching the kids tonight." I answered as if it wasn't a big deal. And it wasn't.

Bruce's scowl deepened, and he added a frown to his expression. He had to know that I hadn't ditched Kenny after Derek had died. I couldn't blame Kenny if she didn't mention how often we talked or when I stopped by. She didn't need to take shit from Bruce.

Willow fluttered a hand by her chest. I had a hard time looking her in the eye. Her doe brown gaze was so much like Derek's. "I don't think she should be doing that."

The scandal in her tone grated on my nerves. "She enjoys being around them."

"Is that what you tell yourself to get free babysitting?" Bruce stepped closer. Before I could tell him to load the fuck back up in his pickup and drive away from my house, he hissed, "Don't you know how hard she took not having a baby when my son died?"

I sucked in a breath. That was low. I had known they wanted kids and that mourning the lost chance with Derek was part of her grief process. Bruce had no right to wield it against me. "She's an adult. She teaches full-time—at an *elementary* school. Or would you rather she stay all alone in her house?"

Willow's hand fluttered again. Derek's parents were hopelessly old-fashioned. Willow jumped when Bruce told her how high. She deferred to him for everything, from what she made for the church potluck to their finances. "It's not that, Liam. We all know you don't plan on staying here. We've heard that Ginny is thinking of selling. Then what? You take the boys away from her after she gets attached."

Kenny was already attached. We were all attached to each other, like a motley crew of Lego figures stuck on the same flat piece. Moving wouldn't change that. Except how often I could stop by her house. And how often I'd have the boys with me when I did. But we could call.

A tiny fissure opened in my chest. A hint of the void that would be left behind when I moved completely out of Coal Haven.

Bruce assessed me. "What are you doing with Kenny anyway?"

I was doing more than telling her "This too shall pass" and encouraging her to give up the job she loved to "take care of herself." The last thing Kenny did during her breakdown was take care of herself. Part of me wondered if she'd have hit bottom so hard if it hadn't been for her well-meaning in-laws. They hadn't held her hand to get her through; they'd smothered her.

Her mom hadn't helped either. She'd been an enabler.

An enabler to do nothing. But her motivations were a little clearer. Kenny had suffered undiagnosed Lyme disease for years before they'd learned what was going on. Her mom had learned to coddle Kenny and couldn't unlearn it.

A "none of your business" wouldn't do me any good. I tried to have more tact than they expected. "She's my friend too."

Willow tsked like I had no business calling Kenny my friend.

My temper flared. I opened my mouth, and to hell with what I said—

The screen door creaked open. "Willow, Bruce, hello! I'm sorry I didn't return your message right away. I was going to after I got the kids into bed." Kenny stepped onto the porch, her expression as pleasant as always, but I caught her quick glance between me and her in-laws like she was judging the level of tension she was walking into.

Kenny standing on my porch fit her better than that cramped, outdated thing she lived in now. The peeling siding didn't look so haggard around her sunny smile.

She blocked the door, keeping the boys inside, rightly noting the animosity swirling around.

"Call us whenever you want." Willow's tone had done a one-eighty to matronly and full of love.

Bruce's glare deepened on me, but he directed his words to Kenny. "I just came to talk to Liam about the fences."

Dread pooled as heavy as molten lead in my belly. "What about them?"

"They need to be fixed. I need to let my cattle out for the summer."

"So fix them." Same argument, different day.

He cocked an arrogant brow. Derek would pull the same move when he was being an ass and I used to mimic it and call him Bruce. His laughing *fuck you* still rang in my ears as one of my treasured memories. "I'm leasing the land; I don't need to fix the damn fence."

"Bruce," Willow gently chastised, her gaze darting to the screen that my kids' faces were pressed against. I hated to soften toward her and her rare lack of accommodation when it came to her spouse.

"You're leasing the land for your cattle," I said in a flat tone, knowing it wouldn't help. "If you want the fence fixed, fix it. Unless you want the seventy-year-old woman to do it."

Grandma Gin would do it too. And then take so many pain meds she either couldn't sleep or would sleep too well.

"If Ginny can't take care of her land, maybe it's time to sell."

My initial reaction was to tell him fuck no, we'd never sell. But this place wasn't mine, and the last few years had shown me that it was expensive to keep. "Let me guess. You'd be the first to offer?"

Seeing me around must have made him worry I would decide to stay and purchase the land. Part of me was tempted to see if I could rearrange my expenses to cover payments and upkeep. Then I wouldn't just be his brother's reminder of a scandalous affair, I would be one of the blocks between him and his siblings acquiring all the land around Coal Haven.

Bruce drew himself to his full height—two inches shorter than me—and planted his hands on his hips. "Then I'm taking the cost of supplies and time off the payment."

He'd gotten a good fucking deal. Grandma Gin's back had been against the wall. She should've had Bruce sign a contract instead of using the handshake method, but she hadn't been able to afford a lawyer. She hadn't bothered me about it.

Kenny's gaze burned into me, a silent unspoken

support. She knew better than I did what Derek's parents thought of me. When she'd first started dating Derek, they'd tried using her to talk him into giving up his friendship with me. Bad influence and all that.

Which might've been true, but half the destructive ideas had been Derek's. It was why we'd gotten along so well. He was a hellion, but he'd been better at blending in, so I'd shouldered a lot of the blame. Kenny hadn't treated me differently or avoided me, no matter how much she'd been urged to.

Birdsongs rang around us, cutting into the tense silence. Kenny was watching us. Eli and Owen were watching and would have a million questions. I wasn't going to leave a mess for Grandma Gin. "Fine."

I'd have to make up the difference with my own money to help Grandma Gin cover expenses. Maybe I could try to sell some of the pieces in my shop.

Bruce's gaze flicked to Kenny. "Make sure you give us a call, Kennedy."

His tone told me what he'd be talking to her about. How I was no good. I was a user. Stay away from me. As if I hadn't helped drag her back to the land of the living. Since my back was to the house, I let my fury flame across my face. Kenny and my kids didn't have to know how upset I was.

Bruce and Willow had lost their son, and I grieved with them. But when it came to my personal life, they'd tried to take away my only friend. It wasn't going to work with Kenny any more than it had with Derek.

Three

KENNEDY

I flopped back on the couch. The ring from the phone call I was making echoed through my earbuds as I crossed my ankles over the armrest and cradled the phone on my chest.

Liam answered. "Did you shower today?"

Laughter burst out of me. "I just did. Want to know why?"

"Because your water heater's working."

I grimaced, but my smile didn't fade. "Too soon."

The water heater was brand new. Bruce had replaced it last year after I had ignored having no hot water—thus not taking showers—and then conveniently ignored the musty smell rising from the basement, thanks to the leaky water heater.

"Umm..." His rumble through the earbuds was more intimate than when I cradled the phone against my ear. "As long as the answer isn't because you haven't showered since I left for Williston, hit me."

He'd been gone for two and a half weeks. My conversation could wait until he got home. Should wait. But messaging back and forth with him was making me antsy. I wanted to hear his voice.

I grinned at the popcorn ceiling. "I started cleaning out the garage."

"You never use the garage. Why would you clean it?" The curiosity in his tone was nicer than the abject surprise I'd expected when he found out that I had chosen to tackle a big project. I wished I could explain this concept to Bruce, that I wanted him to be a part of my life, not take it over, but it was easier to ignore his attempts than to risk hurt feelings from a misunderstanding. Bruce and Willow were grieving, and I didn't want to add to their stress.

But I had to deal with the stress of their "helpful" advice, and the garage was my target. It was a stand-alone building behind the house that opened to the alley and was more a shelter than a usable building. It was full of items discarded by all the previous owners. An old lawn mower. Half-busted garden gnomes. Rakes, shovels, hoes, all with broken handles. Barely wide enough to fit a car decently, it was too uncomfortable to park in it and then wrestle with the heavy door.

"I'm cleaning because there's probably nothing in it that I need to fix." Mostly true. "It's a dump and it's going to stay a dump. But I'll start there and move to the house, and maybe do some of the repairs in here myself."

He whistled. "Kenny gonna get herself an HGTV show."

"You might be surprised." I giggled. I didn't plan to tell anyone else. Derek's parents would offer to do the work themselves. In addition to the water heater and the consequential carpet removal in the basement, replacing the garbage disposal, and lawn care, Bruce had put in a new ceiling fan in the living room and snaked out the bathtub drain in the last year. Not to mention how he'd swooped in to arrange my finances when I'd let a few too many bill payments slip at the worst of my breakdown. He'd have no problem letting himself in while I was at work to fix whatever I mentioned was broken; it was what he'd been doing all along.

My mom would tell me not to do too much too soon. She had a hard time seeing me as anything more than the sick teenager that had turned into a mourning widow. My sister was over me and my drama. And my coworkers didn't understand. They were either single and already doing it all themselves, or married and had at least moral support.

I'd been with Derek since I was a junior in high school. He'd been a year older than me and had gone to college an hour away in Bismarck during my senior year, but he'd spent every free moment with me. I'd gone to the same college and stayed in the dorms. We married right after I got my degree. The world would witness me moving on, going back to work, and—maybe someday—dating again. It didn't need to see me trying to live on my own for the first time in my life.

"Nah," Liam drawled. "I won't be surprised by what you can do."

Warmth, like a cozy fire on a cold night, spread through my gut, but it kept going until I was flushed. Heat pooled in my belly and I squirmed, trying to find a more comfortable position.

Was it that time of the month? My periods were always sporadic. I didn't know if it was from my illness as a kid or another problem. I fanned my face. I had called Liam for more than compliments. "Hey, I was hanging out with Grandma Gin and the boys while you were gone."

His deep laugh stoked the heat. "They told me, believe me. I think you're a superhero in their eyes."

Easter was weeks ago, but we had colored eggs and did an egg hunt anyway. I put money and candy in the eggs and didn't hide them in any gimme spots. The kids had had to *search*. "I had as much fun as them."

I tried to be at peace with the quiet nights at home. But I was torn. Sometimes it felt like I was using Liam's kids to get me through my healing process until I could cope on my own. I was pretty sure it was more than that, though. I loved being around them, and they didn't feel the need to do anything more than spend time with me.

I'd grown up with Mom fluttering around me, worrying about the constant pain I was in from chronic Lyme disease, how tired I was. Fretting over whether the next doctor we saw would believe I was more than a drama-prone young lady. I had slept while my older sister did my share of our chores.

I'd met Derek shortly after I started treatment. He'd given me massages. He'd carried my backpack in high school, and then had carried in the groceries after we were married. I'd been coddled by everyone in my life.

I hadn't realized how dependent I was until I wanted to do a project by myself and faced well-intentioned concern from my mother or found that Bruce had already done it.

The last thing I wanted was to seem ungrateful. At least, that was until I thought about the phone call with Willow and the way she expressed her concern that Liam wasn't a stable presence in my life. To top it off, I'd been brave enough to mention to Bruce that I'd like to mow my lawn, only to come home from work last Friday to find it done. My chest was heavy, like I was getting smothered, a feeling I wasn't used to.

I was capable, dammit. Which was why I called Liam. "I'm actually calling for a reason."

"Aw, Kenny. You never need a reason to call."

"Well, you're a single guy in oil country. I don't want to interrupt...stuff."

He chuckled, and his voice lowered. "And what *stuff* would that be? Specifically."

Fire raged along my cheeks as images of Liam's strong body entwined with some faceless woman's blazed through my mind. I sputtered before I managed to grit out his full name. "William Robert Barron, if you make me describe anything, *specifically*, we're both going to regret it."

His deep laughter anchored me in the comfort zone. His unrepentant personality and those two little boys of his had been my light at the end of a long, dark tunnel.

"There are a lot more eligible guys here than women," he said. "And I'm a lot choosier than I used to be about who I'll mess around with. Payton taught me that lesson."

Something like relief rushed through me. Was I afraid I was bugging him when he was with a woman? Or was I afraid he was with a woman? I didn't want to be a selfish friend. Liam didn't have the support network I did. Maybe I was just protective of him.

Derek and I had been there through the Payton debacle. Nothing but drama from the beginning. Payton wanted a sugar daddy. Liam hadn't admitted it, but he'd wanted someone of his own. His grandpa had been sick, in and out of the hospital. Grandma Gin had been at her husband's bedside. Liam worked a new job, away from a town that acted like it didn't want him, and he'd been lonely. Ripe pickings for someone like Payton.

Liam wasn't in a much different situation now. I'd hate for him to get used again.

I shamelessly turned the conversation to safer ground. "I

wanted to talk to you about Eli. I really think he'd benefit from speech therapy."

"But he's five. Isn't the way he talks normal?"

"To some extent, but some kids can improve a lot with early intervention."

He was quiet for a moment. Had I overstepped?

"You really think it's something?"

"Yes, I really do." I had noticed Eli's inability to say several consonants correctly, but I hadn't been in the headspace to mention anything. I was doing little more than surviving. But now, for the first time since I'd gotten the Lyme disease diagnosis in high school, I thought I could flourish. Help people instead of always needing it.

"Would he get teased when he goes to school in the fall?"

"I mean, some kids would never notice, much less tease him. Other kids could be brutal. You never know. For his own ability to communicate, though, I think he should at least get a screening. Then we'll know if he falls below standards before he starts school in the fall. You'll be able to communicate with his teacher from the get-go."

"Is it something Grandma Gin can do, or that I can do when I'm home?"

I knew exactly what he was worried about. His limited time had so many demands on it already. "So, I've been thinking—"

"Nothing good ever came from a woman saying that."

"Do I have to use your full name again? You did not just go there." His laughter made my lips twitch. He was a shit, and it was one of my favorite things about him. Always had been. "Anyway, insurance often pays for therapy. Maybe you can try to get him screened in Bismarck before you move the kids to Williston. I'm sure they have services too, but if you start in Bismarck, I can help take him to appointments or entertain Owen while you or Grandma Gin take him."

Liam snorted. "That might be more critical." He let out a breath. "You'd do that?"

"Of course."

"But you have your own job."

"By the time he gets screened and evaluated, it'll be summer. I applied to teach summer school, but those classes are in the mornings." And they were a hot job opening for those who didn't stay home with their kids or work a second job in the summer. There would be a lot of applicants.

Liam and the kids had helped me wander back into life, but a large motivator had been the finances. Bruce had mentioned moving me in with them when the life insurance money ran out and I couldn't cover mortgage payments. I was an independent adult and it'd been time to start acting like it. The paraprofessional job helped cover the cost of living, but it didn't pay as much as a full-time teacher, and it didn't pay over the summer. I needed the money.

"Thank you, Kenny," he said quietly.

"We're kind of a team," I said lightly to cover how his appreciation nearly brought tears to my eyes. This guy. He did so much for the ones he loved. I wanted to return the favor.

"So, I've been thinking..."

"Uh-oh," I mimicked. "Nothing good ever came from a guy saying that."

"Ha ha, smart-ass," he said in a tone that widened my smile. "The farmers market. If I did it, I'd want to have more items to sell, to make it look like I'm serious."

My mouth hitched up. "What if we go to Bismarck and hit the thrift shops? See what you can overhaul. We'll bring the kids and take them somewhere fun to eat or go to a park." My excitement grew with each sentence. It was one thing to hang out at my dreary house or his lively place. But to shed it all and go somewhere else?

I calmed myself down. He was probably busy. I had no claims to his time.

"You got yourself a date."

My heart stuttered. "A date" echoed in my brain. *Quit being silly.* "Let me know when works for you."

"Saturday," he said without hesitation. "I'll pick you up at nine. We'll have to get our shit done before we eat. It's the carrot on the stick for the kids. Owen needs incentive."

"Okay. I'll see you then. Oh, Liam." My hand tightened around the phone. I didn't know why I was going to keep talking, but I couldn't stop. I didn't want to get off the phone, but Liam had to know how much he'd done for me in this call alone. He'd taken me seriously about Eli's speech and the farmers market idea. Our relationship was more than one-sided, and he needed to know that. "I've always treasured your friendship, but you really mean a lot to me. Thank you. For everything."

"Same, Kenny. I'm not letting the only other person besides Grandma Gin that doesn't think I'm a piece of crap out of my life." His tone was light, but his words weren't.

I ached for him. He was a special guy, but too many people had made him feel differently. "The people who can't see what a good guy you are don't know you."

"Well, it'll have to be our little secret."

It shouldn't be a secret. He and Derek had gotten into a lot of trouble as kids. Derek had told me all the stories. Off-roading through a quarry. Losing a four-wheeler trying to ice fish on the river. Taking their horses through Tasty Queen's drive-through. When it came to Derek, it was *boys will be boys*. When it came to Liam, he was a good-for-nothing. "See you Saturday."

"Looking forward to it."

He clicked off, but I continued staring at the ceiling. The countdown to Saturday had started in my head. T minus three days. Only, I couldn't tell if I was excited because I didn't have to spend the weekend home alone, or if I couldn't wait to spend the day with Liam.

I stared at the ceiling. A different feeling seeped into my bones. A heaviness, neediness. Heat wicked along my body until it pooled between my legs.

Sucking my lower lip into my mouth, I concentrated on a pattern in the popcorn ceiling that resembled the constellation Orion. Three larger hunks in a tight line with a few more prominent ones spattered around it.

I knew this day would come. The day my hormones remembered I was in my midtwenties and had a sex drive that hadn't been used for too long. A sex drive that hadn't been wanted for too long. The few times it had thought to rear its head, I'd dissolved into a puddle of tears in my bed. I'd refused to do anything about it. The memory of Derek's arms around me, the way he kissed me, the groans he'd made when he came. They'd ripped open the gaping hole inside me.

I waited for that moment. For the tears. For the hole to wrench open wider.

Only a steady throb that made me want to scissor my legs remained. The longing was there. I missed my husband. If I orgasmed, I wanted it to be with him. With him, I'd been safe. Cherished. But he was gone. There was just me, and I was curious what, if anything, worked for me now, and if I wanted it to.

Who was Kennedy Barron, and how did she handle being horny?

Feeling like I needed physical relief brought up more questions.

If I could handle being horny, could I handle dating? Making a profile on an app?

Was I ready?

The latter questions were for another time. Right now, I was going to go with this feeling until I came or I cried or both. Like with cleaning out the closet and the drawers, figuring out how our automatic payments for the mortgage were set up, signing up for health insurance under my name with my new job, I had to do this. On my own.

I rolled off the couch, shut off the lights and went to my bedroom. No matter what happened, I'd go to the cemetery tomorrow and talk to Derek about it. Maybe meet with my therapist. Or both.

* * *

Liam parked outside his garage. His was more spacious than mine, also detached, but filled with so much of his grandpa's stuff that Liam would have a hard time fitting a bicycle in there. There were already at least six. Bob Pewter hadn't been able to throw anything away. He'd been a pack rat, but Grandma Gin hadn't been able to get rid of his more eccentric collections, like bicycles and record players with no records.

Liam, Eli, Owen, and I had spent the day in Bismarck. Liam had picked me up and we all drove down, playing I Spy games from Coal Haven to the interstate. When we returned to Coal Haven, Liam had asked if I wanted to be dropped off at home. I'd said I wanted to unload the items he'd picked up at the salvage yard and we'd selected at the thrift stores. Liam thought he could bulk up his booth with colorful, functional furniture. We'd stopped for chalk paint supplies. I'd added some design ideas, and Liam had chosen the paint colors I recommended.

I hadn't been ready for the day to end. The endless energy swirling around Liam and the kids was a security blanket. It reminded me of having my own classroom, where I was the hub and the others were the welcome chaos. After being so sick most of my teenage years and missing the parties and the sleepovers and the noise, I had fed on it.

Liam killed the engine and twisted around to look in the back seat. "We're going to pay for today."

It was like two tiny little Liams napped in the back seat. The boys were losing their toddler cherub cheeks, and they'd insisted on having their hair cut like their dad's. Short on the sides, longer on top.

When I looked at those two, so peaceful in sleep, all was right in my world. "They're going to be awake until midnight."

"Yup." Liam got out and opened the door on Eli's side. "I'll be back for Owen."

"I got him." I cradled Owen to my chest. His bleary amber eyes opened, but he rested his head against my shoulder. I leaned my face on his head as I carried him in. Muscles I hadn't exerted in a while, or ever, protested.

I could start working out or, at the very least, going for walks like I used to during the summer when I wasn't teaching. I could start yoga again. When I made it a regular habit, the residual ache in my joints from having chronic Lyme disease didn't bother me as much. I could find some online videos. I'd had an emotional breakdown, and much of me lived in fear of another, but I could prevent a physical one.

I'd never joined the gym on our limited budget, and it wouldn't be happening now that the mortgage and benefits were coming out of my paycheck. Derek's life insurance had gotten me through the worst of the grief, but what little was left needed to last until I got a higher-paying position. Anything left over was my only safety net.

Liam laid Eli on one end of the couch, and I put Owen on the other side, grateful I hadn't dropped him. Both boys stayed asleep. I pushed my hair back, a sense of accomplishment prompting a smile.

"Ready to unload?" Liam's eyes sparkled. The end table and two-drawer chest were the lightest items we'd brought back. The rest were steel rods and chunks from the scrap yard.

Anyone other than Liam would encourage me to wait with the kids. But Liam would probably turn it into a race just to see how I'd hold up. So I beat him to it. "I'll race you." I darted out of the house as quietly as I could.

His chuckle drifted behind me. Outside, his long strides caught up to me, and he tapped me on the shoulder. "Gotcha."

I slowed to a walk, giggling. "It was worth a shot."

"I don't need to spend my ten days home nursing a sore back. I'll pull around to the shop. You wanna open it up?" He tossed me the keys.

I let out a delighted squeal when I caught them and shared a grin with Liam. The way the green glinted in his eyes made my heart stammer. His laughter sent a flush through my body. I whirled around, willing my hormones to settle down. I'd given myself one orgasm. Was my body going to start reacting to a man? This wasn't an appropriate time—or an appropriate guy. Liam was a good person, but he was a friend.

I unlocked the entry door, flipped the lights on, and punched the button for the overhead door. It creaked open. The sound might be enough to wake the kids. They'd either stay asleep while Liam and I unloaded, or they'd watch as much TV as they could sneak in before Liam made them turn it off. Either way, I'd be alone with Liam.

The thrill of our unfinished race lingered along with the

lick of heat. Would I need to go home and get myself off again tonight? I was comfortable with what had happened. The orgasm had been a release I hadn't known I needed. It was like I'd been handed sixty years back, like *here, you're not a withered crone.*

I waited just inside the shop as Liam backed the pickup in. Unloading was just the distraction I needed from my X-rated thoughts. We worked side by side. I missed being this comfortable around someone. Just existing together. Doing activities next to each other without the *what should I say?* awkwardness.

"We're working up an appetite," Liam said, brushing the back of his wrist across his brow. "I'm gonna hafta feed you again."

My stomach rumbled as if the pizza I'd had at the alien-themed restaurant in Bismarck had burned off as soon as it hit my stomach. "You don't need to feed me."

He hefted long bars of steel, his biceps flexing and veins protruding in his forearms. It was the last load, so I leaned against the side of the pickup and crossed my arms over the top. My gaze stuck on his muscled back as he carried his load into the shop. His shirt was untucked and the hem made a one-sided frame above his butt as it flexed with each step.

I blinked and ripped my gaze away. These hormones.

This longing.

Should I get serious about dating? I'd caught myself staring at Liam too often today to deny that I was moving into another phase of my life. I couldn't have this affect how I was around Liam. My online Sexy, Young, and Widowed support group would have good advice.

He stopped by the back of the pickup. The scent of his aftershave wafted between us. I'd always liked that he didn't douse himself in cologne. He'd said he'd sweat it off anyway when he got to work. "I have to feed the boys. You know they're going to wake up starving."

"Because they talked all the way through their meal about the games they wanted to play in the arcade?"

He chuckled and leaned against the tailgate of his pickup, facing me. "They're going to be up late, so it's no problem to eat before we run you home."

I did want to stay longer. I loved being around Liam and his kids and witnessing what a naturally good dad he was after the piece of crap he'd had for a father. I also loved his place. Sounds of crickets, frogs, and birds mingled and soaked into my bones. A light breeze ruffled my hair and cooled the exertion from unloading the bed of Liam's truck. I turned around, propped myself against his pickup, not caring if I was going to get a backside full of dust, and dropped my head back.

"It's so peaceful here." I used to love going to Derek's place after we started dating. I let out a soft exhale. I loved my in-laws. But it was easier to enjoy the peace of country living when I was at Liam's than when I was at Bruce and Willow's.

I opened my eyes and looked at Liam. His steady gaze was on me, his expression unreadable. He was respecting my time. He could tell I was enjoying the moment. Energy zinged between us, an awareness of him I wasn't ready for.

So I brought up a topic that doused that spark. "What was with the whole fence thing? They don't want to fix any of it?"

Irritation flashed through his expression. He didn't bother to cover it. Another thing I appreciated about him. He didn't feel like he had to hide from me. "They want Grandma Gin to sell sooner than later, and to sell to them."

"But they're nearing their own retirement years. What would they do with more land?"

His smile was grim. "The Barrons have always tried to gobble up land. It's why they don't get along with the Grangers. But Grandma Gin heard Derek's brother mention his interest in moving back home. I'm sure Bruce thinks he can hand over an empire."

"Evander's moving home?" Why hadn't Bruce or Willow mentioned anything? Derek and his brother hadn't been close, but his parents' relationship with Evander was even more complicated. Maybe they didn't know what to think themselves.

"Who knows?" He shifted his stance, his boots grinding in the gravel. "I just know I don't want to sell to my father or any of his siblings or my cousins, and I don't want them to make it hard to sell, period."

The way he frowned as he said it made me wonder if he wanted to sell at all. He'd been optimistic about the house, but now that Grandma Gin had given him a rough deadline, he hadn't been as enthused as before.

"Would you sell it to...yourself?"

A moment of longing passed over his features before he shook his head. "I could never afford it."

"Never?" I prompted, no idea why. He'd been open about his pay and how he could cover his rent, Grandma Gin's, and not much more. But this was Liam's childhood home. His kids loved being here. I enjoyed having them here.

"I mean...maybe I could get a loan, but for the house and land? I dunno." He adjusted the brim of his hat, a move he made when he was frustrated, irritated, or conflicted.

"You've thought of it though?" He had, and he didn't want to admit it. It was written across his tight shoulders and in the set of his jaw. I'd gotten to know Liam better in the last year and a half and could do more than admire his looks. I could read his body language.

He pinned me with his intense hazel stare, the vivid green of his irises captivating me. "What if nothing's changed?"

I didn't want to encourage him to stay if he'd be miserable, but selling the place was clearly starting to weigh heavily on him. I didn't know what was best. "You've changed. You don't have to tolerate being treated like you were."

"There's the issue of getting a job. If I start applying to the coal mine or the power plant, my dad might find out and interfere again."

Damn Cameron and his asshole ways. It probably wasn't just him, either. After a few family dinners Cameron and his wife, Naomi, had attended, I'd assumed she was just as much of the push behind driving Liam away as Cameron was. Possibly more, since she'd been the humiliated new mom that had been cheated on. "It's been a few years. Your record of work should speak for itself."

"I don't trust people not to listen to my father and stupid rumors."

Cameron and Naomi were woven into the community. Liam was on the fringes. They thought he was the kid who'd burned down the barn and cost his grandparents their ranch. Grandpa Bob had accidentally set the fire when he'd tried to quickly weld something into place, and Liam had been content to let the rumors fly about him rather than his grandpa. I suspected Cameron had used the story to keep businesses from hiring Liam.

He was a twenty-seven-year-old single father who supported his grandma but got treated like he was seventeen.

Liam grinned, a wicked glint that sent tingles down my spine to my toes. "I could be ornery and let the Grangers know before we officially list it, ask them if they want to make an offer."

Hearing the Granger name made me want to shudder. Laney Granger had been a blunt-speaking force in our teens. I hadn't met her parents, but I'd heard she was a milder version of her mom. Milder? Laney could draw blood with her words. I wasn't a timid high schooler anymore. I was a timid twenty-six-year-old, and I hoped I didn't cross paths with her now that she was back in town.

Then guilt curled through my lungs, making it hard to breathe. I wasn't the only one suffering. Laney was home for a reason. Just like Derek's brother, Evander, was coming home because Derek wasn't going to be the kid who kept the ranch going after Bruce and Willow were gone. Laney's brother could no longer take over their ranch. She'd moved back to do it.

"Now that Laney's home," Liam continued, "she might want a place of her own."

Laney living in Liam's home? The wrongness sank into my bones. No one should be living here but him or Grandma Gin. Another woman? My stomach cramped. It didn't feel right.

Liam pushed off the truck and walked toward the house. I did the same to keep myself from staring at his swagger as he wandered off. "No matter what, tomorrow I'm fixing the fence."

"I thought Bruce did it."

"He did. But I went out last night after I got home. There's another section that needs repair. If I do it, he can't take the money away from Grandma Gin."

"Want help?" I wasn't terribly productive today. We'd had fun and had gotten supplies. But being out of the house the entire day with people I enjoyed being around was exactly what I'd needed. One day wasn't enough. Especially if Liam really was moving.

"I don't want Bruce and Willow to give you another grinding down, but you're always welcome to help."

Right. Bruce worked every day, driving here and there and checking on his land and cattle. He might very well see me helping Liam stretch wire. "I don't want to make trouble for you either."

Liam opened the door to the house. Voices drifted from the living room. The boys were awake. "One thing I can guarantee, Kenny, is that none of the trouble in my life is caused by you."

Four

~~~

</div>

LIAM

I cut Eli's pancake into squares. He'd speared a sausage link with his fork and was chewing on one end. Silverware clattered around us. I'd grown up coming to this diner with Grandma Gin. Grandpa had never come to town with us. I thought he hadn't liked the food. Then I'd gotten older. Saw the looks people gave us. Saw the tightening in Grandma Gin's shoulders when we went to the bank or to the store or the tractor supply place on the edge of town. Her friends worked at the diner and she'd felt comfortable here. Everywhere else, I was Cameron Barron's bastard, and the gossip about the night Mom died never went out of style.

I set the knife down. "There. Don't drown them in syrup." I glanced at Owen's plate. He'd ripped his pancake in half and speared it like Eli had the sausage. "Put that down. We're not cavemen."

Eli screwed his face up as he dumped Log Cabin all over his plate. "Cavemen ate pancakes?"
~~~

A large shadow loomed over us. "What are you teaching your kids, Liam?" Holden swung into the booth, bumping Owen over with a grin.

"Holden!" Owen and Eli said in unison.

My cousin was like a celebrity. I wasn't sure if it was because Holden treated them like his buddies, only smaller, and with cleaner language, or if it was because I didn't bring many people around. I might suffer assholes that were usually my relatives, like I was paid a million a year to do it, but my kids didn't have to.

Holden ruffled Owen's hair like a soft noogie and lifted his chin to Eli. The waitress who'd served me when I was the kids' age stopped over. "Usual for you today, kiddo?"

Holden was as tall as me. His heavy shoulders took up most of the forty-year-old booth. Only a five-year-old could fit next to him. But Holden grinned the same way he probably had when he was five and Jocelyn had waited on him. "Yes, ma'am."

She gave him a sweet smile that made me wonder if she was going to muss his hair like he had Owen's, but she hurried away.

I dug into my everything omelet. Holden eyed it. "Thought you'd be sick of eating out."

"I don't eat out much." At his raised brow, I explained. "I pack sandwiches for lunch. Sometimes I buy a few subs to get me through the week cuz I get sick of packing lunch. When I leave in the morning, I grab my lunchbox, a Pop-Tart, and a banana. By the time I get off work, I'd have to go shower before I went to a place with decent food or go through fast food." I poked my fork at him. "Drive-throughs got old after the first year."

Holden grunted. "I'm not used to living in a place with more than a Tasty Queen that's open only in the summer." The only drive-through place in town. Fast food in Coal Haven was that or the Hot Stuff pizza in the gas station.

"I miss home-cooked meals. If it doesn't come out of a box and can't be grilled, I don't make it."

"I cook. You've gotta come over. Bring your wingmen."

Eli's wide eyes turned on me. "Can we go to Holden's, Dad?"

I studied my cousin. Who was he trying to piss off by having me and the boys over? The guys I worked with and around in Williston were either single and out looking for hookups, or they had families and were like me. When work was done, we shot home as fast as possible. Some guys were a mixture of both, and I tried to stay away from that drama waiting to happen. My life had been affected enough by a cheating husband.

A lot of the guys I went to school with had moved away. That left the relatives that had nothing to do with me. And Holden, when he liked to get under his mom's or uncle's skin. I hadn't been invited anywhere, unless it was a woman's place. Half the time, they wanted a quick fuck in the back seat, skip the awkward *time to leave* stage, and go our separate ways. Add in the kids, and there were no *hey, you should come over* invites.

Derek and Kenny had been the exception.

"You serious?" There was an edge of warning in my voice. He could kid around with me in that superficial way of his, but Eli and Owen wouldn't understand.

Holden lifted his brows. "Why wouldn't I be?" He shrugged. "I mean, I *know*, but I'm a grown-ass— Uh, a grown man. I don't need my mom's permission about who I hang out with."

He glanced at Eli and awareness brightened his eyes. Holden wasn't an idiot. He acted like it sometimes, but it was just that. An act. I had no idea why. "Look, the things we get told as kids, we accept. We don't know any different. Then we grow up and think about that information and realize there's more to the story. And we don't necessarily agree with how people were treated."

"Not everyone thinks the story has more than one point of view." It felt like we were speaking in code. If I were to buy the house and land, Eli and Owen would learn soon enough what it was like to be different from the other Barrons in town.

"Not everyone is able to distance themselves from certain people." Like Cameron and Naomi. "Not everyone got a front-row seat to the shi— Uh, crap show that went down. It was messed up, what happened."

"Yeah, it was." Mom had confronted Cameron. She'd pissed him off by naming him as the dad on the birth certificate and giving me Barron as a last name. She'd already lost her job. Fucking the married boss and getting pregnant with his kid tended to do that.

But she hadn't been able to let it go. Scorned by the guy she'd had the bad judgment to fall in love with. Hated by the town, thanks to the vitriol spewed by Naomi. Broke and living with her parents, she'd left me with Grandma Gin and confronted Cameron at the street fair. He'd told her off in front of everyone. Accused her of being greedy, luring him away from his wife—as if he were some unwitting sailor at sea and she was a siren when he'd been the CEO of the oil refinery and she'd been his young personal assistant. He'd demanded she leave him alone and claimed she needed to seek professional help. Hadn't she damaged his family enough? Wasn't she satisfied with what she'd done?

I knew all the details. People had filled them in over the years. The town could be super helpful like that.

Mom had left, distraught. Sobbing. Shaking. And she'd accidentally driven headfirst into a grain truck on the narrow highway heading out of town. So... Shit show was an accurate description.

My father couldn't own up to his role in his infidelity. He'd chosen to be harsh and mean, and I'd lost my mother because of him. Messed up? Completely and utterly fucked up.

"Anyway, my new place is done, and it's just me there," Holden said. "But I can pick a night when Mom's out of town with her new man if that'd make you feel better."

Holden's house was on his mom's land. My great-grandparents on the Barron side had gotten serious oil money and had used it to buy as much land in the county as possible. Once they'd passed, Cameron, the oldest, had let the others buy him out of their shares so he could become a big deal at the refinery that had become the largest employer in the area. He had a lot of power.

Meanwhile, I was twenty-seven but still planning to go to a friend's house when his parents were out of town to keep from getting into trouble.

"Sure." Might as well agree. It wasn't like it was going to happen in the short time I was home before the boys and I moved for good. And refusing might make it seem like I wasn't open to being congenial with any family not being an asshole to me. It wasn't like my life was overflowing with friends. "I leave again in a couple of days, but maybe one of these times when I'm home."

Owen started peppering Holden with questions about his house. When Holden said he ranched, there was no saving the man from the next hundred questions about cows, horses, and heavy equipment. He answered patiently, but he seemed to like talking about his life. This was what it would be like if my kids had aunts or uncles.

Technically, they had one of each. Stetson was older and ignored me with simmering hostility whenever we crossed paths. His younger sister, Isla, had watched me like I was a bug she'd been warned was venomous. Did they even know the kids' names?

I shouldn't care. But sometimes I did.

I paid for our meal and Holden's, too, though he stayed behind, chatting with a couple of old farmers having coffee. I gathered the boys, and outside they each jumped over cracks in the sidewalk on the way to my pickup. "Hey, we're not loading up yet. Just grab a toy for when I'm talking with Mr. Hart."

My insurance agent's office was right next to the diner on Main Street.

Owen opened the back door of my pickup, and they each dove inside to find the toys I'd made them bring for when we were running errands today. I could do a lot online and over the phone, but sometimes, in person was the only way. And the only way I did business anymore was with kids in tow.

The door to the law office next door to the insurance agency opened and Laney breezed out, her eyes flashing and her red lips in a mutinous line. When her gaze landed on me, surprise replaced anger. "Liam."

"Hey, Laney." I didn't bother to ask what was wrong. Laney would tell you what was wrong and what your role in it was.

It was warmer out than the last time I'd seen her, but she was dressed for cooler weather, tucked into a green hoodie with black leggings on her long legs. Her pale hair was up in a ponytail. Except for a worldly gleam in her eyes and the weight of the adult world on her shoulders, she looked like she'd walked out of high school.

She noticed the flurry of activity in my vehicle. I waited for the rant of what had pissed her off, but it never came. "You're getting carjacked," she said wryly.

"They'll take a lot, but they can't drive off. I have the keys."

"You leaving town again soon?"

"Tuesday."

She folded her arms and cocked her hip out. "And you're back…"

"At the end of the month."

Her eyes widened. "That's a long time."

It got exponentially longer each time I was away. "A little over twenty days."

"You gonna let me know when you get back so we can meet up?" Again, I couldn't get a read on her tone. She was almost shy, like she was asking me on a date and was afraid I'd turn her down. But there was a hint of desperation. As if the same thought I'd had when Holden invited me over also ran through her head. Having a friend in town would be welcome.

I was thinking it now. Other than Grandma Gin and Kenny, I didn't have anyone. Holden was a maybe. Laney and I were still neighbors. Maybe I could get a read on whether she'd be interested in buying my place.

I didn't like the idea of selling. Kenny had read me accurately about that. But I liked the idea of having other options who didn't share my last name. "Sure. Yeah. I'll find a sitter."

"Great. You've got my number." She sauntered away. Confident. Mysterious.

I'd been thinking about real estate. What if Laney was interested in more than catching up? Shit. Had I just agreed to a date? My omelet sat like a steel ball in my gut. My thoughts stuck on how I was going to tell Kenny. It shouldn't matter, but when it came to Kenny, everything mattered.

I had twenty days to figure out what the hell I was going to do.

* * *

Kennedy

Grandma Gin stepped onto the porch, her arms folded and her face tipped to the sinking sun. I parked in front of the house. The click of buckles sounded moments before the back doors of my car flew open. Eli and Owen raced out, bombarding Grandma Gin with details of our day in Bismarck.

She nodded, but only had to listen for a few moments before the kids raced into the house. She glanced down at me. "Thank you for taking both of them."

"Not a problem. It was fun."

School had let out for the summer last week, and Eli had had his speech screening in Bismarck. Owen would've been beside himself if his brother had taken a trip to Bismarck by himself. I'd brought them both and run them through a park to wear them out for Grandma Gin.

She sniffled. "Well, I appreciate it, and I know they had fun." Her voice was rough, like she wasn't feeling well, or like she'd been crying.

"Everything okay?"

She waved me off. "I think I caught a little cold. Those two bring home more germs from the playground than Liam ever did."

I chuckled. "I got a cold every other month my first two years of teaching. Derek said he should've bought stock in Kleenex. Call me if you need anything. I'm around all day tomorrow."

Since the day out with Liam and the kids, I'd been inspired to do something, anything, and I couldn't rely on Liam to entertain me. No matter how much I liked being with him, I had to learn to live with myself. And to prove to myself that I was capable on my own, I had a date with a leaky faucet. But I'd be here in a heartbeat if Grandma Gin needed me.

"Eh, not the first cold I've had. How'd the screening go?"

Grandma Gin might not get terribly sick, but she still had two five year olds to take care of. I'd call her tomorrow. I leaned against my car. She would invite me in if she wanted me to stay. If she wasn't feeling well, she probably wanted to relax on the couch while the kids watched a show.

"They recommended an eval so they can make a therapy plan. I set one up for next week, and Liam needs to send them his insurance information." We talked regularly while he was gone, but I only seemed to find more reasons to talk to him. Sometimes he called instead of messaging, and I gladly abandoned whatever DIY tinkering I was doing to answer. And I was really starting to enjoy improving my house.

Grandma Gin nodded, matter of fact. I'd always gotten the impression that she took the cards life dealt her and neatly tucked them into her hand.

Failing ranch. Stick that next to the jack of spades.

Daughter dies in the most-talked-about accident in Coal Haven's history. Put that by the queen of diamonds.

Single-dad grandson who works out of town. Goes by the king of hearts.

Eli and his speech difficulties were getting placed. Grandma Gin played the hand she was dealt. She didn't ask for a re-deal.

"I've got a casserole in the oven. You're welcome to stay." Her invitation lacked all energy.

"Thanks, but I need to stop at the hardware store before I go home." I hated the anxiety that wound around my stomach. It was my first trip by myself to the hardware store. Mom had never gone there when I was growing up—that was what her various husbands had been for—and I'd gladly let Derek do those tasks. But last night, I'd watched videos, taken notes, and made a list. I was going to make that faucet my bitch. "I'll talk to Liam and let him know everything."

She gave me a tired smile. "Sounds good. Drive safe, Kennedy."

I drove to town and scurried into the hardware store. Cleaning the garage was one thing. Scrubbing the floorboards another. This involved tools and a system I knew nothing about. I felt exposed, like a floodlight had spilled over me and highlighted only my ineptness. I recognized the lady paying the cashier. She worked at the grocery store. The guy taking her money had a shock of white hair and wasn't much younger than Grandma Gin. I thought he owned the store and refused to quit working the counter.

I looked at my list. Last weekend, I'd lugged Derek's toolbox in from the garage. I had attacked it with paper towels to clean the grime it'd collected from sitting so long and had done an inventory. I'd found all the tools I'd need for the sink. All I needed were sink parts.

Was there a sink section in the store?

I didn't bother with a shopping basket as I wandered down the first aisle. Some of the items hanging on the hooks and piled on shelves had pictures of vehicles on them. Wrong aisle. By the time I turned down the next one, the man from the register was waiting for me with a pleasant smile. His name badge said Carlton.

"Can I help you with anything?"

Everything. I needed help with everything. In the day and age of strong and independent women, I had missed the train while sitting in the waiting rooms of doctors' offices. And I hadn't tried to hop on after I'd met Derek.

I held out my list. "I have a leaky faucet."

He dug dark-framed readers out of the pocket of his red polo shirt and put them on. "Oh, yes." He gave me another grin. "You're close."

He spun and hustled to the next aisle. I almost had to trot to catch up.

Peering through his readers at my list, then looking over the glasses to select from the shelf, he handed each pick to me. "Here's the washer. And the cartridge. Oh, yes, sometimes it's easier to buy a new aerator if it's an old faucet. The outside might be okay, but the insides could be corroded."

"The outside is pretty corroded."

Another pleasant smile as he looked over his readers. "Sure you don't want to replace the whole thing?" The trepidation must've shown in my expression. He chuckled. "Nothing wrong with trying to fix it first. Sometimes we need the win before we tackle a bigger project."

Tears pricked the backs of my eyes. I needed the win. Sweeping the garage could be done by anyone, but I wanted to fix the damn sink. *I* wanted to fix it. I didn't have the money to hire a plumber. I didn't want Derek's parents to rush over. I didn't want Mom to make Benji drive from Fargo for a seemingly simple task. Liam would help and it wouldn't matter if he was out of town, but Carlton was right. Sometimes we need the win.

I gathered myself before it was time to check out. Going to the hardware store was such a monumental hurdle, and I had a little bag of supplies to show for it.

When I got home, I parked next to the garage, then ducked in through the side door. Last weekend, I'd swept the floor and organized the trash that might be someone else's treasure into piles. The broken-down lawn mower had gone out to the curb on spring cleanup week. Someone had claimed it during their curbside shopping before the dump truck came by the next morning. Same with the old-school grass cutter that ran on manpower and was full of rust.

I had a pile of metal somethings in the back corner. They were large and heavy and strange. The garage light didn't work. I'd hauled out a ladder and changed the bulb, but no luck. Enough ambient light was coming through the two dingy windows that I could get pictures with a flash.

I aimed and shot a few pictures, then sent them to Liam. **Can you work your magic with whatever these are?**

I thought he was still working, but my phone rang. I answered.

"Those are old tractor seats, Kenny."

I tilted my head to view the parts from a different angle. "Seriously?"

His deep laugh had become one of my favorite sounds. "Yeah, I'll take them. Some people collect them. Maybe I can make 'em pretty, like a lawn ornament."

"Like one of those for the garden where it looks like a lady bending over?"

"They'd probably sell faster than the lamp."

The lamp was gorgeous. I'd rather have that than an ass to put next to my sweet peas, but people's tastes differed. "They're yours. I can bring them next time I go to your place."

"Just let me know. I'll make sure the shop door's open. How'd Eli's screening go?"

I passed along the information. "I'm calling Grandma Gin tomorrow. I don't think she's feeling well."

"She'd never admit it if she wasn't."

"No, that's why I'm going to be a pest. You don't mind,

do you?" Days like today, I felt like I'd come out of a grief fog and barged into Liam's life. "I can offer to sleep over if she's really under the weather." Liam's place had four small bedrooms. The kids' room was upstairs, and Grandma Gin preferred to sleep across from them in the other upstairs bedroom. Liam's bedroom was on the main floor along with the guest bedroom he kept ready in case his grandma wanted to quit doing stairs.

"My house is your house, Kenny."

"The future Mrs. Liam might have something to say about that." My smile died, replaced by a scowl. I was protective of him. That was all.

"I'd have to date to get married. But—" He cut himself off so quickly, I frowned. He might not be dating, but he could be having sex.

My pulse kicked up. Liam and sex in the same thought sent my body into a whirlwind and left my thoughts tumbling.

"Is there someone?" Anxiety like I'd had before going into the hardware store squeezed around my stomach. I pressed a hand to my belly. I must be hungry or something.

"No. It's just... Laney Granger asked to meet up."

I sucked in a breath. "Oh." Laney. Sexy, smart, and capable. Cowgirl turned city girl who came home to save the family ranch. She'd probably put in a new faucet in her sleep and give me *that look*. The one she'd given me in high school that said she was trying to determine what the big deal about me was and couldn't for the life of her figure it out.

Back then, I hadn't cared. Like my mother when she got a new husband and life was good again, I'd had Derek.

What if I lost my friend to Laney? I could envision Laney's smug karmic smile. The vise around my insides cinched tighter.

"It's not like I can get a babysitter anyway," Liam said.

"I can watch the boys." I toed a loose pebble that I'd missed sweeping. It skittered across the concrete as I stared. Offering was the right thing to do. Liam had done so much for me.

"You'd watch them so I can hang out with Laney Granger?" Quiet shock resonated in his question.

"Why wouldn't I? High school was a long time ago." But when I thought about Laney and Liam dating, high school seemed like yesterday. "You should be able to date. You're too nice of a guy for me to keep to myself." I chewed on my lip. I wasn't keeping him to myself. He kept to himself and I hung around with him. That was different.

"I mean, sure. I don't know if it's really a date, but yeah, if you don't mind?"

A little sliver of hope hooked on *I don't know if it's really a date*. Was my urge to smash the phone and pretend I'd never offered only because it was Laney Granger? "Okay."

"Okay." Silence stretched on, but I didn't know what to say. My mouth was dry and my stomach hurt.

Liam broke the silence first. "You'll let me know if Grandma Gin's not doing well? She'd never tell me."

"Yes." I struggled for something else to say.

"Hey, congrats on getting the summer position."

He'd been the first one I'd messaged. Not only had I gotten the summer teaching job and relieved my money worries until the fall, but it was one step closer to proving I could be in charge of a full classroom again.

"I knew you would." There was a smile in his voice that chased away some of the earlier turmoil.

"Thanks. I wasn't sure, but it shows they're willing to give me another chance."

"You'll get the next open teaching position. Don't worry about it. Just have fun."

It would be fun. My body slowly unclenched while talking about work. "I'll start a week after Memorial Day, but I'll still have time to take Eli to his appointments."

"We'll figure it out, Kenny."

"You always do."

We hung up, and loneliness settled around my shoulders. I liked being around Liam and his kids. But if he was dating again—and apparently, I was helping him—then I had to learn not to be dependent on him. I knew he planned on moving, but I'd conveniently forgotten he also had a life to live and that my place in it was as his friend.

Five

KENNEDY

It was Memorial Day weekend. Most people were going on picnics, heading to the river, or relaxing. I was fixing a toilet. As the sink dripped behind me. My win had been temporary. The faucet repair had gone well, but it had resumed leaking two days later.

My water bill was going to cost as much as it would've to hire a plumber. Instead, I'd gone back to the hardware store and hit up Carlton. He sold me a faucet, gave me a few tips, and when I mentioned that my toilet wouldn't quit running, found an insides kit for me.

An entire week of how-to videos. I'd dreamed of how to replace the innards of a toilet tank and install a shiny new faucet. It was time to make it real.

If real meant I was red-faced and sweaty and had said more swear words in two hours than I had in my entire life, then it was real.

I sat on the floor and puffed a lock of hair out of my face. I needed to redo my topknot but my hands were grungy. They'd only been in the toilet tank, but the level of intimacy I'd had with the toilet was all over my clothing.

I flexed my hand. My modest wedding ring glittered under the bathroom lights. There'd been a few times I'd thought I should take it off while I was working in the toilet tank, but I couldn't bring myself to do it. The square diamond was less than a quarter carat. The wedding band had six diamonds in a line.

I remembered how hard Derek had worked for this, taking extra jobs around his college schedule. I'd thought he was saving for a house, but he had saved for this. One night before the ceremony, Derek had confessed that Liam had helped him buy it. Derek had paid him back by then, but he'd talked about how the jewelry store had a two-week-long sale. Derek hadn't saved enough by then, but Liam had kicked in the rest.

I admired the ring that the two most important people in my life had worked hard for. Wedding rings were symbolic, but this one meant so much. Tonight was the first night I'd considered removing it, even just temporarily.

Would I ever be ready?

My phone rang.

Dammit.

Upbeat music flowed from a speaker on the edge of the bathtub, but I needed to switch to motivational podcasts. Another one about finances and empowered women— sometimes both in the same podcast. Bruce had set up the bill pay to be automatic based on advice from a banker friend of his, but I needed to know about more than keeping my account in the black.

My phone chirped again. I glanced at it. My mom.

If I didn't answer, she'd keep calling. If I still didn't answer, she'd make Benji drive three and a half hours to check on me.

I hurried through a handwashing and put the call on speaker. "Hey, Mom."

"Oh, Kennedy. I was afraid you weren't going to answer."

"I was in the middle of something."

"Oh?"

I chewed the inside of my cheek. There were micromanagers, and there were micromommers. She was going to want to know exactly what I was doing. "I'm working in the bathroom."

"Is something wrong?"

"No." I made my voice as light as I could. "Just a leaky sink. I've got it covered."

"Are you sure? Benji's real good with plumbing. He's done all of the repairs in the condo." The condo had been built five years ago. This house was fifty years old. "Benji!"

"No, Mom!" I took a breath. I hadn't meant to shout. "It's fine. I've got it."

"It's no problem. Benji can pack his tools and—"

I grasped for a way to keep my oasis from getting invaded by my smothering mother. "Carlton's helping me."

Mom stalled at the mention of someone—not me—who was involved. "Carlton?"

"He owns the hardware store, remember? Between him and YouTube—"

"Benji!"

"Liam's helping me," I blurted.

"Liam's there? Oh, good." Relief poured over the line. "How is he?"

"Doing well." Other daughters might feel bad for lying to their mothers. It wasn't like having a caring parent should be a hardship. It was that Mom still viewed me as the sick kid she had to fight the medical world for. Mom was ready to battle the rest of the world for me too. "I watched the kids a couple of days last week when Grandma Gin wasn't feeling well." Once she had spiked a fever, I'd shooed her out of the house and stayed for two nights. The days had flown by as the kids and I played games, watched movies, and explored the pastures.

"He's asking you to watch his kids?"

I closed my eyes at my mom's exasperated tone. I should've kept my mouth shut. "I offered."

"Do you think it's wise?"

"Why wouldn't it be?" I was a teacher. But this was Mom. She was probably stuck on how I couldn't continue teaching after Derek's funeral, and she hadn't seen me since Christmas, since before I went back to work. She'd occasionally flown back to Coal Haven to dote on me, but never to just visit me.

"Liam shouldn't be using you for free childcare after all you've been through."

"Like I said, I offered."

"Mmm. Are you sure I shouldn't send Benji over?" Her *Mmm* was so much less satisfying than Liam's. "It might be a little too much too soon for you."

Benji would do what Mom wanted. Stepdad number four had been around the longest, and truthfully, I liked him the best. But he wasn't a father figure, and I didn't really want to make awkward small talk with him.

"Nope, Liam's almost done." I hated that the way to get Mom off my back was to let her think that a man had fixed my problems. I wasn't a Disney princess. Those princesses also had networks of friends. I hadn't quite reached the level of little birds doing my laundry. "I should probably go."

"Oh, okay. Goodbye. Call if you need anything."

And she'd send Benji over. Got it. "Love you, Mom."

I disconnected and wrestled with the toilet for another half an hour. The flapper was taut but not too tight. Before I'd started, I'd taken pictures of the float valve and adjusted the new kit. Thanks to at least three how-to videos, I was prepared to adjust more. I leaned over it and peered inside. I didn't know what normal looked like, but it looked pretty damn good if I said so myself.

I was about to turn the water to the tank back on when my phone rang again. My sister. I dropped my head and my hair flopped over my forehead. "For fuck's sake."

Good thing I didn't keep a swear jar. I washed my hands again and answered. "Mom told you to call."

"Something about Benji's plumbing and Liam's kids," Cassidy said dryly.

Cassidy and I weren't close, but it wasn't like we didn't get along. She was six years older than me, and we hadn't gotten much of a chance to be sisters before she had moved halfway across the country. "God. I had to tell her that Liam fixed the sink to keep her from shoving Benji in the car and pointing him west."

"You fixed the sink?"

"Yes," I said defensively, disliking the surprise in her tone. "No. I mean, I did, then it started leaking again. I think I need a new faucet. It's old. Right now, I'm about to turn on the water to the toilet and see if I fixed that."

"Damn. And you're doing it yourself?" Unlike me, Cassidy had made it her mission to prove she could win the award for Most Independent Woman Ever. While Mom was taking me to doctors' appointments, Cassidy was fixing the overhead garage door or changing oil. Cassidy and I were adults, but I didn't think she'd gotten over her conflicted feelings about me. The way she'd needed to show how competent she was because I'd received all the attention for being sick, to being resentful that everything had fallen on her shoulders—especially when Mom had been between husbands.

Times like this, Mom still turned to Cassidy to fix things or to check on me. Cassidy never called otherwise.

"I don't need help. I wasn't lying about Liam being around. He's home and will come over if I get into trouble." After our last conversation, I had stuck to messaging him. Something about him and Laney going on a maybe date had left me raw. He was home for his ten-day stretch, and he hadn't stopped in either. Totally normal, but somehow this time felt different.

"So what's with you and his kids? I couldn't understand Mom."

Cassidy probably hadn't listened to half of what Mom had said. "I've been helping Liam's grandma with them because I want to. He's my friend and I like his kids, but he's moving soon, and Mom's afraid I'll get too attached to Eli and Owen."

"Is Liam only a friend?"

"Cassidy."

"What? It's an honest question."

"I'm—" I was about to say married, but that wasn't exactly true. The knife twist to the gut was there, but not as damaging as it usually was when I thought about my marital status. "I'm not on the market?"

"Are you asking me or telling me?"

"I'm just trying to stay off the couch every day."

"Sounds like you're past that point, Ms. Fix-it."

This was what it was like to talk to Cassidy. Others in my life had treated me like I was a precious figurine. Cassidy acted like I was a snow globe, breakable but still needing to be shaken up. She challenged me to do more than what was expected of me. When I was younger, talking to her made me defensive. Not every girl had to conquer the world before she could be soft and wear pink.

My world had crumbled. I didn't need to conquer it. I needed to rebuild it. And Cassidy's comments that made me question my worldview didn't unsettle me like they had before.

"It's too soon to date." Because the thought of dating gave me palpitations as strong as the thought of Liam dating.

"Is that what the widow's rule book says?"

"Cassidy!"

"I'm not sorry, Kennedy. You lower yourself to everyone's expectations. It's your default, and I get that you were sick for so long. But when you lost Derek, you were healthier than you'd ever been, yet you shattered so badly I thought the next time my phone rang I'd learn that you were gone too."

I pressed my hand to my lips to hold in my gasp as tears sprang into my eyes. Cassidy never talked about feelings. Never. For her to admit that she feared for me meant she'd been terrified.

"So, you need to quit defining your life by rules other people set."

That was what it felt like. Other people's unspoken rules about what I was capable of. "I just have to follow your rules?" I asked wryly.

"Yes. And I'm older, so you have to listen."

I smiled. "You can report to Mom that I'm fine."

"Don't be surprised if she and Benji show up. She could've handled home repairs or you watching Liam's kids. She can't handle both."

That was how weak Mom thought I was. "I've been fairly warned. They'll have a brand-new faucet to wash their hands with."

"Right on. Love ya, kid." That was her only endearment, but it wasn't as automatic as it used to be. I should call her more often. We didn't even message, other than wishing each other happy birthday. I had assumed she resented me. What if she thought I was okay on my own? That'd be one less person I had to prove it to.

I hung up, set the phone down, and took a deep breath. I gave my wedding ring another look. There was no rule book. I slipped the ring off and went into my bedroom. With the work I was doing, it made sense to take it off. Take some of the emotion out of it. There were no rules. I could put it back on after I was done with the bathroom.

It was time to turn the water on.

* * *

Liam

My phone rang. I pushed my stool away from the lawn mower I was changing the oil on and wiped my hands off. I hit answer, and the song I had playing through the speaker died down. "Kenny, you shower today?"

"Oh my God, Liam. There's water everywhere, and I don't know what to do. I tried to fix—"

"Whoa." I hated stopping her, but if she was in her house, an explanation could wait. "Where's the water coming from?"

"Under the sink. I tried to turn the water off to it and—"

"Okay, go downstairs." I rose and hit the button to close the shop doors before I stepped outside. Grandma Gin had taken the boys to lunch and a park so I could mow the lawn a couple hours quicker than it'd go with them around.

"What?"

"Shut off the water to the house. The valve is downstairs."

"What if that springs a leak?"

"Then we'll call a plumber, but I can guarantee that's been turned more than the one under your sink." Kenny's house was a starter home. Couples moved in, made some money, and found something bigger. Each time they moved, I'd made sure the water was turned off until the new owners moved in.

"I just used the one under the sink last weekend." Her voice was hitched. She must be going down the stairs. I hated sending her to the musty basement of that old house, but it had to be done.

"They're old, Kenny." I crossed the driveway to my pickup.

"Okay, I'm downstairs. Now what?"

"In the furnace room, you'll find a valve sticking out of the wall. Lefty loosey, righty tighty." I slid behind the wheel of my vehicle.

"Okay. Hold on."

I heard rustling, a small grunt that made me smile, then more shifting until she spoke again. "I think it worked."

More heavy breathing as she jogged up the stairs. As much as I loved hearing her sigh into the phone, I said, "I'm on my way."

"The door's unlocked."

The drive seemed like it took three times longer to get there, but I was antsy. I hadn't seen Kenny since I'd been back. Eli told me all about his speech and Owen told me stories of Kenny's sleepovers every day since I'd been back. The way I rolled my eyes each time Owen launched into a Kenny story, I'd think I was jealous they got sleepovers and I didn't.

I had wanted to see Kenny as soon as I'd gotten into town. But she'd watched the boys for days and had taken them to Eli's appointments. All while landing a new job and fixing up her place. And she'd offered to babysit so I could go on a date. Or at least meet a friend, but she probably would've offered if I'd had a bona fide date. Kenny was fully in the land of the living, and maybe I had felt a little left behind.

I pulled up to her place and hopped out. I didn't bother knocking. Since she wasn't in the kitchen, I headed for the bathroom. The light filtered into the hall.

I rounded the corner and stopped. Kenny was half buried under the sink, her butt in the air. It was the finest ass I'd seen. Round, firm, and swaying from side to side as she mopped up water with a towel.

My gaze was glued to her backside when she sat on her heels and popped her head out. I blinked and shook my head as if it could reorient blood back to my brain and away from my dick. "So, tell me again what happened."

She jumped and twisted around. My lips quirked. She was a mess. Half her shirt was soaked, part of it plastered against her breasts. I tried, hard, not to look at the way her nipples fought the constraints of the material.

Her appearance didn't change how my body was reacting. Her hair spilled out of a bun and stuck to her face from either the water or sweat. She was flushed and breathing heavily, as if it wasn't hard enough to keep my eyes above her neckline.

"I'm so glad you're here." She pushed off the floor and dumped the wet towels into the bathtub. Sticking her hands on her hips she gestured to the sink. "I fixed that damn thing. Remember I told you I did it? And then it started leaking again. So I thought I'd put in a new faucet, cuz now

I'm a superwoman or some shit. Only I fixed the toilet first. See?"

She flushed, then winced. "I forgot the water was off, so you can't witness the tank refill, but it will. And it won't leak."

I didn't fight my smile. This was rare Kenny. Rambling, flustered, and a little pissed off. "So high on home repairs, you turned the water off again under the sink, only it started leaking?"

She brushed the back of her wrist across her forehead. "That's about right. I noticed a small drip after I turned it back on last weekend, but I watched a video and it said to just tighten it. That worked, or so I thought."

"Sounds like you need to repair the stem."

"I haven't watched those videos yet." She crossed her arms. "I suppose that's another trip to the hardware store."

A tiny tendril of guilt snaked through my mind. I'd been sulking because she was being *superwoman or some shit.* Yet I was still the first one she ran to—because we were friends. I was wasting what time I had left in Coal Haven avoiding her. "I can run and get them. Then I'll walk you through rebuilding the shut-off valve."

"Where are the boys?"

"Grandma Gin took them to the park. I think she feels bad for being sick so long, like she has to earn her money."

"That sounds like her."

"Hey, uh..." My throat worked over my question. Why was it hard to ask her? A part of my brain suggested this was the reason I hadn't come to see Kenny. "I've been messaging Laney since I've been back. Any chance you can babysit tomorrow night?"

She blinked at me, her normally expressive dark brown eyes unreadable.

"I'll pay," I rushed to add. Was the awkwardness my

imagination? Was it that I was meeting Laney and neither Kenny nor I knew what to think of that? Or was it that I didn't want to date anyone and I didn't want to uncover the reason why? I was a single twenty-seven-year-old man. I should be wanting to get laid as much as possible, by as many women as possible. Yet, there was only one woman on my mind.

"No. Oh, no. Yeah, I can do it. I can even stay overnight, you know, so you don't have to worry about curfew like when you were a teen." She leaned in, her smile not like her normal ones that brightened the whole room. "And you don't need to pay me."

"Yeah. Okay. I don't think I'll be overnighting anywhere, but it'd be nice not to watch the clock." She nodded like it made sense. I nodded like it made sense. Nothing about her watching my kids while I was out with another woman made sense. "Well, I'll go grab the stem kits. We might as well replace both."

Her smile was stuck in place. "Sure. I'll keep sopping up water." She rolled her eyes. "It actually wasn't that bad. I panicked, sorry."

"Don't be. Happy to help." Happy to be here. With her.

"I'm happy you're helping too."

I was happy to forget the stilted babysitting talk. I fled the bathroom. I waited until I was parked in front of the hardware store to let Laney know we were on for tomorrow night. My fingers stalled over the buttons, and I swallowed hard.

I messaged Grandma Gin first to let her know that I wasn't home and why. Then I tapped out **Tomorrow night, Rattler's?** to Laney and hit send.

I stared at our message history for a moment before I tucked the phone away as if the last few minutes had never happened and climbed out of the truck. I didn't know what would come from going out with Laney. What was she looking for? Was I only looking to gauge her interest in my grandparents' place?

Right now, I wanted to prove that the erection I'd fought away in Kenny's bathroom was only because I hadn't gotten laid in a while and not because I found my best friend's widow incredibly sexy.

Six

KENNEDY

I dug through my purse, looking for a stray Tums. I'd never needed them before, but I'd picked them up this morning to fight the random stomachaches I'd been getting the last twenty-four hours.

Was I suddenly allergic to dairy or wheat? Was something about Lyme disease still affecting me? Was it stress? I started my new job in a little over a week. I was at the same school, but my role would be different. The kids would know me even if I'd never worked with them in their classrooms before.

That must be it. The summer job and how critical it would be to getting a full-time spot.

Liam's house loomed over me. He was in there. Waiting for me so he could go on a date. With Laney Granger.

Did she know I was watching his kids so she could go out with him?

Did it matter?

I got out, hitched my overnight bag over my shoulder, and went inside. Eli was racing a fire truck against Owen's police car across the floor. Nimbly stepping over the imaginary racetrack after getting hugs from them, I went to the living room. I was deciding between sitting on the couch or hovering like this was my first time at the house when Liam emerged from the hallway.

My breath whooshed out. His jeans were nicer than what he usually wore. Expertly faded in all the right spots. His long-sleeved dark blue shirt hugged his body and made his shoulders look wider. He'd styled his hair so most of it was brushed off his forehead except for one stubborn lock. And he smelled good. Like sunshine breaking through a dark forest.

"Kenny." His arms hung loosely at his sides, like he was facing a reckoning. "Thanks. You know. For coming."

I forced a bright smile, like I had yesterday when he'd asked about tonight. "Of course. What are friends for?"

He was my friend, but that didn't mean I was the only person in his life. I couldn't be the girl he helped all the time while sacrificing his own dating life.

I also had to remind myself to breathe again. Air in. Air out. He just...looked really good. He'd been in a tux at my wedding as Derek's best man, but other than joking that I'd done the impossible and gotten Liam into a tux, I hadn't dwelled on it.

I was dwelling now.

Liam nodded. I nodded.

He went to run a hand through his hair and stopped. He dropped his arm. "You sure it's okay that I don't know how long I'll be out?"

Neither of us mentioned Laney's reputation after Derek had broken up with her. She'd chewed through guys, making sure she'd earned all the small-town gossip. I had no idea what she was like now. All I knew was that if I were on a date with Liam tonight, I wouldn't want to be home by eleven.

"It's fine." I lifted my gym bag that had never seen the inside of a gym. "I'm prepared."

"Okay. I'll say good night to the boys." His expression flickered, but before it settled on an emotion I could identify, he disappeared into the kitchen.

I stood in my spot as he gave the kids hugs and went out the door. I gazed out the window as he drove away.

Owen popped his head into the living room. "Can I have a snack?"

His question got me to move my legs. "Yes. Then you two can help me make muffins for breakfast."

"You're staying over again?"

Activity in the kitchen stopped and then Eli appeared next to Owen. "Is Dad going to Williston?"

It took me a moment to understand what he asked. "No. He's...out. Didn't he tell you?"

Owen shrugged. Liam could've told them twenty times, but they were five and hadn't cared until now.

But an explanation didn't easily come to my lips. "I said I wanted to stay over again. Your dad is going out with...a friend." I winced, grateful for no other witnesses.

"Holden?" Owen asked.

"No," I said grimly, wanting this discussion over. It wasn't my place to talk to them about Liam's dating life. "What do you have for snacks?"

I shamelessly distracted them with food, baking, and bath time. But when those activities were done, I was again bombarded with the reality of why Liam wasn't home yet.

After the first two years of their lives, when Payton had moved them all over Williston, leaving them with friends and acquaintances, they thrived on a predictable routine.

Eli melted down at the bottom of the stairs. I'd been trying to herd them up the stairs for an hour. Owen ran through the house like I'd given him 5 Hour Energy instead of milk for supper.

Something was going on. I had slept over before, but that was when Liam was working. Their dad was home, but he wasn't *home*. "Would you feel better if you slept in your dad's bed tonight?"

Eli sniffled and rubbed his eyes. Both boys nodded.

"I'll lie with you until you go to sleep."

It didn't take more than one story before both kids were asleep. I lay in the dark and stared at the ceiling. I was on top of the comforter, a boy on each side under the blankets, but Liam's scent surrounded me. It was more delicate than his freshly showered smell, but it soaked into my clothes.

What was he doing right now?

Had he and Laney kissed yet?

Heat blazed in my belly. Jealousy?

No. I was lonely.

I rolled up so abruptly, I worried I'd awakened the kids. They shifted but stayed asleep.

I crawled off the end, wishing Liam's scent stayed in the bed. In the guest room, I undressed down to my underwear and threw on my nightshirt. I kept a pair of sweats on the nightstand in case the kids woke up in the night.

I got between the covers, which smelled less of Liam and his aftershave. I closed my eyes, but they popped back open. I flipped to my back. Restless. Unsatisfied. *Needy*.

Questions about Liam's night tried to rise in my mind, but I quashed them. They were replaced with the comment my sister had made about dating.

I had told her I wasn't ready. But I was in bed wishing I was on a date instead. My mind rebelled, but my body thought it was a fine idea. Heat pooled between my legs like it'd been doing so often lately. The more active I was, the more my body continued to remind me that I was a mature woman who got turned on. Who thought about sex. Who wondered what it would be like to sleep with someone other than—

I chewed on my lip. The first time I'd thought that, it'd felt scandalous. Sacrilegious. Like I was a cheater. Each time after only made it easier to ponder.

I shook my head, my hair brushing against the pillow. I could dwell on sex as much as I wanted in my own house. This was not the place.

But somehow it was easier here. I wasn't in my own bed. I wasn't in the home I'd shared with my husband. Here it was easier to think about what I felt and what it meant— and not have the answers. For once the answers didn't depend on someone else. They depended on me.

* * *

Liam

Laney's bare leg brushed mine again as she tilted on her barstool, closer to me. "And then Papa says that he went and called them. Canceled everything without consulting me." She rolled her eyes and took a pull of her White Claw.

"Pissed you off?"

"Fuck, yeah. Partnering with a genetics company for our seed bulls would ease a lot of expenses, and we could charge so much more a head."

Well, that finally answered my question. If she was worried about the finances of her family's ranch, then she wasn't looking to buy more land or land and a house.

We'd been here for hours. I didn't think I could feel my

ass anymore, but I couldn't bring myself to get up. Then we'd have to decide. Did I cut Laney loose and explain to her, and somehow to myself, that even though I hadn't been laid in months, jacking off in the shower like it was part of my routine after shaving, I wasn't interested in doing anything more than knuckle bumping her and going our separate ways?

The first part of the night had been safe territory. My story after graduation. She'd heard it differently from her parents, which was probably how the rumors blew through Coal Haven. I'd knocked Payton up, fucked my way through Williston while she was pregnant, and then she got sick of my shit and dumped the kids on my doorstep. Accurate, except for reversing our roles up to the part where she couldn't relinquish her rights fast enough once she'd realized I wasn't her free ride.

Laney said she'd moved to Texas and gone to college for marketing. She didn't say that she moved nearly as far away from her family as she could without jumping oceans. She also didn't comment on what she'd done after school. And there was one glaring detail I'd noticed about her, but if she wasn't bringing it up, neither was I.

She actually didn't talk about herself that much. She was a good listener, and that wasn't a trait I'd remembered.

She rested her elbow on the table, her body angled toward mine. "Sorry to hear about your grandpa."

"Didn't think I'd hear a Granger say that."

She flashed a grin. "Ma isn't nice to anyone. Don't take it personally. They've tried to hire on help, but she's not the type to be patient and teach someone how to do things her way. She just unleashes hell and storms away." Her mouth flattened. "Yet she's surprised at what happened. Go figure."

"How's Kane doing?" I asked about her brother with as

much sincerity as possible. Kane was a couple years older than me. Good at everything. Football. Women. Ranching. The whole town had been stunned to learn that he'd shot himself. Laney's parents would've preferred no one had learned what had happened, but between the ambulance, a small-town ER, and the Life Flight helicopter landing in the middle of the highway, it would've been impossible to keep it a secret.

"He's alive. Beyond that, anything else is a bonus, I guess, right?" She couldn't hide the stress wavering under her expression. "I mean, it was a miracle the bullet didn't penetrate his skull, but I guess it happens. Low caliber whatever. Anyway, he's got lingering...issues. He wants to do something besides ranching. I'll see to it he gets where he needs to be."

"How are you doing?"

Her quiet chuckle was full of scorn and resignation. "I'll tell you a secret." She tapped the bar between us. "And I'm only telling you because you and Derek were ride or die and he trusted you with everything." When I nodded, she licked her lips and glanced around. "If my life had been twenty-four-karat gold in Texas, I wouldn't have come home. But when Ma called to tell me about Kane, I dropped everything. It was then that I realized how little I really had. Ugh." She flicked the tab on her can. "I wish this was stronger than pond water."

"I'm sorry." The leg brush, the way she was sitting...I had worried she was hitting on me. But they hadn't been practiced calls for attention. She sounded like she wanted someone to talk to. I had Kenny. Who did she have?

"Well, I brought it on myself, so..."

"You know, when you first asked me out, I wasn't sure why. You were usually irritated that I took your time with Derek."

She put her head in her hand and swiveled close to me. "You thought I wanted to fuck you?"

Her purr should've gone straight to my groin. She was in tight white bottoms that stopped below her knees to show off defined calves. Her pink top fit her slender body and accentuated her breasts without showing one inch of cleavage.

"Honestly? I am quite a catch." I cocked a brow. She laughed, an easy sound that reassured me that she had been looking to mine an old acquaintance for more, but not to the point where clothes came off. "But I think you and I both want an ally in a town that seems to judge us harder than anyone else."

She snorted softly and straightened on her stool. "You win the lottery for being my only friend. Ever think that would've happened?"

She didn't clarify that I was her only friend in town. What had happened to her in Texas? Or had she been surrounded by fake people, and, when tragedy struck, they'd scattered?

"A lot has happened since we graduated that I wouldn't have imagined."

"Yeah," she said quietly. "You and me both."

Our hands weren't close together, but I stretched a pinky out and aimed it toward her left ring finger. A fading tan line circled the digit. "That bad?"

She held her hand out as if the ring were on it. She closed it into a fist and glanced around, like she was worried someone had noticed. "It wasn't as good as I thought."

Or she wouldn't be here alone.

Beckoning the bartender, she asked, "You want to stay and talk and have another? I really don't want to go home yet."

I wanted to go home. Kenny was there. The kids were

probably in bed. We could actually talk without being interrupted with arguments or show-and-tells.

"I'll have one more." Then I was leaving. Would Kenny still sleep over or head home? It'd be fun to have her there in the morning. Chat while I was making breakfast. Play with the kids together. Try out the chalk paint and see if I could get more items together for the farmers market.

"Is your sitter old enough to drive, or is your grandma watching them?"

"Kenny's staying over."

Laney stared at me. "*Kennedy?*"

I nodded.

"Staying at your house?"

I nodded again.

"Does she know you're out with me?"

"Why would she care?" I was asking more to see what Laney thought about Kenny all these years later.

"Because I dumped my soda all over her new winter jacket, which was actually an accident, but no one believed it. I backpack whacked her at least once; that wasn't completely an accident. And I told her that Derek likes girls with brains, not girls who can't decide which shoe to tie first without a man to tell them."

"Shit, Laney. You said that?" Kenny hadn't said a thing, but that was so her. Derek hadn't hated Laney, and Kenny wouldn't interfere with that. I hated that she might not have mentioned it because she believed what was said.

She cocked her head. "That was probably the tamest. I was seventeen and had just been dumped by the guy I'd been dating since before I got my period. Think I was a little pissed?" A new White Claw was delivered. She spun the can in a slow circle. "How's she doing?"

"Better."

"Papa said she fell off the face of the earth for a while. Must've been hard."

I couldn't get past my protectiveness toward Kenny. I wouldn't be the one spilling her business. "Well, I think she starts with tying her right shoe now, so…"

Laney laughed, but it died quickly. "I wish I could've come to the funeral."

I'd noticed she wasn't there, and at the time, I had thought that Derek had hurt her that bad. "Why didn't you?"

She wiggled her ring finger. "It's complicated."

Whatever that history had been, it had tempered Laney. I missed her fire.

"So you two are close, huh?"

I ducked my head. "She's never thought I was a piece of shit like the rest of the town."

Laney's lips lifted. "I didn't think you were, but I hated that Derek wanted to rebuild an engine with you instead of make out in my bedroom."

"Fair." That engine had never worked again. Grandpa had sold the car for scrap. "She's just a friend."

I didn't know why I felt the need to clarify. *Friend* wasn't a strong enough word for what Kenny meant to me, but I didn't know what else to call it.

"I'm sure you'll be there to vet the line of men that are going to appear when she starts dating again." She flashed a smile and tipped the can to her mouth.

A wildfire of rage swept through me, jacking up my pulse. I ground my teeth together. Men were not going to line up for Kenny, thinking she's an easy target.

Laney's smirk was the blasting hose of cold water I needed. "Just a friend," she muttered and took another drink.

Seven

KENNEDY

The creak of the front door got my attention. I hadn't been able to sleep. It was just after midnight. I sat up and waited for Liam to tiptoe down the hall.

"Liam," I whispered.

A big shadow stopped in front of my door. I'd left it open so I could hear the kids if they called for me or stumbled to the bathroom.

"You awake?" he asked quietly.

"Yes. The boys are in your bed."

Liam eased the door farther open. "Mind if I come in?"

I nodded, but it was too dark for him to see. "Not at all."

I was in only a T-shirt and underwear, but Liam had seen me when I hadn't showered for a week. I was clean, and it was dark.

He stepped in and closed the door behind him. "There,

we don't have to whisper," he said quietly and perched on the end of the bed, twisting toward me.

I took a deep breath but couldn't smell clingy perfume. "How was tonight?" My heart hammered waiting for the answer.

"It was different."

I wished I could see his face. What was his expression?

"Nothing happened, if that's what you're asking."

"Oh, no. It's none of my business." Not sleeping together on the first date didn't mean they weren't going to in the future. Would I offer to babysit for those too? I didn't want to.

"My business is your business. But no, it wasn't like that. Get this, she said I was her only friend."

"What?" Laney had been the alpha of the girls in her class, the hot girl that others were a little bit in fear of. Kids tried to be her friend, desperate to not be her enemy.

"Yeah, and maybe keep this to yourself, but she's divorced."

"*What?*"

I could see him nod in the dark. The old blinds on the window didn't let in much of the yard light. He was a big, comforting shadow. "Tan line where a wedding ring used to be. She's different, Kenny. Still Laney, but I could talk to her. I don't know if she regrets any of her behavior in high school, so maybe not that different. But she admitted to being young and pissed and jealous."

"That was obvious," I said dryly. "No one knows she was married?"

"I don't know. We all say Laney Granger's back home, unless she didn't change her name. She doesn't wear her ring. I barely noticed the tan line, but we were sitting next to each other at the bar at Rattler's."

"She didn't come to the funeral." I'd had the where-withal to notice, if only to be hurt on Derek's behalf.

"She didn't say why. Just said it was complicated." He fell quiet for a moment, and I soaked up the company. A big, dark house with two kids hadn't been scary. This was nice. Really nice. Talking in the dark like I had a partner again. "How'd the boys do tonight?"

"The change in routine upset them, I think. I finally suggested your bed. I didn't think they'd go willingly to theirs. Eli wouldn't go past the first step."

"Shit," Liam said softly. "I shouldn't have gone out. I'm sorry."

"You're allowed to have a life, Liam."

"Mm."

That little sound was more powerful in person. "I'm serious."

"I wasn't really feeling it."

"Feeling what?"

"Doing the whole dating thing. Anyway, it turned out not to be a date, and I got to know Laney again. She's not my only friend, but it's nice to have one more person on my side."

It turned out not to be a date.

My relief was short lived. One day it would be. Liam was too good of a catch to be alone. I didn't want him to be alone; I wanted him to be with me.

I sucked in a breath and shoved that thought out of my head. I reached for a different subject, any subject. "Did you talk to the farmers market director?"

Much safer territory. He'd messaged that he was going to try if he got a chance on one of his breaks. I'd forgotten to follow up, caught in my sinkcapades.

"No."

"Call them tomorrow."

He clamped a big hand over my ankle under the covers. "All right, Kenny. I'll call the director. For you."

Heat shot through my body. He wasn't even touching me skin on skin. "Thank you."

I lay back. I had to move, do something. His strength soaked through the fabric, and God, I missed that.

"I should get to bed," he said, his voice gruff. "They'll be up early."

"Where are you going to sleep?"

"I dunno. Maybe one of their beds? The couch? I don't dare touch Grandma Gin's room. She doesn't even let the boys inside."

He'd leave and take his heat and his strength and his company with him.

"Just sleep here."

"Here?" Disbelief resounded.

I tried to sound casual when inside my head I was screaming *I can't believe you said that!* "We're adults. I'm under the quilt. You can sleep over it."

He was quiet for a moment. This time I was grateful I couldn't see his expression. There was no reason to be embarrassed. I wasn't hitting on him. It made sense. His kids were close by, and it was late. He might wake them up when he was finding blankets for the couch.

It was a practical offer. He was fully dressed, and I was under blankets. A practical offer shouldn't make my heart race and my body flush with heat.

"All right," he said. "But if you snore, I'm kicking you out."

I swatted his rock-hard shoulder as he lay back. "I was here first."

His deep chuckle traveled through the bed right into my body. So much better than over the phone. My eyelids drifted shut and I stole a second of pleasure. I was a woman, and I appreciated a deep voice. That was all it was.

It didn't feel like that was all, but I fell asleep faster than I had in months.

* * *

Liam

I woke with the strongest erection of my life. It wasn't quite morning yet. I shifted, and my hip bumped against a solid body and the soft smell of roses and vanilla filled my nose.

Kenny. I was in bed with *Kenny*.

I rolled to my side to give her more room, but like a dumbass, I went the direction that ended up with me facing her. Weak. I was too weak to roll away from her.

A soft moan escaped her, and I opened my eyes. She was facing me, the blankets kicked off. The room was warm, thanks to the door being closed.

I could let her sleep, but this was... It was just... It was intimate. And I didn't know how she'd feel about it.

Because one thing had become startlingly clear.

I'd been lying to myself. I didn't know when it'd started, but it was recent. Sometime after the flush returned to Kenny's cheeks. When she started eating like she wanted to live again. When she laughed and talked to me in the dark in the middle of the night.

Kenny was important to me, but she had become so much more than a friend. She'd transitioned from a sweet and sexy friend straight into my dream girl. She was kind, great with my kids, and she respected me.

I had to wake her up and get her back under those covers. The last thing I would do was let her know I was interested in her. She was too important to me. I couldn't risk her shutting me out, appalled and upset that I would cross the line.

"Kenny?" I gently rubbed her shoulder.

"Mm? Liam?"

"You're not under the covers anymore."

"No." She let out a soft sigh. "I'm not."

We both remained still. She made the first move, pressing her hand against my chest, increasing the pulse in my nearly painful hard-on. "God, Liam. Lately, I've been... I'm just... I really miss—" Another moment of silence. "I just *need,* and I'm tired of it."

The ragged desperation in her voice was the only reason I rolled closer. "What do you need, Kenny?"

"I want to feel close to someone again."

I wanted to be the one close to her, but I shouldn't. *Someone* was not me. "Do you need me to leave?"

"No, Liam," she said, and her hand lifted to my cheek, her touch light. "I want you to stay."

Stunned, I didn't know what to say. I'd do anything for Kenny. But this wasn't cracking jokes or replacing a headlight in her car. We were at a precipice, and the next minute would determine the future of our friendship. "Kenny."

She flipped to her other side, her back pressed to my belly. I tensed. There would be no hiding what her ass was pressing against, yet she didn't jerk away, and neither did I. Her slight body fit perfectly with mine, and we stayed like that for a few moments. I was afraid to move, afraid to put my hand on her like I wanted to.

Her wiggles were slight, growing in strength, her legs bending and straightening. "Liam? Can you touch me?"

The vulnerability in her voice was enough motivation. "Where?"

She reached behind her and grabbed my hand. I held my

breath as she placed it over the sweltering apex of her thighs. Her grip weakened, like she was going to fling my arm away and run, but then it firmed.

I couldn't move. She was in the same place I was. Wanting this, but questioning how wrong was too wrong. "Are you... Are you sure?"

"Please? I did this the other night, and it was so lonely."

She'd gotten herself off? If it wasn't for the heartbreak in her words, I would've come right there in my jeans.

I whispered in her ear as I splayed my fingers wide. "Tell me to stop and I'll stop."

She writhed under my hand. "Just make me feel good. Make me feel whole."

That awkwardness over the phone when talking about my maybe date. The way it had been so unlike us. How she'd looked at me tonight before I'd left, her expression a mix of yearning and like she'd sipped a sour beverage. This attraction wasn't one sided. But it might be as sudden for her as it was for me. My concern for her didn't stop at the bedroom door.

"I've got you, Kenny."

I brushed a soft kiss over the shell of her ear. A shiver traced down her body. So responsive, it was humbling. Slowly, I slipped my hand under the waistband of her underwear. Her breath hitched. I didn't stall but every nerve was tensed to stop at her command. I wouldn't have noticed the slight stiffening of her body if she weren't pressed so close to me, but her hips rolled ever so slightly into my hand.

I slipped a finger through her soft curls and hit her wetness. I held in my groan. She was aching, needy, her wet heat inviting me and wrapping around me, coaxing me to stay. I'd never touched something so soft, so warm. I never wanted to leave.

All I did was slide my finger back and forth, coating it in

her juices, giving her time to get used to another hand besides her own. Giving her time to get used to having a hand down there at all. Giving me time to get used to who I held in my arms. Time to admit how badly I'd lied to myself about wanting this.

I stroked a small circle around her clit and she whimpered, her legs widening.

"I've got you," I murmured into her hair, soothing myself as much as her. Letting us both know that was natural, that she wasn't the only one who wanted to feel whole.

She didn't let go of my wrist, squeezing like she was just as conflicted as I was, probably more, her grip a clamp over my skin as I worked her. Her breathing quickened, her squirms grew more demanding, and I held her in the cocoon of my arms. I circled, alternating pressure depending on how she responded. Her hand held mine to her like she was afraid I'd pull away, or so she could fling me off when it got to be too much.

My erection pounded behind my jeans, but I had no intention of dealing with it. What was happening was more special, more critical, than any other intimate moment in my life. I never wanted this to change. Kenny in my house. Kenny in my bed. I wanted her as my friend, and more.

I didn't shut my eyes. As faint light dawned behind me through the window, I watched this woman I'd grown so close to in the last couple of months writhe.

"More," she whispered as if she was terrified to ask. I held her tighter, switched my thumb to her clit and slipped a finger through her wet heat, pushing inside.

I knew she'd needed more but had waited for her to ask, to tell me so I didn't record scratch this moment between us. I relished the ragged moan she pressed into the covers. So fucking tight. Once her body had something to clamp around, once she could ride me with her short hip thrusts, she blew apart. Rolling toward the covers, she smothered her face and cried out.

"I've got you, Kenny. Let it go. I've got you."

Warmth flooded my hand as she rode out her orgasm. I did nothing but hold her, staying true to my word.

As she panted through the final tremors, I withdrew my hand but rested it on top of her underwear. She wasn't going to feel abandoned by my arms.

Emotions whirled inside of me, mingling into a twist until there was a tornado wreaking havoc inside my chest. I'd gotten Kenny off. I'd touched her where I suspected only one man had touched her before.

Kenny had been off-limits since I'd met her. She was my best friend's girl, and we'd just been intimate. Worse than that, I wanted this again. I wanted her. I wanted *everything*.

What kind of ass did that make me? Should I have rolled away and pretended there was nothing between us? That we hadn't grown closer because we'd lost someone critical in our lives?

If I could go back in time, knowing the conflict that raged inside of me, I'd do it all over again. I'd be selfish and tell myself that I was here for her. That I was here for anything she wanted. I'd ignore the fact that Kenny had become the only woman in my life that I'd ever want to be with.

* * *

Kennedy

Strength and heat surrounded me. My shoulders ached from keeping quiet. I'd been all too aware that there were kids sleeping nearby, just like I'd been all too aware that it was Liam behind me and not my husband.

It wasn't Derek that held me. It wasn't Derek that had whispered to me in the dark. It wasn't Derek that I had fallen apart with. And at no point had I convinced myself it was.

Liam felt different. He smelled different. His voice and his touch were different. It was all wrong, yet so achingly right at the same time.

A hot tear leaked out of the corner of my eye. Then another. I ferociously blinked it away.

I wanted to push Liam off the bed and run. Terror raced through me at the thought of upsetting him until he went away too.

I couldn't lose Liam. But I'd lost my husband. And I'd just begged for his best friend to get me off.

I squeezed my eyes shut. A war raged in my head and in my heart.

What did I do? How did I act? How had blame and regret and relief piled up on my chest?

I clenched my legs together. Liam moved his hand to rest on my hip. A solid, heavy weight that warmed me more than any blanket.

I had no idea what to do.

The heat that had stoked my desire until I'd grabbed a man's hand and put it on me changed, morphed into an invisible choke hold.

"Are you okay?" His words were nothing more than a whisper, but his breath feathered my hair, reminding me about what was so startlingly clear. I was in his arms. He was curled around me like he was protecting me, but my brain was formulating an escape.

It'd be easy enough for him to tell Eli and Owen that he'd come back early and I'd gone home. No one knew that I was here. No one knew what had gone on between us.

My throat grew thick, and pressure built behind my eyes. Liam had seen me like no one else on earth had, but he wasn't witnessing me cry after he'd stroked out one of the quickest, most relentless orgasms I'd ever had.

It wasn't fair.

I rolled away from him and sat up.

It wasn't fair that he wasn't my husband, and it wasn't fair that he was so good at getting me off. There was no bumbling, no testing, no guessing. Liam had touched me and known exactly what to do.

It wasn't fair that I wanted more and I wanted it from him.

It wasn't fair that he was leaving too.

I fought back a sob. My mind was a mess, but my body wanted more. My clothes were piled on the end table. I threw the T-shirt I wore yesterday on over my nightshirt.

"Kenny, we should talk about this."

"Not right now, Liam." My voice was hard from holding back tears. Emotion built inside me until I feared I'd explode and take the county with me, but none of it had seeped into my words.

I stepped into my leggings. Fuck my socks. I wadded them up in my hands and stood. My legs quivered. I had Jell-O legs from a simple orgasm.

Simple? I huffed out a scornful laugh. This was the most complicated thing that had happened to me.

I lifted my overnight bag and rose. "I need to go."

"Kenny." His voice was soft, like I was a skittish pony primed to bolt.

I was exactly that. I opened the door, heedless of the noise it'd make, and beelined for my shoes by the front door.

His presence loomed behind me. He'd followed me out,

but I couldn't look at him. That didn't stop me from picturing his rumpled sexiness. The shirt he'd worn last night that made his eyes bright and teased me with how wide his shoulders were was probably untucked. His hands were likely stuck in his pockets as he watched me. Tall, straight. So very much here.

I managed to get one athletic shoe on a bare foot. I danced around, wrestling with the other. When that was done, I gripped the handle of the door. "I'm sorry."

The floor creaked as he took a step. I whipped open the door and swept down the porch stairs. I didn't pause when I got to my car. I started it and pulled away. From the corner of my eye, I saw him leaning in the open door. His strong body propped against the doorframe. Exactly how I'd pictured.

My hands clenched the wheel as I drove. I didn't go home right away. I went to the only place I could seek solace.

I parked in my usual spot and ignored the early morning chill that was still around this time of year. Dewy grass kissed my shoes as I strode to my target. Five headstones in, two to the right from the flare of the dirt path that allowed me to park without being in anyone's way.

I didn't stop until I was facing a reddish-brown granite headstone that read *Derek Barron*.

Dropping to my knees, tears streamed down my face. "Derek." My ragged cry cut through the early morning peace. "Something happened."

Eight

KENNEDY

I managed to stay off the couch.

Maybe I should've parked my ass on the couch. I'd been a cleaning fiend since I'd come home. The pile of junk in the garage had gotten rearranged. Again. Then I'd come inside and vacuumed. Swept the floor that didn't need sweeping. Scrubbed the already clean bathroom. Now I was pushing a mop around the tiny kitchen floor, wishing I had another thousand square feet to go over.

Fatigue dogged me, clinging to my eyelids, making them heavy. At first, I'd thought it was from the early morning teary confession at my husband's grave. Eventually, I realized that I hadn't gotten much sleep last night. I wasn't ready to think about why.

Liam had sent me a message. All it said was **Please call me when you're ready**.

Would I ever be ready to face him? What did he think of all this? How did he feel?

How did I feel? Would I have the guts to call him before he left town again?

I'd have to. I couldn't hide from him, and I'd promised I'd help with Eli's speech therapy.

If it weren't the weekend, I'd call my therapist.

The doorbell rang. I spun around, my heart clambering into my throat. Was he here?

I set the mop handle against the counter, but left the audiobook streaming over the Bluetooth speaker on the counter, and went for the door. The handle slid out and clattered on the floor. I yelped and jumped. Putting my hand to my chest, I rolled my eyes. I was a little strung out.

I peered out the little window in my door. Two heads were waiting on my doorstep and neither of them wore a navy-blue Drillers ball cap.

The disappointment was staggering. I ripped the door open, attempting not to scowl at the two people who were not Liam on my step.

I focused on the woman: my height, primly styled hair that was my color only highlighted within an inch of its life. "Mom?" I switched my gaze to the wiry man only a couple of inches taller than us. "Benji?"

I tried to be happy to see them. I tried. But today was a bad day, and they weren't here just to visit. Mom's expression said as much. Her eyes flared as she studied my appearance. Sweaty. Rumpled. My nightshirt was still under the shirt I'd worn yesterday, and dust from working in the garage was smeared over my leggings.

"I couldn't quit worrying about you being all by yourself and the house falling apart around you like another water heater incident." Mom embraced me before I had a chance to invite them inside. "I'm so sorry we couldn't come earlier. Benji had to work yesterday."

"I was busy yesterday," I mumbled. The water heater incident had been all on me. Water in the basement, and I'd ignored it until Bruce stopped by and noticed the smell. *The smell.* I had worried it was me. The relief that it was the basement was the first sign to myself that I had descended too far into my melancholy. The reality of my finances was the final tug up.

She released me, giving me a *sure you were busy* look and ushered me into my own house. "Benji brought his tools. I know Liam probably fixed the sink, but if there's a leaky faucet, there's probably more going on."

"I fixed it." With Liam's guidance. Liam and the way he towered over me, making me more self-conscious of being spread out beneath him on my bathroom floor than I'd ever been in my life. Liam and the way he'd held me, like I was a fragile treasure that he didn't want to let go of. Liam and the way I'd left him behind.

Benji followed us in and shut the door. "Did you call Thorson's? The faucet's not the only part that's old."

"No," was all I said. Thorson's was the plumbing company in town. The one I hadn't needed because of Liam.

Guilt crept in, not just for how I'd jetted on Liam, but for being so curt with Benji. He treated Cassidy and me like people, not like kids he had to be buddies with in order to win Mom's affections. But he also treated me like Mom did. He'd met her when I had started my treatment for Lyme, so I had still been ill and weak. He'd been with Mom when they'd dropped in to check on me throughout last year, and it had looked like nothing had changed since high school. Yet, when Mom thought I might need help, he'd grabbed his toolbox and left town with her.

"Hungry?" I asked, going to the mop. My stomach rumbled. I'd skipped breakfast. My appetite hadn't dared rear its head after all the other feelings I'd dealt with this morning.

"You look tired, dear." Mom fluffed my limp hair. I hadn't brushed it yet today either.

"I am tired." I shouldn't have admitted it. Mom had no idea why I was emotionally and physically exhausted, and I'd never tell her. She'd try to ban me from Liam forever just because he'd cost me some sleep.

"Why don't you lie down? Benji and I can run to the store and come up with an idea for supper."

"Are you staying overnight?" Please say no. I loved Mom, but her smothering wasn't going to make working through what had happened in the dark this morning any easier.

"No. I open the customer service desk tomorrow. But we'll make sure you're fed first. I'll freeze some leftovers."

Mom was an amazing cook. I didn't know how I would've survived after the funeral without all the hot dishes from her and my neighbors that were frozen for later.

She gave me a kiss on the forehead. "Get some rest. We've got it."

I succumbed to the mommying. She only wanted to take care of me, and, suddenly, I wanted to be taken care of. "Thanks."

I trudged to the bedroom. I'd shower when I woke up.

Have you showered yet?

I sank onto the mattress and eyed my phone on the nightstand. I wanted to talk to Liam, but I wished it could be like before. Before I'd gotten front-seat insight into how good it was with him, and before the guilt and shock had taken over.

I couldn't avoid him forever. I shouldn't. I had to figure out how I felt. What he thought. Was he feeling just as guilty? Had he done it out of pity? A sense of duty?

I've got you, Kenny. I've got you.

Mom and Benji weren't staying over, and Liam was leaving tomorrow afternoon. I sent a message.

Can you meet me at the park at 10 tomorrow? The boys can play and we can talk.

I stared at the screen, afraid of his answer. And after his message of **I'll be there** popped up, I stared at it longer.

That was done. I had until tomorrow to figure myself out. But I also had to wait until tomorrow before I knew whether I'd blown the closest friendship I'd ever had.

* * *

Liam

There she was. The boys piled out of the truck and sprinted toward Kenny. I took my time, soaking up her beauty and how she embraced the kids.

Her hair was pulled into a ponytail and a wide cloth headband circled her forehead. She smiled easily at the boys, and the knot inside me loosened, but just a hair.

My boots hit the grass of the lawn and muffled my steps. We weren't the only ones here. Two women sipped coffee on the other side of the park while their children played. I counted three others on the playground besides the two babies in the strollers by the women.

I knew why Kenny had chosen this park. I was leaving town today and didn't want to be away from my kids. They could play where we could see them, and they couldn't sneak up on us and accidentally hear what we were talking about.

I set a tea down by her. She used to drink coffee but had quit shortly after she'd broken down. First, I suspected she'd lacked the will to make coffee. Then I figured she wanted one less thing to be dependent on.

She rose, brushing her hands down her workout pants. They were leggings, but shorter and with brighter colors. Her shirt was some sort of athletic wear too. The material hugged her body. It wasn't appropriate to notice her lush curves and remember the way she'd felt against me, but I did.

She straightened as the kids ran to the digger toys in the sand pit next to the play equipment. Her soft brown eyes met mine. "Hey."

"Hey." I'd never been this nervous around a woman. Since I'd gotten her message, I had distracted myself as much as possible. I'd worked in the shop and taken the boys fishing.

There was nothing as distracting as trying not to be impaled with hooks randomly flying around and constantly adding new bait. Add in the thousand questions I fielded about fishing, the river, and how many fish I'd caught in my life, what kind they were, were they slimy, and did they taste good, and I was lucky to remember my own name by the time we'd gotten home.

"How are you doing?" I asked. My biggest worry was that she'd have some sort of setback. I knew she'd been seeing a therapist, and for most of that year when she didn't leave the house, I'd wondered what the hell good it had done. But I'd been grateful she had someone to turn to since she hadn't been doing much talking to me. I didn't want to return to that. I wanted her to be okay, and it seemed like a big ask, but I wanted her to be okay with us.

"Better." Her frank answer surprised me. She gestured to the picnic tables under the shelter. We'd be far away from everyone and still have full sight of the playground.

We sat on the bench of a picnic table, side by side, facing

out. Like buds. Not like two people about to have a personal conversation.

"I'm sorry I put you in that position," she said.

Dejection hung heavy on my shoulders. She regretted it. "I'm sorry I didn't stop us."

She gazed at me, but I couldn't meet her eyes. "Are you?"

I sensed fear and sincerity in her question. I could lie and say yes. Tell her that I shouldn't have been in the bed in the first place. Tell her that we're only friends. Confess some shit about how we were in the moment, that we weren't thinking.

But I'd never been good at keeping my mouth shut. "No, Kenny. I'm not sorry. Truth is..." This time I looked at her. The open and searching expression on her fresh face encouraged me to keep going. I didn't see regret. "I don't know what to call how I feel about you, but I passed the just-a-friend stage at some point before I stretched out in the bed next to you, only I tried to deny it."

Her eyes widened, then narrowed as she inspected me, but I kept going.

"And I'll be honest. Yes, I feel like shit, and I don't know what to think because you're my best friend's wife. I can't imagine what you're feeling like and that piles on the shit even more. Because the one thing I never, ever, want to do is hurt you, Kenny. You're just too important."

I ripped my gaze away. If I was going to get rejected, I'd have to hear it. I didn't have to see it too. Eli was dumping sand in Owen's hair. I should tell him to stop—the women across the playground were looking at us like I should tell him to stop—but it was early in the day. It wasn't like Owen was going to stay clean until his bath tonight. Might as well get dirty now.

"I talked to him," she said quietly.

I clenched my jaw. I had known that was where she was going as soon as she'd left my house. Running to Derek didn't bother me. It brought her comfort and helped ease her transition to living without him. That I was the reason for her visit and any tears ripped me apart inside.

"I told him everything." She twisted her hands together. "I don't even remember what I said. I probably looked like a rabid mess, sobbing in the wet grass, spilling out random confessions."

"I'm sorry."

"I'm not."

I whipped my head around to look at her.

This time she couldn't meet my gaze. "I crossed the just-a-friend point somewhere too. I think it was before you asked Laney out. That *bothered* me."

"Jesus, Kenny, if I'd known I wouldn't have—"

"No." She shook her head. "I think we would've both kept denying it." Her hands kept twisting. "Here's the thing though. I feel like crap. Like it was wrong. Like I'm a bad person. But once those initial feelings died down... I wanted to do it again. And that's fucked up."

"No. It's not." What was fucked up was hearing that she wanted to do it again, when she'd just told me how shitty she felt. She shouldn't have to be in that position.

"It is. And after spending hours lurking in Sexy, Young, and Widowed, I realized it's my world. This is my new normal. I'm going to want to be close to someone again, and it's going to feel shitty, and it's going to make me think things very few people can understand." When she met my gaze, her eyes were watery. "But I know that if you want to do it again, so do I. I really like you, Liam. I *really* like you."

Hearing that from another woman might mean a blush or a coy glance. I'd be thrilled or nervous. Kenny was near tears. The confession had taken a lot for her, yet she'd said it.

For me. To keep from making this harder for her and adding more pressure, I simplified my feelings. "I really like you too."

We sounded like two school kids confessing their crushes, but the subject underlying our words was anything but elementary. It was heavy. It was hard. It was ugly. But if I were going to stick with Kenny through this—and I wanted to—it was us.

Her hand twitched like she was going to reach over and squeeze mine. I almost made the move for her. The urge to touch her somehow, some way, was strong, but we were in public, and the boys had switched to the rocking toys closest to us. Eli was on a rhino and Owen's was a lion.

"So now what?" I asked. The ball was in her court, where it would always be. I just hoped to be in the same game with her.

"I'd like to keep doing what we're doing. I'll take Eli to his appointments. Bring Owen along and give Grandma Gin a break."

I nodded. It wasn't exactly dating or walking hand in hand, but I wouldn't lose her in my life. "Thank you." I hated having to be gone again for so long. The need for money paled when my presence at home would help in times like these.

"And...whatever we do, I'd like to keep it between us."

"I understand." I wasn't lying. A girl like Kenny would make me want to puff out my chest and show her off. This classy lady wanted me. Yet, I knew the shit she took for being my friend. If the people closest to her learned of my more-than-a-friend role in her life, she'd take the heat when she was still healing.

"I mean Grandma Gin. My mom and sister. Everyone," she tacked on softly.

"I won't tell anyone." It'd be hard not to tell Grandma

Gin. She'd be the only one I'd care to talk to, but this was new. A new level of emotion. New territory for me and Kenny. So, yeah. I'd keep my mouth shut. I brushed the backs of my fingers along her shoulder. Quick and discreet. "And, Kenny, we'll take it as slow as you need."

Her smile was small, but I counted it as a win. Her gaze darkened and swept over me, from my cap down my face, my torso, to the tips of my boots. "You're really sexy."

I think I blushed for the first time in my life.

I wasn't the only one. Pink dusted her cheeks. "I've always thought you were good-looking, but I can't help but notice it a lot lately. I thought I'd start by seeing if I was brave enough to tell you that."

She worried the corner of her lip. Anxiety or mortification? The Kenny I knew in high school wouldn't have been so bold. Derek had made all the moves. He'd told me things, but not everything. Enough to know that Kenny had been shy and inexperienced. She'd made him wait until she was close to her own high school graduation. And he'd gladly done it.

I hadn't lied to her. I felt like shit for what had happened between us, but once she'd admitted she had wanted it, my attitude immeasurably improved. This thing with Kenny wasn't superficial. I wasn't playing around when it came to her.

"I've been noticing you a lot more lately too." I leaned to the side. "Especially your ass."

"Liam." She peered at me. "Seriously?"

"Why would I be joking?"

"It's not like I've been working out. Though I'm going for a walk after this." She flipped her ponytail. "I might even run."

"Kennedy Lillian Barron. Outside?" She rolled her eyes,

but I nudged her with an elbow and pressed on. "Does your mother know?"

In high school, anything more than yoga and gentle stretching had made her mother fret about her joints and nerve pain.

"She surprised me with a visit yesterday. Her and Benji."

As if yesterday hadn't been hard enough to deal with for her. "How'd that go?"

"I napped. She cooked. Benji couldn't find anything to fix, so he went to the basement and swept and dusted."

"That was nice of him."

"Yeah. Overall, it was a nice visit."

I heard the sigh that she didn't let out. "But?"

Her mouth quirked as she rolled her eyes to me. "But... I wish she'd come and visit just because. I wish she'd quit treating me like I'll break."

"She worried about you for so long, she probably doesn't know how not to. Hard not to take it personally though."

"I didn't tell either of them I plan to replace the kitchen and bathroom floor." She sounded like that information would make them think she was loading what possessions she could fit into her car and going to join the circus.

I winced. She might prefer to join the circus once she saw how much more work some home renovations made. "If you mess up with the bathroom floor, you might as well install a new toilet. Remember when I had to do that in my house?"

Her grimace was adorable. "I might need help with that."

"I have no problem watching you work." The playful grin I shot her brought her flush back. Laughter sputtered out of her, and I chuckled. I was now free to think about the day she'd been tucked under her sink with her ass sticking out, but if I continued to do so, I wouldn't be able to stand. I wasn't going to sport an erection at the park. "The boys are going to ask what's for lunch in five minutes. Want to grab a bite with us?"

Her expression grew solemn. "I don't want to intrude on your day with the kids before you go."

Was she kidding? I enjoyed seeing her with my kids. "I want you to. They want you to. Do you want to?"

The corner of her mouth kicked up. "Yeah. I do."

Triumph beat through me—not because she was joining us only for lunch, but for the entire damn day. "Then I know the perfect little diner."

She chuckled. "Hmmm. That must be the only little diner in town. I love their fries."

I relaxed for the first time in days. I hadn't epically fucked up. Kenny said she wanted to be a part of something again. In her own time, she'd realize that she always had a place with me and the kids.

Nine

I banged out of Liam's house behind the boys. He'd returned only yesterday, and the first farmers market was tonight. We'd kept in touch the weeks he was gone, but my days had been blessedly busy. I had summer school in the morning. A couple afternoons a week, I took Eli to his therapy and read books to Owen in the waiting room or took him on a walk on the bike path beside the center.

At night, I ripped up old laminate. It was sweaty, dirty work. Between my home improvement project and the walks I took in the morning before work or with Owen, my muscles were peeking out where I hadn't seen them in, really, ever.

I'd been looking forward to mowing my lawn, but Bruce had done it while I was teaching one morning. I'd asked him not to again, tacked on that I liked lawn care and the smell of freshly cut grass.

He'd done it anyway. Claimed that since I was working

now, he wanted to make sure I didn't have additional stress. Sweet, but frustrating.

He didn't realize that being in my yard decompressed the stress. One of the local pastors and her husband next door chatted across the fence with me if we were outside at the same time. The elderly couple on the other side weren't moving around as well as when I'd last seen them, and the wife, Ruth, had invited me in for tea after I helped her put all her potted petunias back upright. The wind had knocked three pots into my yard. She'd recommended easy-to-care-for flowers when I'd admitted to being a newbie with plants. A seventh grader I'd taught two years ago lived down the street, and he'd stopped to tell me all about middle school.

I liked being outside and wanted more reasons to hang out in my yard.

Bruce must've noticed my efforts with the lawn. He razed through the beds with a small tiller and destroyed any annuals that might've bloomed again. I knew he was doing what he'd do for Willow—till up the beds before her annual greenhouse shopping spree, but I had different plans. Ruth had lived here long enough to know everyone's flowers. She named them and told me how to thin them out. She'd noticed they were thick last year, but I doubted they'd grow back after Bruce's attempts to help.

His heart was in the right place. That knowledge tempered my anger. But June was my new favorite month. It used to be December. Cozy with Christmas, giving presents, getting gifts from Derek. The last two Christmases had been brutal, and while I was optimistic for it this year, I was all in with June. Lawns were green, and rain showers washed away all the dirt that had collected over the snow in the winter.

Flowers bloomed in my neighbors' yards and around town. I couldn't afford to drop a ton of cash on new flowers. I guessed I'd have to see what I could do with a couple packets of seeds and Ruth's knowledge. Life was happening again, and I wanted to be out enjoying it.

After I had planted a few bucks' worth of wildflower seeds, I had started demolition on the kitchen floor, directing all my irritation toward old laminate.

I banished thoughts of my in-laws when I found Liam in the shop, loading his pickup. "Is that everything?"

We had slipped into our good-friends routine since he'd returned. We discussed our daily lives and the farmers market, but we hadn't done more than that. Our talk in the park hadn't hit reset, but we hadn't had the opportunity for more either. It wasn't the relief I'd expected. Part of the feelings I purged with the flooring might've been the needy desire that reignited every time I remembered the solid wall of him behind me and the way he seemed to know my body better than I did.

He put a hand on the tailgate, his expression pensive. "You think she'll be there?"

When Liam had learned that the director of the farmers market was his half sister, Isla Barron, I'd done the footwork for him to reserve the booth. No use starting drama if there didn't need to be any. I hadn't exactly lied, but I'd put my name down as the contact for Pewter Creations. He'd decided on the name, honoring his grandparents, but also as a play on the metalwork he offered. His items weren't pewter, but the locals—and, more importantly, his half sister—wouldn't initially put the two together.

Isla was a gentle soul as far as I'd heard. A little bit of a pampered princess, but sweet. She might not hinder Liam's ability to sell his wares, but Bruce and Cameron would. They were so close to successfully driving Liam away for good, they wouldn't give up. Liam hadn't listed the house yet. Since the Barrons were likely going to be the buyers, wanting the house in case Evander really did move home,

Grandma Gin had said to wait, just as long as it sold before winter. It'd give her more time to stomach *that family* living on the land she'd cared for most of her life.

"If she is, she'll be professional. And if your booth is a success, it'll make her look good. It'll be fine." It had to be fine. This was my idea. I didn't want to be the one who thrust Liam headlong into needless conflict. Maybe we should've tried a market in a different town. Spent the extra time and gas money to keep him from getting hurt.

He flipped his hat off and scratched his head as he considered the load in his pickup: the barstools, two individual stools made from the tractor seats, the end tables, and my favorite lamp. "I don't have much to offer."

"The evening market is only a couple of hours." I smiled at him. "Enough time to show off Pewter Creations."

"Enough time to get run out of town."

"There are plenty of non-Barrons here who will love to buy this stuff."

His dubious look made me wonder for the hundredth time if we were doing the right thing. I gave myself a mental shake. The right thing was letting others enjoy his beautiful work. It shouldn't matter what his last name was.

"This is your town too," I added stubbornly. For a little while longer.

The corner of his mouth lifted. "Then I guess it's time to show them that I'm a lot like my dad. Cocky and full of denial."

I barked out a laugh. The boys ran into the shop.

"Load up," Liam told them.

My nerves rose the closer to town we got. I'd packed sandwiches for the kids. Liam and I would eat after we got home. He didn't admit it, but his nerves would probably make any food taste like wood.

We didn't see Isla. The young supervisor we were

directed to was barely out of high school. When Liam gave her his name, she blinked. Hopefully, she was too young to realize Liam was *that* Barron.

After we were shown where to set up, he backed his pickup up to his booth. We got cursory glances from the rest of the sellers. The June market wasn't loaded with produce yet. I recognized a few people from around town. One booth had several varieties of lettuce and leafy greens that must have been herbs. The couple working the booth had two kids in elementary school, but I hadn't had them in class. Another booth displayed various soaps, many made from goat milk. There was a flavored-popcorn booth—all organic, and another with products made from honey: glosses, lotions, and balms.

We stood back and stared at the setup. Simple. Understated. Like Liam. He kept the pickup backed up to the booth and left the tailgate down. Other booths did the same, only the canvas overhang and walls hid the vehicles. We had a table and the iPad Liam set up for transactions.

"This is it," he murmured.

Engines buzzed around the park. We were on the opposite side from the playground where Liam and I had talked about us.

Us.

When we'd talked, I didn't think about him leaving. All I could think about was not losing him. But his plans to move hadn't changed. What did that mean for us? Was there enough of an us for him to stay? For me to leave?

Familiar panic clawed into my throat. The same as when I'd realized that if I couldn't afford the house, I'd have to move. That old house was my first real home. Mom had moved us around fairly regularly and Coal Haven was the first place to feel like home.

Bruce and Willow were like a second set of parents. Just

as smothering and overbearing, but they loved me. If Evander was home, maybe the guilt of leaving them wouldn't weigh so heavily. But I was getting ahead of myself. Liam and I had time to figure us out.

The first customers arrived. A teacher from the high school and his wife. She worked in another town. For the next two hours, shoppers wandered through, several stopping to admire Liam's work. Several people recognized Liam. A few knew his story. A few others gave his booth a wide berth as if they feared their livelihoods depended on it. If they worked at the gasification plant, then they probably did.

Charlotte Garcia stopped and discussed a custom job with Liam. She had several horseshoes that had been her dad's and she didn't want to throw them out. Liam discussed a few options, and they settled on a firepit. I had no idea how he got a firepit out of horseshoes, but she was thrilled, and because of her reaction, I was thrilled.

By ten minutes before close he'd sold the barstool set, both end tables he'd painted, and had an additional custom order to make before he left to go to Williston again.

Liam scanned his notes. "These will take some time. Good thing I decided not to finish fixing up the house. If Bruce wants it, he can deal with a new porch."

In this case, I sided with Liam. He lit up a lot more when he welded for fun and sold his work than when he thought of selling his childhood home.

Eli and Owen played in the back of the pickup, throwing large bouncy balls onto the lawn to see who could throw the farthest and who had the biggest bounce on the grass. Customers were dwindling as the last ten minutes ticked away.

Liam was chatting to the soy candle couple next to us

when I heard a man say, "You two need to knock it off before you hurt someone."

Liam's conversation cut off, and we both spun to find the source.

A tall man in a black suit with cowboy boots I hadn't seen since Derek's funeral glowered at the boys. Eli's face was scrunched up like he was figuring out why they were in trouble, and Owen's eyes were wide and fixed on the translucent blue ball in the man's hands.

Cameron Barron.

His hard amber eyes landed on Liam. His lip curled like an automatic response, but his gaze swept the market, probably afraid his wife, Naomi, would witness him breathing the same air as Liam.

I was afraid Naomi was close. That woman was toxic.

"William. I should've known they were yours." Cameron's mouth changed from a sneer to a flat line. He had this thing about calling Liam by his full name. Derek had once asked Liam why and Liam had recited Cameron's exact words. *It's the name your mother put on your birth certificate.* Insinuating he didn't agree about Liam's full name, especially his last name, and he'd had no say.

Liam took a few steps away from the pickup and lowered his voice so the boys wouldn't hear. "Yeah, you should've, but we all know why you don't. What did they supposedly do now?"

Cameron tossed the ball to Liam. "They were throwing this at people."

"Nuh-uh," Eli said. "He just walked by. It hit his boots." The lisp made Cameron wince. If Eli wasn't in the bed of the pickup, I'd put a protective arm around him.

"He should've seen me," Cameron said succinctly. "And he shouldn't have thrown the ball."

"It was Owen," Eli countered.

Cameron didn't look at him. "Perhaps you should be teaching your kids how to take responsibility for their mistakes."

Liam lifted a brow. "Pretty lofty standards for a guy who could never do it."

His father's face flushed. "You and your—" His hostile gaze slid toward me. Animosity drained and his eyes widened. "Kennedy?"

"Hi." I stuffed my hands into the back pockets of my shorts as if I could pretend this was a nice normal night and my worst fear of what would happen wasn't occurring this very minute.

The sneer returned and was aimed at Liam. "I heard you were using her for free childcare."

"That's me." Liam spoke while I grasped for words to defend myself. "A user like my dad. Goodbye. I'll tell Grandma Gin you said hi."

Cameron's eye twitched. The boys were quiet, but sensing the hostility between the two men wasn't hard. I would have been surprised if the whole market wasn't staring at us.

"Don't come back here, William. Sell your garbage somewhere else. Isla has worked hard to build this up. She doesn't need trouble." He spun on the heel of his leather boot and strode off. I spotted Isla at the far end of the market, talking to another vendor. She lifted her gaze, spotted her dad, read his expression, then found us. Her mouth formed an O and she rushed to her dad.

She'd found out and told him? I'd expected better of her, but then saying hi to someone at family picnics didn't mean I knew her.

"Who was that?" Owen asked, incensed that the man had interrupted his good time.

"No one." Liam flipped the case on his iPad closed and

tossed it into the cab of the pickup. "Just a mean man with nothing better to do."

His jaw was set as he started loading the items that didn't sell into the back of his pickup. The soy candle couple watched us, their gazes full of sympathy. If they hadn't known before, they'd figured out who Liam was to the great Cameron Barron.

I got the boys loaded and buckled by the time Liam was done. The supervisor was wandering by, oblivious to the drama. Liam thanked her for the booth. Her surprise seemed genuine when he canceled the rest of his reservations.

"Was there something wrong?" she asked.

"No," he said grimly. "But if I keep coming, then there will be."

We packed what was left and drove away.

"I'm sorry," I said quietly.

"Nothing you did."

I had done everything. I'd encouraged him to come. I'd used my name instead of his. Putting his name down might've prevented the confrontation from being public. "It shouldn't be like this."

"I shouldn't have thought it'd be any different."

He was talented. He had a good eye for design and the creativity needed to do work that wasn't for an oil field. I hated that the Barrons thought Liam was using me. He was the most generous man I'd ever known. But a family that hadn't acknowledged him since before birth and pretended as if he and his kids didn't exist wouldn't understand anyway.

* * *

Liam

. . .

The drive to my place was quiet. The boys sensed something was wrong. I didn't want Kenny to feel bad. The only person I blamed was Cameron.

Once I'd become a father, his behavior had seemed more bizarre. My situation hadn't been identical, but there'd been similarities. My mom had latched on to him, gotten big ideas in her head. Thought she was what he'd be willing to leave his family for.

As the only child of a couple who struggled to get into the black with ranching, my mom had envied Cameron's wealth. Third generation oil money. Land. Siblings with land. A high-paying job handed to him because of the status of his last name. His wife drove a Lexus. My mom had wanted to be Naomi. She'd wanted to be in a family that didn't have to mend clothes ten times before they purchased new ones. She'd wanted to be the wife that drove to Minneapolis to shop. The wife who'd had the entire refinery lighted for her when she'd given birth to Stetson.

Then Cameron had showed her how he'd really felt. Hell, maybe he'd been remorseful. Maybe his affair with Mom had really been a bad decision in an overly stressful time of his life. But the way he'd handled it! A life growing up as the revered oldest, getting whatever he'd wanted, hadn't made him sympathetic to the emotions of others—especially when he'd been the one to cause the hurt.

With Mom gone, he had no one else to blame. No one to shove a finger at and claim *look what she made me do*. But I'd been around. And I'd gotten older. Worse, I had his height, his build, and the same brown in my hazel eyes.

I also had my mother's tendency to not care what people thought...or at least pretend like I didn't. I had my maternal grandparents' tenacity. When times got tough, I tucked my chin down and barreled forward. But I didn't have Cameron's money. And I didn't have a huge family backing me.

I'd do anything for my kids. Was that what Cameron was doing? Shunning me so thoroughly to protect the feelings of his kids, Stetson and Isla? Was he creating the illusion that an affair had never happened and his marriage to their mother was faultless, and whenever he saw me that illusion was shattered like the windshield my mom had flown through?

I wouldn't feel empathy for him. He was a selfish asshole, no matter what his motivation was.

When I reached home, I backed up to the shop and stared at the house. The place where I'd grown up. The property and the land that Grandma Gin didn't want to sell. The first place my kids experienced real stability and unconditional love. Eli and Owen had been two when I'd moved them here and started commuting. They'd been with me for a few months before that as we'd crammed into the room I rented.

I used to have to drop them off at day care an hour before my shift started so I could sit on the floor with them while they had a chance to calm down. Now, they loved having their own bedroom to share in a house that was always the same, and Grandma Gin was the perfect mix of unconditional love and consistent discipline. *Say thank you and please. Pick up the toys on the floor before you brush your teeth.* Bedtime was the same every night.

Coal Haven had driven me away, but it had become a sanctuary for my kids. Was I really prepared to do everything for them?

"I'll open the shop door." Kenny grabbed the keys from my console and slipped out. She probably thought I needed a moment to calm down. I did need some time, but I was calm as hell.

"What's for supper, Daddy?" Owen asked.

"We already ate, remember?" Yeah, the evening had felt that long for me too. "But you can have a snack after I'm done unloading."

They both piled out and ran to the house. Once the shop door was open far enough to get the pickup in, I finished backing in. I'd just leave it inside tonight.

Kenny had the tailgate down before I was out. "I can't believe this lamp didn't sell. It really is gorgeous."

I had liked it before, but Kenny had bought a translucent cream lampshade that allowed the twist of the lamp to become the centerpiece.

I had regretted loading it earlier and had been relieved when interested shoppers had moved on. "That's because it's yours."

She smiled while her fingers danced along the shade. She glanced at me and did a double take. "Are you serious?"

"Of course."

"I can't take this. You can sell it and put it in your Grandma Gin fund."

"And if Grandma Gin found out I sold it for fifty bucks to save for her when you really liked it? You want to get me into trouble?"

"Liam, I..." She eyed the lamp, her brow furrowing. "This is the first thing I've brought home that's just...mine."

It'd never be hers and Derek's. Just hers. She hadn't bought more than groceries and the necessities since he'd died. The faucet was for the house. All the home improvements were more about the activity and not so much the new material she used for repairs.

"I can hang on to it until you're ready to take it home," I offered.

She hugged the lamp to her, the shade cocking up against her head. "No. It's time. I haven't even bought new underwear." Pink flushed her cheeks. "TMI. I'll put this in my car. Be right back."

I'd finished unloading by the time she returned.

She twisted her hands together as she approached me. "I know I apologized before, but I'm so sorry about tonight."

"I'll never blame anyone else for the way they treat me, Kenny."

"I know, but—"

I put my fingers on her soft lips. We hadn't kissed yet, but I dreamed of it every night. "No, I've made a decision. I'm not letting them drive my boys from their home. I'm going to talk to Grandma Gin. Then I'm going to the bank and having a long chat. And then I'll call the school."

She blinked her big brown eyes. I'd been so sure of my decision, but her reaction meant everything to me. Yes, I wanted to stay for her too. I wasn't wasting more time working in a different town away from everyone I cared about. There had to be a job near Coal Haven but out of Cameron's reach.

She didn't answer for so long, nerves knotted my stomach. "What do you think? Seriously? Think the boys will just relive what I went through? Think this decision is stupid and impulsive and maybe I'm just trying to piss off my dad? Tell it to me straight, Kenny."

She twined her arms around my neck and drew my head down to hers. Was I imagining this?

Our lips touched, tentatively at first, then she increased the pressure. I let her lead, too afraid she'd stop. Until she opened for me. I had to know what she tasted like. I licked into her mouth, and she timidly met my tongue, stroking it like she was exploring. I gripped her waist, flaring my fingers to touch as much of her as possible. Lush flesh under my hands. A warm mouth on mine.

All too soon, she was pulling away, gazing at me from hooded eyes, her pupils fathomless.

"Was that to shut me up?" I asked, my voice husky. My body was rock hard from head to toe. This woman wound me up tight in all the best ways. "Was that your way of telling me it's an awful decision?"

She pulled her red lip between white teeth. "I wanted to know what it was like to kiss you and thought celebrating you sticking around Coal Haven was a good time to find out."

A slow grin spread across my face. I probably looked like a giddy turned-on clown. "And? How was kissing me?"

She ran her teeth across her lower lip again. "I mean, I think I need to experiment more before I know for sure, and it sounds like we're going to get more time together."

A soft chuckle puffed out of me. I was drawing her closer, dropping my head down, when the screen door banged.

We stepped apart.

The backs of my legs hit the bumper. "They're waiting for a snack."

"Later, then?" she asked, almost shyly.

"Promise." A day I thought was ending like shit had turned out to be one I'd never forget for all the right reasons.

Ten

KENNEDY

I was sweeping the last remnants of my kitchen floor demolition when there was a knock at the door.

Liam hadn't mentioned coming over this early. He was going to have a long talk with Grandma Gin and then take a hard look at his income and what jobs were available in the area. After the kids had gone to bed last night, we'd brainstormed all the places welders would work around Coal Haven and the surrounding towns. I gave him the information to register the kids at the school. And we'd made out. A lot. My body had wanted more. And *maybe* I was mentally ready, but it'd been *a day* for Liam and he hadn't needed to deal with my reaction to sex with him, whatever it would be.

The knock sounded again. I kept my audiobook about managing money and investing running. I didn't need to know about maintaining a budget. Me and a budget had become quite friendly. If I missed some of this chapter, that was fine. As I walked to the door, I admired the floor. It was cleared down to the subfloor and clean. I'd ripped out the laminate and hauled out the disgusting pad underneath.

I opened the door and smiled, managing to hold it in place when I saw it wasn't Liam on the other side. I should've known. When he was bringing the kids, each boy had to have their turn knocking or ringing the doorbell.

"Bruce, hi. What brings you by?"

It was Saturday. Give Cameron one day to tattle to his brother that I was hanging around Liam, and here was Bruce.

"I talked to my brother, and we're worried about you."

I refrained from rolling my eyes, but anxiety burned in my gut. "Why? I'm doing really well." I didn't wake up every morning wondering how I was going to make it through the day. Even more, I was productive. I was hopeful. I was happier than I thought I would ever be again.

"We know how Liam can be."

I cocked my head, confused that he couldn't see his ignorance. "Do you?"

Bruce's gaze flickered over my shoulder. "Can I come in?"

The fatherly concern in his eyes made it hard to say no. I knew my father's name and that he wanted nothing to do with me beyond paying the child support he'd resented. Benji wasn't exactly a father figure per se, but a guy who supported me because he loved my mother.

Bruce stepped inside, and I shut the door. He stared at my floor. How could I keep him from interfering with my remodeling?

I twisted my hands together. This was my current pride and joy. I went to bed sore and worn out, but with a sense of accomplishment. The new wood planking I planned to install was stacked in the garage. Installation seemed simple enough, and I planned to find out this weekend.

"What's this?" he asked.

I went to where I'd set my phone on the counter and shut off the audiobook. "I'm making some updates. It's brighter in here already, don't you think?"

"You're doing this?" The surprise wasn't unexpected, but the dismay was.

I nodded and went to twist the spot where my wedding ring had been. I hadn't put it back on, but I still looked at it sitting in its black velvet jewelry box every day. I covered the bare spot with my other hand. I didn't want Bruce to notice while I was still getting used to going without. "It's been fun." More fun than messing with the plumbing. I didn't have to worry about a flood.

His mouth tightened in a line. "This is what I'm talking about. That boy wants you to work for him—for free, but he can't help you do this."

"He helps when I need it." I stressed the last part of that statement.

Bruce lifted his brows. A move Derek used to do when he wanted me to elaborate. I'd found it endearing with him. With his father, it bordered on maddening. Why did I have to explain?

But I did. "I call him with any questions. He's happy to help. I want to do this."

"You don't need to do it alone though."

"Well"—I kept a light tone—"I don't want someone to come in and take over."

His gaze softened with more than a touch of sadness. Oh, crap. I made him feel bad. "It's supposed to rain tonight. Are you sure I can't help you mow?"

The yearning in his voice sapped the willfulness out of me. Taking care of my lawn was his way of coping. "How about you mow, and I'll keep going with the flooring? I've been watching videos, and I'm excited to try what I've learned."

A beat of relief went through his expression. His gaze landed on the floor, and I wanted to shift to the side to block his view. It was just a floor, but I was high on the sense of accomplishment. I couldn't wait to walk into the house, see a pristine floor, and know that I did it.

His expression hardened into resolve and I was afraid to know about what. "I can let Willow know that I won't be home 'til later."

I wanted to avoid the next part, but I wasn't going to be home all day either. "Actually, I was just going to shower and then I was going out." I forced myself to say the rest. I shouldn't have to hide everything about my life. "With Liam and the boys. They're taking me fishing." I'd hide only the part where I was taking the monumental step of moving on and it was with Liam.

"He wants you to keep the boys from hurting themselves while he messes around." His tone was matter of fact.

I couldn't keep the sigh out of my voice. "He's a good dad, Bruce." I left the *better than his own* out.

Bruce grunted. "Ginny's the one raising them."

"Helping doesn't mean someone has to do everything." Hint, hint.

Bruce leveled a flat stare. "He'd have to be here in order to make me think that Ginny isn't doing everything."

A rare moment of defiance straightened my spine. "Then too bad the circumstances of his birth prevented him from finding a job around here."

"It's never been about his birth, Kennedy. It's about how he conducts himself." I opened my mouth, but he put a hand up and that gentle expression formed, the one where I had to double-check that I was twenty-six and not six. "He's an adult now, yes. But he's also a single dad. He chased the mom away and he's making his grandmother raise his kids. As for the job hunt when he was younger, well, no one wanted to hire the welder that burned down his barn."

"It was an—"

"Kennedy." That placating tone ignited a fire I hadn't known existed, but I wasn't sure how to deal with it. "I know you think the way you do because of my son. I take responsibility for that."

I know Liam didn't want his grandpa blamed, but it wasn't his fault people put two and two together and came up with five instead. "Bruce—"

"Derek had a blind spot a mile wide when it came to that kid. I'm sure it's cuz we were strict and the Pewters weren't." I almost laughed. How could he know Grandma Gin and think she was a pushover? "But I'd like to save you from the headache a guy like Liam can cause. You've been through enough."

I'd been through enough of this conversation. I pressed my fingers against my temples. I was about to reiterate how Liam had been nothing but supportive when Bruce noticed what I was doing.

"Dammit, Kennedy, I'm sorry." Bruce shoved a hand through his graying hair, his expression distraught. "I didn't mean to upset you. It's just that I'd never forgive myself if you got hurt and I didn't do anything. Without Derek around, I just want to—" He made a strangled sound and his eyes misted over.

I'd woken up full of energy and optimism. Now I was tired, and I didn't want to make Bruce feel worse, but I wanted him to leave. The fastest way to achieve that would be to let him do what he'd come here to do. "Thanks for doing the lawn. I need to clean up and maybe lie down for a while."

I regretted the white lie, but if he thought I was resting, he'd be quick and go.

"I'll make it quick. You lie down," he said in a fatherly tone. Bruce might be a little overbearing, a bit old-fashioned, and too unthinking when it came to what Cameron demanded, but he was the closest thing to a father I had.

"Thanks, Bruce. Tell Willow hi."

He was on the way to the door when he stopped. "She'd like to invite you over for supper. When's a good night?"

This was what I realized was missing with my relationship with my mother. A simple invite over. "How about Wednesday?"

"Wednesday it is. Get some rest."

I went to the bedroom to message Liam and ask if we could postpone for an hour to give Bruce time to clear out. When it came to Bruce's opinion of Liam, we couldn't agree to disagree forever, but I couldn't tackle the argument when Bruce's grief was still so acute.

* * *

Liam

The steady lap of the water against the shore sank into my bones, relaxing my tight muscles. I had hiked us around the campsites of Hazen Bay on the edge of Lake Sakakawea. We set up our fishing area where there was enough sand for the boys to play in and find the occasional mussel shell and large rocks for them to climb but no drop-offs. The water was shallow, so they could wade on the edge when they got bored with watching their bobber. They were like little tops, twirling from spot to spot. Kenny was in a folding camp chair, holding the fishing rod for Owen. I was knotting a hook onto Eli's line for the third time since we'd gotten here. When it was secure, I helped him cast, then he ran to where Owen was digging for worms.

I squatted next to Kenny, my gaze brushing along the satiny skin of her bare legs. "Eli's appointment is at two on Thursday, right?"

"Yes. Want me to come with?"

The corner of my mouth kicked up. "I won't say no, but it has nothing to do with thinking I can't do it myself."

"I know." Her shy smile confirmed she wanted to go with me just because. Never in my life had I gotten gooey over a woman, but here I was, insides turned to mush, ready to hand my balls over on a silver platter.

The sun peeked out from behind a cloud. Her deep brown eyes brightened and golden highlights scattered across her hair. She wore a tank top that covered as much as a T-shirt except for the upper parts of her arms. My fingers twitched to stroke along her flesh, but the kids were nearby.

If we weren't hiding our intimacy, what would I do? I didn't have much experience with long-term dating. My time with Payton was a drama-filled roller coaster, and we'd hung out at the bar a lot when we weren't fucking. Watching movies and going fishing was a level of intimacy I hadn't attained with a woman. I enjoyed it and wanted more. But I'd have to settle with touching her in private. Kenny didn't want to handle the emotions of others if they learned about us, but I also didn't want to upturn the stability my kids had finally found by confusing them about Kenny's role in our life.

Didn't mean I didn't think about all the ways I wanted to touch her in private.

I sat in the chair next to her before I did something foolish like steal a kiss. I slowly reeled in Eli's line and tried to forget how yielding her lips had been under mine. Casting, I didn't worry about Eli getting upset that he'd missed his chance. He had dug out his truck, and Owen was making a racetrack around a large boulder. They might be interested in fishing again in the next twenty minutes, but building a dirt jump for the toy truck was more important right now.

"Did you take pictures of the floor?" I asked. I'd had my phone ready in case she called with questions. She hadn't. I'd almost called her just to hear her voice, but I didn't want to seem like another overpowering force in her life.

"No, I forgot." She started reeling Owen's line in, her gaze on the bobber in the water. "Bruce stopped by."

I nodded, grinding my teeth together before I forced my jaws apart. "The hour delay?"

"He insisted on mowing. I was hoping to get in a workout when I did it tomorrow."

"Did you tell him that?"

"Not the workout part. He said it was supposed to rain tonight, and then he saw the kitchen and said he'd install the flooring too. So I told him I had a headache and needed to lie down."

Kenny wanted to think the best of him, but I didn't get my stubbornness solely from my mom's side. "He's going to be back tomorrow to do the floor."

"I doubt it." She squinted at me. "You think?"

I jerked the rod up to keep the hook from catching in the pebbles and weeds by the shore. "He thinks you need to be taken care of. And I'm sure it keeps him from feeling guilty about Derek."

"I agree that's part of it, but he and Willow welcomed me into the family. I'm like a daughter to him." She set the rod down and slumped in the chair. "Willow's a lot like Mom. I know how to handle her. But with Bruce... I don't know. I feel bad even complaining. He's done so much."

"Relax, Kenny. It's me, remember? Having a Barron as a father—or even a father figure—isn't easy." We were leaning close to each other, our heads tilted in, and it had nothing to do with keeping the kids from hearing us. I couldn't help wanting to be close to her. "Evander left home after graduation for a reason, and Derek always complained about the pressure his dad put on him to take over the ranch."

Derek had used Kenny as an excuse to create distance between himself and his parents as much as Kenny had used Derek to keep her mother from being a helicopter mom into adulthood. Love had been the biggest motivator in their relationship, but they each had wanted to claim their own version of happiness. I'd been more than happy to see them do it. But the problems between Derek and Bruce had gone unresolved, and Bruce was going to try to do what he did best—control his loved ones.

She brushed her fingers along my arm. An innocent touch with a hint of promise that made me want to groan. I met her gaze, her need reflecting my own. "Enough about my in-laws. How'd the talk with Grandma Gin go?"

"Short of her slapping me upside the head and asking what took me so long to realize that I had as much right to a happy life in Coal Haven as the rest of my family, it went well." I shared a wry smile with Kenny, grateful for the warmth and acceptance. The two people I cared about the most in the world wanted me to stay. "She did ask what changed my mind."

"You told her about the farmers market?" Kenny asked, seemingly clueless that she was any part of my motivation. It'd stay that way. This thing between us was so new, I didn't want to scare her off.

"Yes. Told her I realized I'd rerouted my life because of my dad, and my kids shouldn't have to do the same."

"I'm proud of you, Liam."

My chest damn near puffed out. But I lowered my voice to a purr. "And you find me really sexy, right?"

She laughed, tipping her head back, making me wish I could nibble along her slender neck. "News flash: most women find you sexy. But yes, I do."

"Good. Cuz you're sexy as hell."

Surprise lifted her brows. "I'm not—"

I silenced her with a hot look. She bit her lip. Owen rushed over. "Did I catch anything, Kenny?"

Her cheeks were flushed when she switched her gaze to my son. "Not yet. Should we cast again?"

She stole another glance, one that said she wanted me to prove what I meant later. I'd do exactly that.

Eleven

KENNEDY

I stayed on the couch while Liam tucked the kids into bed. I had given each of them a hug. I usually loved getting them to bed and witnessing their wily minds slowing down for the night, but I'd helped the other night. If I did it too often, they might start to ask questions Liam and I weren't ready to answer. Instead, I had taken our mint chip ice cream bowls to the kitchen and loaded the dishwasher before waiting in the living room like a nervous date.

The stairs creaked as he came down. When his gaze landed on me, he chuckled. "They were both asleep by the time the first story was done. I think we need to go fishing every day."

"I'm not sure it was fishing as much as racing up and down the shore for hours with their toy trucks."

Liam and I had given up with the rods, only putting a line in the water when a boy popped over wanting to cast.

Eli was disappointed they couldn't teach me how to fillet a fish, but I was okay not knowing what the guts of my food looked like.

Liam sank onto the couch next to me. I continued flipping through shows on TV, enjoying the heat radiating off his body. Having him sit near enough that I could curl my legs to the side and tuck my feet close to him was a different sort of intimate. The thought of kissing him again sent my belly tumbling, but cuddling also ignited my nerves.

"What do you feel like watching?" I clicked through more options, trying to be casual. This wasn't me testing the waters of touching and sex. This was us being a couple. This was me wondering if I was moving too fast or too slow into another relationship.

I concentrated on the screen, flipping through action movies. Horror movies were definitely a no. There were a lot of young adult series options, but Liam wouldn't be interested in those. I stayed away from romance. I had my own to weather.

"I feel like taking you to the bedroom and making out." My startled gaze jumped to him. He glanced at me out of the corner of his eye, quirking a brow. He hadn't been joking. "No pressure, Kenny."

Heat flooded my body, but my flight response had kicked in at the word *bedroom*. I had thought I was ready for more, but thanks to my toes tucked under his powerful thigh, I was back in uncertain territory. Having sex with Liam meant I was navigating new territory and he was there to support me. We'd talked about moving beyond friendship status, and we'd done things that were more than handshakes, but this relationship was blooming faster than I had expected. My mind had a hard time keeping up.

I licked my bottom lip. Neither of us wanted a repeat of me fleeing his house. "I want to be ready for more, but I'm not sure I'm ready for everything." Sex had never been casual in my life, and this thing between us was anything but superficial. I didn't want to mess it up because all of me wasn't on the same page.

"We're only doing what you're comfortable with." He dropped his hand onto my calf, and my body lit up like the night sky. "We can watch a show too."

The choice between watching a show and making out with Liam was absurd. Who wouldn't want to be held by him? Yet, I was tempted to tell him that I could find something on TV we'd both enjoy.

He gave me time. The internal struggle probably played out over my face and in my eyes, but he didn't back away. He didn't get frustrated and tell me to forget it. He waited, and I could tell he'd be fine with another kissing session or just a night full of screen time.

I wouldn't be, though. On that simple point, I was clear. I rose and held out my hand.

A ghost of a smile passed over his full lips—lips I wanted on mine.

I struggled to draw a breath as I led him to the guest room. This room had become neutral ground. My house was loaded with emotion. His bed promised more intimacy than I was ready to handle. The guest bedroom didn't smell like him. The bed was made and not rumpled from his strong body. His clothing wasn't lying on the dresser or piled in the laundry.

I stopped just feet from the bed, and he closed the door behind us.

He tugged me into his embrace, but like he'd been doing, he took it slow. Shadows draped over us, giving me space to hide, time to ease into this moment. He lowered his head and grazed his mouth across mine.

Soft, with a hint of firmness. My lips parted. I'd watched

those lips for years: smile, frown, joke, discipline. The touch sent tingles down to my toes. I lifted my head and met his light pressure with more force. He was warm and safe and, for the moment, he was mine.

Wrapping my arms around his wide shoulders, I encouraged him. More. Faster. Harder. He answered each demand, prodding my lips apart until my tongue tentatively danced with his. He made each move deliberately, waiting for me to take it further.

Electricity swept through my body. I angled my head, took him deeper. Tasted the mint chip ice cream on his breath. Soaked up the heat from his body. Relied on his strength to hold me up.

When he moved, I was ready to go with him. He backed me to the bed. His strong hands gripped me around the waist, and he lifted me. My surprise didn't stop me from twining my legs around his waist to keep the kiss from stopping.

I clung to him as he laid us back. I didn't release him to relax into the mattress. I couldn't let go, but the easy compliance from earlier was receding. I needed a moment to adjust. His weight was on me, over me, yet he supported me. He kept most of the pressure off until the tension leaked out of my body, then he eased his weight onto me.

His jeans held back the erection that pressed between us, but my awareness centered on the length, the thickness, how hard he was. For me. With my legs around him, I cradled him, getting used to the idea that someday soon we'd do this without clothing between us. My body reacted, and I rocked against the hard ridge.

A growl left him, and his kiss increased in force and matched the rocking of his pelvis. Sensation swept me away. I unhooked my legs to press my heels into the mattress and use it for leverage. Need piled on top of desire, wrapped in demand. I writhed. I whimpered.

He backed off the kiss and murmured, "Do you need more, Kenny?"

"Yes," I pleaded, trusting him not to go too far.

His hand landed at my waistband as he kissed a path down my neck. I rocked up, urging him to go faster. I hated that he had to put space between us for him to undo my jean shorts, but when his warm fingers pressed against me, I was lost in pleasure. I knew nothing but his touch. His hot lips at my neck. His expert fingers stroking me.

Within minutes I went off, lightning exploding behind my eyes. He smashed his mouth to mine and swallowed my cries and my whimpers and my moans. When I settled, he withdrew his hand and muffled that moan too.

He'd taken care of me, like he had before. Who would take care of him? I'd take all the pleasure he was willing to give, but I didn't want to be selfish. I brushed my hand across the hard erection behind his jeans.

Liam curled his fingers around mine and rolled to his side, tucking me in next to him. "You don't have to do that."

I blinked from the sting of rejection until I noticed the restraint etched into his expression. This had nothing to do with how I thought I might bumble my way through a hand job compared to the more experienced women he'd likely been with. He was protecting me. "I want to."

"Next time." He dropped a kiss into my hair. "But I'm ready to explode, and I'm afraid it'd be too much too soon for you."

Energy vibrated under our hands. He had to be uncomfortable, but he held me as relaxed as someone ready to fall asleep.

The fog of lust waned, and awareness returned. He was

right. I was growing used to us, but how would I react to stroking him off, to being the one responsible for him coming apart in my arms?

I liked the idea, and the reality would probably be better. But this wasn't just me. It was important to Liam not to push me. So I wouldn't push him.

I caressed his face. The rough stubble that had sprouted up during the day ran under my hand, a texture I hadn't felt for so long and wanted more of.

I pressed a kiss to his lips. "You mind if we stay like this for a while?"

He rewarded me with a sweet smile and wrapped his arms around me. I was safe in his embrace.

* * *

Liam

Eli was telling Grandma Gin about our fishing trip with Kenny from a couple of days ago, so excited he forgot to use the new skills he'd been learning in speech. She smiled and nodded along as we sat around the table, eating our meal. I'd missed seeing her with the boys, these times when she could enjoy herself and didn't have to cook and clean up after them.

I'd invited her over for supper. I had grilled, and the steaks made up for the lack of flair with the rest of the meal, which consisted of frozen green beans I nuked in the microwave and box mac and cheese. She'd played with the boys, and I'd stared into the flames, thinking about how good it had felt to have Kenny shatter in my arms. That night hadn't been like the first time I'd gotten her off in the guest room. She'd held me in return, and she'd wanted to do the same.

I'd wanted nothing more than to have her explore my body. God, had I been fantasizing about it. But if so much as one of her little fingertips had touched my dick, I'd have been coming like a beast. So I'd asked her to wait, and my dick still hated me for that decision.

Eli wrapped up his tales of the weekend and gobbled down his food. Owen shoveled orange macaroni into his mouth. He'd devoured the meat I'd cut up for him as Eli had talked.

"You two can go play," I said. "Just take your plates to the counter."

The boys did as I asked and ran outside. I'd taken them each riding around without training wheels on their bikes. I'd put the trainers back on and had drawn a chalk racetrack on the concrete pad in front of the garage. They'd been riding their bikes around it all afternoon.

Grandma Gin pushed her empty plate to the side and shifted in her chair until she was facing me. "Have you done some job hunting?"

"I've found a few openings." It'd taken longer than expected to comb through them. I kept staring at the screen and thinking about Kenny's heat flooding my hand. Goddamn, I had it bad. "My resume's all polished and ready."

I met her gaze. She read right through me. Not about the Kenny stuff. I'd stuck true to what Kenny had asked. But about the job stuff. I'd left a lot unsaid, and Grandma Gin had heard every word.

"Worried about the can of worms that might open as soon as you hit the apply button?"

"Word's going to spread like wildfire." And a trail of gasoline led right to Cameron. But this time I had seven years of welding experience and a handful of supervisors and managers that could recommend me as both a welder and an employee.

"It always does." Her scrutiny stayed on me. "The fence along the north end looks nice. Did Bruce do that?"

"I fixed it. The kids had fun helping."

"He was an ass about it?"

About the north side? No. That had been the west side of the fence. "Bruce was busy taking over Kenny's flooring project the last couple of days."

She'd called, exasperated. She hadn't had the heart to shoo him away, but at least she'd insisted on helping. Only, he'd made her the tool bitch. Just like I'd been with Grandpa Bob when I was five. *Hand me the hammer. Hold the flashlight. Grab a glass of water, will ya?*

"I take it his help wasn't welcome?" Grandma Gin asked.

I took my plate to the counter and peered out the window above the sink. Eli was halfway around the track, and Owen was lying in the middle hollering something at him. He probably wanted his brother to try to jump him with the bike. "The problem is he doesn't help. He takes over and makes Kenny feel inept."

"Then Kennedy should say something to him."

She wouldn't. She had a soft heart, and Bruce was the closest thing to a father she'd ever had. "She tries, but you know how they are."

Grandma Gin grunted like she didn't believe Kenny really tried, but also like she could believe Bruce ignored her. She brought her plate to the counter and reached for the faucet. I stopped her. "I've got the dishes. Me and the boys wanted to treat you tonight."

She smirked and glanced outside. This time it was Eli lying in the middle. Owen was drawing an outline around him with the chalk. It would look like a crime scene by the time they were done.

She turned her back to the window as if she didn't want the kids to hear. She wasn't afraid of the kids suddenly learning to read lips. She'd put her back to the Barrons' land. We couldn't see their house from the window, but all the land in the distance was theirs.

And I was filled with satisfaction that the pastures surrounding our house wouldn't be.

"Can you meet me at the bank tomorrow? Deano will go over everything with us." Dean Bateman. Forever Deano to the over-fifty crowd in Coal Haven who remembered him as the pitcher who'd almost made it to the minors. "I told him ten and warned him that kids will be there." She ran her tongue along her front teeth. "If the bank wants our business, they'd better not say a damn word about it."

There was no other bank in town. So if we didn't want to drive, they'd get our business. But Grandpa Bob had always liked Deano, and my father had long outgrown doing his banking in Coal Haven. Grandma Gin and I wouldn't worry that Cameron had Deano's ear.

"I'll meet you there. I'll treat you to lunch after?"

She patted my shoulder. "You don't have to spoil me. But one of my friends wants to rearrange her living room, and we're all trying to talk her out of it. She's eighty. If we're not done moving furniture by the time we're eighty, then I don't know why we bother getting that old."

I chuckled. Grandma Gin had likely already volunteered me. She wanted to get in good with her senior living complex. There was nowhere else to go from there. Leaving this house had been hard enough.

"Thanks for the food." She rubbed my back, and I curled an arm around her for a half hug. I walked her to her car. Watched her give the kids hugs.

I didn't want to lose this. The talk with the bank had to go well. I had to land a job closer to home. I was prepared for a drop in pay, but I'd been brainstorming ways to make it up. Thanks to Kenny, I had a few ideas. The farmers market wasn't a bust. It'd shown me that I could sell my wares, and Coal Haven wasn't the only option.

I just needed everything to fall in place.

Twelve

KENNEDY

"Oh, don't worry about that, Kennedy dear. I'll set the table."

I'd been at Willow and Bruce's for a half hour. Thirty minutes of Willow clucking all over me about the summer school I was teaching. *Do you really think you want to go back full-time? Isn't that a lot of pressure? I remember Derek talking about the stress you were under.*

Yes. No job was stress-free. I wanted to be in charge of my own classroom. I wanted to get to know my students' parents again. I wanted to be invested in their education. I could be that as a para, but not on the level I craved. The teacher designed the lesson plans, and I did what she told me to. It didn't matter that I disagreed that Demi needed extra reading lessons. I suspected she was dyslexic. But Marion was in charge, and she made the final decision. She had put her in Title I, and Demi returned from the specialized lessons with her little shoulders hanging and red-rimmed eyes.

Since I wasn't involved in conferences, I hadn't been able to intervene when the Title I teacher accused the parents of not reading to Demi enough. Never mind that Demi's two older siblings read just fine.

I would never have told a parent it was their fault. And I wouldn't have turned down the offer to order specialized chairs for the fidgety kids when the principal came around to discuss budget. But I wasn't in charge of a classroom. The old-fashioned teachers, like Mrs. Z, who had taught Liam and Derek in kindergarten, were still in power and vetoed the newer ways of thinking. I itched to challenge them, to add to the voices that got ignored because they lacked seniority at the school.

Willow took the plates out of the cupboard.

"I can get the silverware at least," I said. My ass was hurting from sitting too long in the hard wooden chairs at the dining room table.

"Not at all. I've got it."

I mentally sighed. Willow was like this, and I shouldn't take it personally. She'd done everything domestic since she'd gotten married at nineteen. With two sons out working cattle and fixing fences, she was used to having no help and used to no one wanting to help her.

But after merely fetching tools for my coveted flooring job, it stung.

It didn't help that my attitude was sour. The school year was approaching, and no jobs were opening up. Last night, I'd sat at the table and calculated my expenses compared to what I would make another year as a para. The expenses had won.

I hadn't talked to Liam about my concerns yet. He'd told me about the bank appointment and his plans to sell his work to supplement what he could make from a job in the area. While I was with Bruce and Willow tonight, he'd planned to apply for jobs. I joined him in worrying that between the bank visit and the job applications, word would get back to Cameron and he'd start shit.

And I had no one else to talk to. Not about my concern for Liam. Not about my own job prospects. Not about a mortgage that was suddenly so much harder to pay on one income. Combine that with visiting Bruce and Willow, and I missed Derek. He wasn't here to smirk when he knew I wanted to roll my eyes. He couldn't tell me everything was fine. And he wouldn't be on the drive home when we could talk about the good and bad parts of the visit.

Willow bustled around me, setting out plates, forks, knives, and glasses. I had to do something, so I filled the water pitcher without asking. Willow disappeared into the kitchen and returned with a steaming glass dish. Chicken and rice. Derek's favorite.

Acid climbed up my throat. I set the water pitcher down and took a long breath in and out. Why was chicken and rice hitting me so hard right now?

"Smells delicious." I'd made chicken and rice before, but it was one of those dishes that never tasted the same when I made it, and it didn't matter if I used identical ingredients.

"Thank you." She beamed. "It was Derek's..." She pressed her lips as she set the dish down. I had my hands plastered on the top of the table. Her gaze landed on my ringless finger, and she paled.

I spread my fingers. "I was working on something and didn't want it to get wrecked. I haven't put it back on because..." I couldn't go back in healing, and right now, that was what it would signal.

"You don't have to explain it to me," she said gently, but her eyes shone as she scurried away.

Should I go to her? Tears burned the backs of my eyes. I rapidly blinked. Why was today so hard? Just because I was a little stressed?

Bruce walked through the side entrance from the garage. Perfect timing. If he hadn't, I wasn't sure I'd win the battle against the tears.

"Smells good." He glanced at me, his eyes crinkling in the corners, thankfully oblivious to my inner turmoil. "Sorry, I had to change a tire on the Ranger."

"It's no problem."

Willow reappeared and acted like nothing had happened. We chatted through supper. Willow asked about the floor. I showed her pictures and threw in the ones with the faucet and the inside of the toilet tank.

Her eyes went wide. "You fixed that? All by yourself?"

I didn't want to get into a discussion about Liam, but a burn of betrayal ignited as I left him out. "I watched videos, and Carlton set me up with the right supplies."

Willow's smile was serene until her gaze landed on Bruce's. Concern filled her eyes and her gaze darted to me.

I tensed. Now what?

Bruce cleared his throat. "I couldn't help but hear what you were listening to when I showed up on Saturday."

"My audiobook? I'd been waiting for a month to get that one from the online library. I can see why there was a long wait." I was waiting for a couple more on easy DIY projects I could do on a budget.

"If you need help, I can look over your finances—"

"No!" I hadn't meant to shout. "No, thank you. I've got everything under control." I wanted my growth to include all aspects of my life. Not just getting off the couch and showering. I wanted to be competent around the house, with my money, my job, my vehicle. Everything. I wasn't going to be carried through life anymore.

"Kennedy, I know it's all new to you: the mortgage, insurance, utilities. I can take over paying the bills again, figure out a monthly budget now that you're working again. And"—he exchanged another glance with Willow—"we can help out. You know, if you need it. I know being a para doesn't pay as much as your previous salary, or Derek's."

Willow's encouraging nod didn't help the dismay mushroom clouding in my chest. Because of my breakdown, Bruce had rescued me. He knew all about my bills, and it was a small town. A few well-placed questions and he'd have a rough idea of a para's hourly wage.

I glanced between the two of them. They wanted to take over the budget and give me an allowance? Did they realize what they were asking? Did they realize the independence it would take away?

I was a twenty-six-year-old widow. An allowance? "I appreciate the offer, but I have it under control. If I can control a classroom of third graders, I think I can handle it." My nervous chuckle landed in their silence.

"It'd take a lot of pressure off," Bruce said gently, like he was talking to a skittish mare. "Really, we want to help. I'd never forgive myself if you were struggling and I didn't know."

The unspoken *again* echoed between us.

That damn water heater. I hadn't realized how badly it had scared Bruce and Willow. The leak must've happened right before Liam had left town for his twenty days. Not only had I ignored my hygiene because I didn't have hot water and had told everyone I was fine, but my wet basement had been growing who knew what. If Bruce hadn't stopped in, I might've gotten sick from the stagnant, mold spore-ridden air and my house's foundation could've been ruined. "Honestly, I'm doing really well. I listened to that audiobook so I can get better, not because I can't do it or because I'm in trouble."

"Just think about it. We're here for you." Another shared look with Willow.

Were they listening? Anger at them draped around me like a suffocating plastic bag. Fury at myself for being so out of it during my breakdown joined in. How could I blame my in-laws for worrying and offering help when they'd had to hold my hand until I could stand on my own again? How could I prove to them that not only was I standing, but I was ready to run? Or did they even want that?

What if doting on me made them feel closer to Derek?

I pinched the bridge of my nose. And that was why my attitude had taken a dive. Times like this anchored me back into being Kennedy the Widow. I was a widow. That would never change. But I was embracing my other roles. Kennedy the teacher. Kennedy the DIY home repair hobbyist. Kennedy the girlfriend. And I really wanted to explore that last role. Because one of the lessons I'd learned as a widow was that life was short.

"Are you feeling okay?" Willow peered outside. "Oh, it's getting dark. You can sleep over if you'd like. There've been several deer hanging out in the trees by the bend. I wouldn't want one to jump in front of you on your way home."

I saw my out and snatched it. "I'd better get going, then. I feel fine; don't worry." They'd worry, but I didn't want to deal with that.

I said my goodbyes and did the best driving of my life when I looped around their yard. No deer were getting in my way. I was a woman on a mission.

Making sure not to kick up a dust cloud so my in-laws couldn't see my route, I drove to the next driveway and the familiar copse of trees.

I could take care of my house. I could take care of my

expenses. I could take care of myself. I was free to choose my path, and, when it came to sex, that path led to Liam.

By the time I jogged up the steps, Liam was at the door. "Hey." His warm gaze swept over my face. "Everything okay?"

"Are the kids asleep?"

"I haven't heard a peep from them in an hour."

I put my fingertips on his hard chest and pushed him inside. "I think I'm ready."

He shut the door behind me. "For what?"

"For everything."

He didn't haul me to his bedroom like I wanted him to. "What happened?"

I had told him about having to visit Bruce and Willow tonight. "Same old."

"Revenge sex isn't the answer," he said softly.

This man. Always looking out for me. I cupped his face. "This is because of the way they coddle me, yes, but it's not revenge. This is me realizing that I've come so far in my healing journey that I'm ready for more. I'm ready to be with you."

His pupils dilated, but he leaned down, his hands gripping my wrists. "You sure?"

"I'm not going to lie and say that it'll be easy. Maybe it will be, maybe it won't. But I know that no matter what, it'll be okay." Liam would make sure of it. "So, yes, I'm sure."

He clasped my hand. "All right."

* * *

I was in Liam's bedroom. It was me and him and the closed door.

The light was off. He let go of my hand and flipped on the dull lamp on the nightstand.

He took my hands, leading me to the bed. I sat on the end, spreading my hands out on his stomach. His muscles tightened, but he remained standing.

"I want you to know that I understand." He took a condom out of his wallet and set it by the lamp. He cupped my chin and lifted until I met his gaze. "I know what a big deal this is. I know that you'll think of him. And I want you to know it's okay. I can't think of a better man to be compared to. I'm not jealous. I'm not intimidated."

I fisted my hands in his shirt, my throat constricting. He was right. I'd been trying not to, but with Liam's words, all that pressure drained out.

"I'm with you, no matter what."

"Liam," I whispered. Tears pricked the backs of my eyes. "You're too good to be true." I used my right hand to swipe at my eyes. "I didn't want to cry during this."

"Cry all you need to." He kneeled in front of me and smoothed his hands along my bare legs, his fingers going under the material of my linen shorts. "As long as you're sure."

I nodded and grabbed his face, bent, and plastered a kiss on his mouth. There was no other way to communicate my appreciation and how badly I wanted to be with him because of how amazing he was.

The kiss was sloppy, demanding, but he rose without breaking contact. He leaned me back until I was stretched in the middle of his bed. He kept his mouth on mine as he shoved all the blankets to the side. And then it was just me and him on the sheets.

I melted between him and the cool mattress. The heat of his body flowed into me, waking up nerve cells that had been jittery for weeks. His weight promised that the demands of those cells would be met tonight.

He broke away to slip his shirt over his head. I'd seen him without his shirt over the years, but this experience was different from them all. The way I looked at him was different. His washboard abs and the smattering of hair across his chest sent a wave of pounding desire from my eyes to my center.

I ran my fingers along his skin. I'd never touched him like this. Never imagined I would, but this moment felt as natural as breathing, yet as terrifying as skydiving.

He drew my blouse over my head and tossed it on the floor next to his shirt. I glanced between us. He was cut from stone, and I was more like a dough ball waiting to be kneaded. My gaze strayed to the light, and he noticed.

"I don't want you to hide from me, but if you want it off, I'll shut it off." His gaze stroked over my chest where I filled out a bra that had once been too roomy, then down to my belly. His gaze heated, filling me with confidence.

"No." I might think differently once my pants were off. By then, he'd have seen everything. This wasn't the time to be self-conscious. I had more to get over than whether my cellulite was visible. "Leave it on."

He kissed a path down my neck until I squirmed. He took his time taking my bra off, kissing across the tops of the cups before he tugged them down. Cool air wafted over my tight nipples before his hot tongue licked across the tip.

I arched into him and moaned. He switched to the other side, sliding his hands behind me to undo the bra. In seconds, it was gone, but he didn't go for my shorts. He took his time with my breasts, sucking a nipple into his mouth on one side, then switching to the other.

I was a needy mess, but I didn't want this torture to end. He kept much of his weight off me, but I wanted him pressed against me. I'd been empty so long; I needed more than his heat and his soapy cedar smell. I needed all of him.

He finally traced a path down my belly, pulling my shorts down and taking the underwear with them an inch at a time. The barer I got, the more I tensed. I squeezed my eyes shut. His head was between my spread legs. But the soft kiss he pressed on my pelvic bone, then to the sensitive flesh farther down, and the way he pushed my legs apart—so gentle, but so confident—eased my tension.

"I've got you, Kenny," he whispered as he dipped his head and kissed my clit.

Ultrasensitive, I bowed my back off the bed. He didn't stop, but he didn't attack me. Small increments of pressure ratcheted me higher until I dug my hands into his hair. He'd always kept it longer than Derek's.

My eyes flew open as panic yanked me out of the moment. I'd just thought about my husband.

Liam's reassuring words from earlier floated through my mind, and I sank back into the pleasure. I luxuriated in the silky texture of his hair between my fingers. How my calves rested against his wide shoulders. The stroke of his tongue against me.

My grip had tightened and my hips had set a rhythm, but I was still seeking, searching for more. Sensing my need, he placed a finger at my entrance, but he didn't shove inside. The invasion was steady, lacking all force, as if he measured his movements against the way I rocked my hips. When he was in, I was lost. His tongue. The thrust of his finger. I clamped around him and rode higher on the pleasure. The crest was there; I just had to reach it.

"Liam." His name was a plea. The desire pounding me was stronger than before. It was like reaching for a favorite candy, but it was just beyond my grasp, and I was stretching so intensely it bordered on painful.

He answered my need, and I rocketed to the peak. Seeing him lick me, his shoulders flexing as he moved, my body spread before him, I barked out a cry and slapped my hand against my mouth as I came. Hard. Against his tongue, all over his hand. Stars exploded behind my eyes as my body shook through my release.

He withdrew from me, but stayed close, kissing his way up my body. "You still with me?"

I gulped in air. "I'm not with myself yet."

His deep chuckle, like the ones over the phone that sent shivers through my body, rooted me in the moment. He reached for the condom and set it on the bed next to us. His hair was mussed from my fingers, and he vibrated with unspent energy. He was holding back, like when we were in the guest room. I was safe with him.

I skimmed my hands up his torso. Firm muscle under warm skin. He was still between my legs, but he hadn't taken off his jeans. This time when my fingers landed on his waistband, he didn't stop me. He was poised above me, propping himself up with one hand as he watched me unbutton and unzip his pants.

If I let go, my hands would shake, but I couldn't stop if I tried. The orgasm had been amazing, but now that the aftershocks had passed, I remained unfulfilled. He wasn't on me or in me, and I needed him to be.

I swallowed as I pushed his jeans down, taking his boxers with them. His cock sprang free, long and thick and arching between us.

Oh. He was big. I'd only touched one man before. This was different—so much different—but so was I. I wasn't Kennedy the shy virgin. I was Kennedy, who'd started seeing my best friend, the friend who had happened to be best friends with my husband. If Derek hadn't died, we wouldn't be here.

But he was gone and I was empty and Liam made me feel safe and wanted. He reminded me of what feeling complete was like.

I wrapped my hand around him and gave him a pump. His flesh pulsed under my skin, giving me a heady sense of power. "I'm ready."

I let him do the condom. I had to withdraw my hand, but I watched. The way his forearm flexed as he rolled it on. The way he kneeled between my open legs. How our breathing mingled as we anticipated what came next.

The condom was on. He shoved his pants down the rest of the way and kicked them off.

I sucked my lower lip between my teeth. This was it.

But he didn't lower his hips to line up with mine. He dropped his head and captured my mouth. I opened for him, tasting the mix of him and myself, enough to feel the slightest bit naughty. He consumed me with the kiss, so much that I didn't tense when his broad head prodded at my entrance. I rocked up to meet him, and he thrust in, but not far. We did the same dance—he pushed in, I rose to meet him—until he was seated inside. We were connected. I was full, my walls greedily clamping around him, and it was *good*.

He continued to kiss me like he wanted to devour me. I hugged his broad shoulders, reveling in the pleasure of him filling me. The tremors that ran through his body echoed into me. He was holding himself back. For me.

I returned his kiss, no longer just a recipient, but an active participant; not just responding to the stroke of his tongue, but creating my rhythm.

And he thrust, withdrew all the way, and buried himself inside me.

I gasped, and he swallowed it. Intoxicating bliss built inside me like a pressure cooker. He was over me, in me, and my mind was in the moment. Pure ecstasy. My body was alive, like a wire that had been downed in a storm. It radiated with electricity and all that power had somewhere to go.

Muscles that had been growing stronger thanks to my job and my home repairs flexed and clenched. My belly was tight as I focused on the sheer rapture between my legs. The slide of his retreat, paired with the way he hit when he plunged inside, propelled me up a steep hill, seeking another peak.

The force from both of us was increasing until I had to free my mouth from his to pant in his ear. "Oh, God, Liam."

Another tremor ran through his body and into mine. "I've got you, Kenny. Come for me again."

Our bodies smashed together, the sound of our skin hitting mingled with my rapid breaths. I hitched my legs up. I needed more, deeper, harder, but I couldn't comprehend enough to ask.

Liam read my body language. He threaded his hand between us and did nothing more than rest a fingertip on top of my clit. The motion of our bodies was enough to trigger my explosion.

Pleasure ripped through my body. "Liam!"

He caught my mouth against his and set a punishing pace, stroking out a long orgasm until I was using him to keep from flying off the face of the earth. I clung to him; I cried into his mouth, and I milked him.

His body went tight, and he hammered into me until he thrust one last time. I held him as heat flooded from him into me. I clung to his shoulders while he pulsed against my walls that gripped him.

We'd done it. We'd had sex. I'd had sex. With someone who wasn't my husband.

A chill began to sweep away the warmth.

Liam pushed up, his gaze brushing across my face. "Let me get rid of the condom. Don't leave though, okay?"

I nodded woodenly. When his body rolled off mine, I wanted to snatch a sheet and cover myself. Liam lifted the blankets from the floor. I kept my gaze on the covers, grabbing for them. He was at the edge of my vision. Tall, lean, with a flagging erection, the condom shiny from me.

I bit the inside of my cheek, my throat constricting, and concentrated on straightening the covers as he ducked into the hallway and used the bathroom.

I should use the bathroom, too, but then I'd have to stand up. I'd have to fully acknowledge that I'd come here to have sex. And I'd had sex. And it was good. So damn good. And that if my mind could shut off, I'd want it again. The panic from earlier resurfaced, and my heart rate kicked up.

Liam reappeared, still naked, of course. So was I. I hugged the sheet to my chest.

He got into bed with slow, measured movements. He shut off the lamp, and we were bathed in shadows.

"You okay?" he asked quietly, scooting until he was close to me. I was tempted to find my clothes and run like I had the first time we'd done something together, but I craved his proximity. I needed him next to me.

I twisted my hands in the sheet as weight piled higher on my chest and my breathing burned. "I don't think so."

He embraced me and laid us both back, but I was as pliant as a two-by-four.

"Go ahead and cry, Kenny. It's all right."

I rolled into him and sobbed.

* * *

Liam

. . .

Kenny's head was buried in my armpit. Her fingers trailed across my chest. We'd dozed off and on after she'd finished crying. She was still here. That wiped out my regrets.

I had my own internal struggles. Was I betraying my friend? What would I tell him? How would I tell him? My life hadn't been as entwined with Derek's as Kenny's had been. He'd been my best friend, like a brother to me. But I hadn't spent every moment of every day with him. It'd been over a year since I'd typed out a message to him just to pretend for a moment that he was still there, waiting to answer and call me a jackass.

He'd been the first one I told when Payton announced she was pregnant. The guy I went to when Payton insisted we get married. The friend who reminded me that I was Eli and Owen's father and I had rights, that I was able to not only raise them better than Payton could, but that I knew how to be a good dad because I realized how important it was to be there for them.

When I got custody of the boys, I'd called him. When I was frustrated that Cameron was trying to run me out of Coal Haven by ensuring I didn't get hired within a sixty-mile radius of the town, Derek had given me the pep talk I needed to keep working in Williston and take care of my boys and Grandma Gin.

So, who would I tell that I'd had the most amazing night with the most special woman in my life? That it was someone I'd been friends with for years and had grown immeasurably closer to? That I wanted more, and I'd do what it took to make sure she trusted me with herself? That I'd never experienced this level of intimacy in my life, and I'd instantly craved more?

Kenny broke into my thoughts. "What are you thinking about?"

I could lie, but similar questions were on her mind. "How things have changed between us and that normally I'd talk to Derek about it but I can't."

"Yeah. Same."

Silence settled between us for a few moments, but her fingers didn't stop. I kept my mind off how soft her body was next to me. How she'd responded to my touch. How hard I'd climaxed. And that we were both naked.

"I have to go soon," she said.

"It's going to be a long day for you." I kissed the top of her head. Her body was lined up with mine; we couldn't be touching any more than if I were inside her, but I couldn't help seeking more. "You don't have to come to Bismarck with us today."

"No, I'll go. I can handle one night of hardly any sleep."

She didn't see my smile. It would be different to spend the day with her. There was a helluva secret between us now. "We'll pick you up."

She nodded, her satiny hair rubbing against my skin. I'd been fighting a second erection since I'd pulled out of her. I was losing.

Her touch went from light and distracted to firm and full of intention. "I have a little bit of time."

If she was willing... "I have more condoms."

The sun was starting to rise, lighting the room more than it had in the last few minutes. I snagged a new condom from the pack in my nightstand. I didn't bring women to the house. And I didn't fuck around a lot in Williston, but what I'd done had been just that. Fast, frantic coupling with someone who wanted less of a commitment than I did.

The only reason I was grateful for that experience was that I had protection handy. Kenny had never been on birth control, and I wasn't going to put her through the emotional turmoil of wondering if she was pregnant and if she could become pregnant.

The image of Kenny, her belly round with my child, nearly made me choke. Suddenly, I wanted that. I wanted it all.

I shoved my fantasies into a box in my mind and locked it. Kenny and her figuring out her new life aside, I had my own mess of a life to straighten out.

"Can I?" She lifted the packet from my fingers.

I reclined. I'd been ready to do everything, to take her as far as she could go, back off, and wait until she was ready for more. Reading Kenny was easy. This was a surprise, but it shouldn't have been. She'd emerged from the cocoon of an identity that had naturally formed for her and that she had been happy with, and now she was fluttering around, free to be anything she wanted.

It'd made her bolder. More confident. She wouldn't think of it that way, but she was on the interstate of her personal journey, no longer stuck in a field surrounded by dead funeral flowers.

I held still as she rolled on the condom. Her intense gaze and the way a blush stole up her cheeks made me grin.

She glanced up, and the flush deepened. "I don't want to mess up."

"I've got you."

"I know you do." She touched her lips to mine as she straddled me.

My brows lifted. This was a turn I wasn't expecting. She was taking charge. She sank her body onto me and took me all the way inside. If I'd thought it had felt like I was sinking into heaven before, the way she took over and surrounded me added another level of rapture.

I gripped her hips, my abs tight. I could lie all the way

back, but I didn't want to miss the goddess on top of me. Her bed head was because of me. Her eyelids were half-mast as she adjusted to my size and began a slow and sensual ride.

I took pleasure in watching her. What she was doing blew my mind, but seeing her take what she wanted was nearly as good.

"I can't believe I'm ready to go again so soon." Her brow crinkled, like she was afraid what she said was insulting to Derek.

I brushed my hands up her torso, cupped her breasts, feathered my fingers over her nipples. "It's okay. It doesn't mean anything other than you want another release."

She softened over me. "There's no rule book."

The statement meant something, but I didn't know the story. As long as it helped. Her hands pressed into my chest, and she rode me harder.

I grunted and thrust up harder. She grew more demanding. I placed my thumb against her wet, hot clit. Her mouth dropped open and she kicked up the pace until we were both moaning and grunting. Good thing my bedroom was on a different level than the boys' room.

When I thought I couldn't hold out any longer, my balls drawn up so tight stars ricocheted behind my eyes, she dropped her head back and let out a low moan.

Someday, we'd do this where she could cry out, call my name, and we could have noisy, messy sex. My house wasn't the place, especially when my kids didn't know that Kenny was more than a friend.

When she exploded over me, spilling heat between us, her walls clenching until I could barely move, I let go. Ecstasy carried me higher until lightning raced down my spine. I curled into her, burying my head in her round breasts as I released. She rocked over me, molten, hugging me to her.

When I came down and we both quit shaking, she gave me a tentative smile. "I suppose I should go."

"You can use the bathroom before me."

I helped her find her clothing. She dressed before scurrying to the bathroom. I put on my jeans from last night.

When she emerged, she'd finger-combed her swirl of mahogany hair. She shyly bit her bottom lip. She had zero experience with the awkward goodbye after sex; it was cuter than hell.

I gave her another kiss. "I'll walk you to the door."

"Thank you," she mumbled.

She shoved a hand through her hair, undoing all the work she'd done in the bathroom to tame it.

"Hey." I drew her into my arms when we reached the front door. "It's okay. Remember, there's no rule book. If you need to go see Derek, go see him. Don't worry about what I might think. I meant what I said."

Relief crossed her face, but her eyes misted over. "It's so hard, but it's so easy at the same time. And it's so damn confusing." She kissed the corner of my mouth. "I'm glad you're with me."

I nodded and watched her walk out. I waited until she drove past the house and turned onto the main road.

She was going straight to the cemetery, and I hadn't lied. I didn't mind.

I cleaned up in the bathroom and went back into the bedroom. I found my phone on my dresser. I could barely comprehend what Kenny was going through, but I could understand. I pulled up Derek's number and tapped out another message that was never going to be read.

Thirteen

LIAM

I lifted my newest creation out of the back of the pickup. It was heavy, but I wasn't about to let the fifty-five-year-old woman who had just paid me three hundred dollars for a horseshoe firepit creation lug it around.

"Where would you like it?" I adjusted my hold, grateful I didn't have the boys underfoot. I'd get to Williston later than my normal, but I had to deliver my custom orders.

Charlotte Garcia rushed ahead of me. "I have a place for it behind the garage, but you can set it on the pavement. My daughter's coming by later, and she can help me move it."

My shoulder muscles began to burn. "It's not a problem. Lead the way."

Her mouth formed an O, but she changed direction and opened the gate to the backyard fence. "Right through here."

She pointed to a spot on a patterned concrete slab. I set

it down, made sure it was stable, and stepped back to admire my work. The pattern of the horseshoes that made up the grates was fancier than the straight lines in the pavement. The two complemented each other.

Charlotte had her phone in her hand, snapping pictures. "This is just perfect, Liam. You are a master with a torch."

I chuckled to cover my embarrassment. My supervisors had told me I did a good job, but they weren't the type to gush over my work. "Thanks."

I'd only had a taste of custom orders, but I'd miss this. I'd dropped off my other piece, the cross made from chain links, and that customer had been thrilled. He'd put it right into his garden and done the same as Charlotte for pictures.

Charlotte tucked her phone away. "Did I hear correctly? You're not going to be at any more markets?"

"Not in Coal Haven." I'd been researching the ones in surrounding towns online. They'd be harder to juggle with the kids, and I'd have to make sure I packed my goods well so they weren't damaged in the commute. Steel creations weren't fragile, but if someone was paying me, I wanted them to have my best.

"Do you have a website?"

I took off my ball cap and scratched my head. "No, but maybe I'll think about designing one while I'm away from work." I'd have to buy a computer first, which I could do with what Charlotte had paid me. Shipping items this heavy might be a sticking point for a lot of potential customers. But online sales were an option.

"My sister owns Haven's Furnishings. You should talk to her."

"Thank you. I'll think about it." It would be a risk to do anything more. Charlotte's sister, Hattie, had experienced her own troubles with my father's wife. If Naomi found out

I was trying to sell my work in Coal Haven, she'd make sure Cameron put a stop to it.

The earnestness fell from Charlotte's expression as if she'd read my mind. "Hattie doesn't care who Cameron and Naomi Barron think they are. Naomi tried to force Hattie out of the building her store's in, and it only made Hattie's business stronger. My sister has an eye for quality, and once I send her these photos, her mind is going to churn up all the possibilities. Call her."

This time I didn't brush off the thought so quickly. The Garcia sisters were well known in town, and well respected, mostly because people were too afraid to mess with them. Charlotte had learned her husband was cheating on her. She kicked him out and hauled all his belongings to his other woman's house and dumped them on her lawn. Then she'd divorced him and changed her name.

I'd heard about the location dispute between Hattie and Naomi. Grandma Gin and Grandpa Bob had discussed it around the dinner table when I was in middle school. Naomi had been on the city council, and she'd wanted to demolish that corner and erect a new building with retail on the main floor and condos on the top. Claimed it would revive downtown.

Hattie had launched a campaign and called it Historic Coal Haven. She'd recruited the historical society, the state archives, and surrounding libraries to advocate and provide research on the benefits of preserving the original look of communities. Hattie had also gathered research about how tax breaks and startup incentives revived downtown at a fraction of the cost of demolition and new builds. To top it all off, she'd asked the council if projects like the retail/combo new build would be allowed to be bid on by companies owned by family members of those on the council, like Naomi's brother, who owned a commercial construction company.

The entire downtown was preserved as part of Coal Haven's history, and she'd needed the city council to sign off on it. Naomi had put on a serene face around town. If she had argued, she'd look like a greedy politician—exactly what she was. But acting as if she didn't care about Coal Haven— a town in which she behaved like royalty—would've been too damaging.

If anyone wanted to renovate downtown, they had to stay within certain specifications, but they also received grants and funding from the city, county, and state. The ashes had fallen, and it'd been years since I'd heard of issues between Hattie and the Barrons.

I admired Hattie. As a kid, I'd hung on updates. My father had earned plenty of blame in the way he treated me, but so had Naomi. It'd been recreational to watch her get taken down a few notches from that high throne she perched on. I wasn't ready for an epic battle against her, not alone. With the Garcia sisters, though? I couldn't have better support.

Still, I was reluctant. I had just started applying for jobs. How much did I want to tempt fate? "I don't want to cause more trouble."

Charlotte snorted. "Hattie would tell you that *you're* not causing trouble. Once those Barrons stick their noses into business that isn't theirs is when the trouble starts. It's on them." She laid a hand on my shoulder. "I'm going to have her call you, Liam. You're too talented, and if the rumors are true, you've gotten a raw deal in this town."

"I appreciate it." And I did. Looking through adult eyes at what Hattie had done helped me remember how much of the town had been on her side. My father and his wife held a lot of power, but perhaps not as much as I had thought.

"The Barrons don't have carte blanche to Coal Haven. Your great-granddaddy might've founded this town, but that doesn't mean they own it or us." She shook her head. "Naomi's trying to run for mayor, and I'll sit with every quilt circle in town and shit talk her. You shouldn't have to fight for what's right, but you do, and sometimes you have to fight dirty."

I didn't know if laughing would be rude. Charlotte's flinty eyes made me think she was going to start bobbing side to side like a prizefighter. She wasn't kidding, but I didn't disagree. Hattie didn't have kids, and Charlotte's were grown and gone. They could afford to fight dirty. My kids lived here. They would start school in two months. When they were teens, they'd look for a job. I wanted them to have more opportunities than I'd had. Which might have to start with building my own support base in Coal Haven instead of lying low.

"Just hear her out," Charlotte said, sensing my reservations.

This time I spoke with more confidence. "Thanks. I will. Sorry, I have to go. I still have a long drive to Williston."

I waited until I hit the highway that'd take me to the interstate before I dialed Kenny.

She was out of breath when she answered, her voice floating through the cab. "Hi. You on the road?"

"Yep. I just had an interesting interaction with Charlotte Garcia." I told her the story.

"It wouldn't hurt to hear Hattie out and see if you two can work out a deal. My gosh, that would be awesome."

I knew she'd agree, but her excitement was infectious. "I don't want to get my hopes up."

"I know, but you can't keep letting Cameron and Naomi take away good things. They don't own you. They've done nothing but hurt you. You don't deserve it."

"I know I don't deserve it." I'd spent too much time wondering why as I was growing up.

"Knowing it *logically* is different from knowing it *viscerally*. Logically, you know that Cameron was the one who started an affair with his assistant. Logically, you know that Cameron said hateful things that made your mom too distraught to drive safely. Viscerally, that asshole and his wife have always made you feel like you were the reason everything blew up. That you being born was the catalyst that destroyed everything. Maybe that's why you've chosen to ignore him rather than fight for your spot in this town."

"Damn, Kenny." I stared at the blacktop with the freshly painted dotted yellow line down the middle in front of me.

"Sorry, that just came out." I could picture her biting her lower lip, an adorable line between her brows.

"I'm glad it did." I laughed, mostly to relieve the knot in my chest that her words had created. I had decided to stay for the boys. Yet, I'd been tiptoeing around, afraid of my father's reaction.

Fuck it. I was leaping in with both feet. "I'm going to tell Grandma Gin to start the paperwork with the bank." Word would get back to Bruce that Grandma Gin was selling—to me and not him. That was going to piss off Bruce, and that would make it Cameron's problem. "And I'll work on my side gig while I'm in Williston." I'd brainstorm ideas for when Hattie called, search for scrap metal I could work with, plan new projects, and apply for every fucking welding job in a sixty-mile radius from Coal Haven.

I was a Barron after all.

* * *

Kennedy

. . .

I faced Rattler's. I'd done a lot of firsts in the last five months. All things I might've done before in my life, but they had become significant after my breakdown. My first long walk. My foray into yoga had become routine, like the walks. Sleeping with Liam.

Tonight was girls' night out. Some of my coworkers had invited me along. They had tried for their May night out, but I had passed. This time, when the fifth-grade teacher, Aspen Whitfield, had asked, I'd made myself accept.

I was regretting it. I'd endured grocery trips with the sympathetic smiles. The knowing looks shot my way. The ones who ignored me completely. Those I was used to. Same with gassing my car up or passing someone on the walking path.

I stared at my bare ring finger. My stomach knotted, and I drew in a long, deep breath.

Had I made the right decision? I was growing used to having the ring off, but I hadn't gone out with it off. I'd been around my coworkers, who'd been discreet if they had noticed I was no longer wearing my ring, with Liam, or at home.

Willow's shocked reaction banged around my head.

My hands clenched around the steering wheel. I could go home and grab it. Tuck it back on my hand where it belonged.

Wedding rings were symbols. For a couple, they were a symbol of love and commitment. For a widow, it got complicated, and I instinctively knew that putting it on to buffer me from others' reactions wasn't healthy for me.

Rattler's was packed. The busy supper crowd, full of people who knew who I was and my story. I was supposed to go in there and pretend I was having a good time. I was supposed to go in there and pretend that I was fine twenty-four seven. I was fine at work, but summer school was only a few hours a day, and the kids were oblivious to anything but what I was teaching and the fun their friends might be having without them. Around Liam, I didn't have to hold back.

I forced my hand loose. This was why I had to do new things, go new places, meet new people—without Liam. I couldn't spend my life waiting for him to slide in front of me like the guy who sweeps the ice in front of the curling stone to help me go farther and straighter.

A red car pulled in kitty-corner to me. Aspen grinned and waved.

The spell broken, I hurried out of my car. Entering the restaurant with someone would be easier.

"I'm so glad you could make it." The description of amber waves of grain came to mind around Aspen. Hair the color of wheat hung down her back in soft waves, and her eyes were the color of a cold glass of light beer. She'd been in Coal Haven for a year. The upcoming school year would be her second out of college, and this was her first job. I didn't know much else about her other than she had my old job.

"Thanks for inviting me—again."

"I've been called tenacious, but my momma calls it nagging." She hooked her arm through mine and towed me toward the door. "Marion is on her way. Kelsey messaged me and said she'd be a little late. Something with her kids. I also invited a friend of mine. She works at the clinic in town. The lab, I think. Oh, she grew up here. Of course you know Lyric."

"Lyric, yes." She was Isla Barron's best friend. Hopefully far enough removed from Liam's drama to not make tonight awkward. Kelsey was the school librarian, and it'd be good to see Marion again, to talk when we weren't working. "Sounds fun."

"Only if we do it right." She practically bounced next to me.

I was less than two years older than Aspen, but the gap could just as well have been ten years. Twenty, even. Yet her enthusiasm wound around me and eased the tension of feeling like a blunt stick in a pile of needles. Next to her, people wouldn't wonder what the hell I was doing here. I would be one of the girls.

I hoped.

Inside, the space was lighter than I'd expected. Large windows let in the summer sun, still high enough to keep from glaring through the glass into diners' eyes. The wood beams soaring along the ceiling and the wooden accents lining the bar and trimming out the walls were a light shade of brown...almost gray, but trendy.

Rattler's Brewhaus had opened a few years ago. I had been here on a date night with Derek once. We'd planned to go again.

I sucked in a breath and concentrated on not meeting anyone's eyes. Aspen told the hostess there'd be five of us. We were led to seats at a bar-height table in the bar section.

Marion appeared at our side and gave both Aspen and me small hugs. "Hi, ladies. I wasn't sure I'd make it on time. Dermot asked what was for supper, and that started a small argument." The older woman shook her head as she climbed onto a tall chair. "Like, seriously. When did asking someone to marry you mean that they have to decide what's for supper for the next forty years?"

Other people would tense around me when someone made a comment like that, but Marion and I had worked together for months. She was comfortable with me. A gift I'd never have the guts to thank her for.

Shortly after we ordered drinks, Kelsey rushed in with tales about her daughter's fast-pitch game. I'd had her daughter in school, and now she was going into ninth grade. High school. The last time I'd really talked to Kelsey, we'd discussed her kid's transition to middle school.

I'd been away from work for a year, but I had missed a lot more than a paycheck.

Lyric arrived, also looking different than I'd last seen her. Purple streaks in her brunette hair gave her an edge that hadn't been there before she'd left for college. She wore a deep red bustier top with cap sleeves and skintight white capris. Maybe I needed to get a few tips from her on how to dress in more than classroom-approved clothing.

"When'd you move back to town?" I asked.

Lyric grinned. Her dimples took away her edginess and made her cute. "I finished college last year and there was an opening in the lab. I graduated and moved right back home."

Last year. I used to see Lyric at all the Barron family functions. Where Isla went, Lyric followed. She'd returned to Coal Haven a year ago.

Another reminder of how much I'd missed.

Conversation revolved around work, the activities that Kelsey's kids were in, Marion's grandkids, and Lyric's job. Tension slowly drained out of me. This was no different from the break room at work. People left me alone, knowingly or unknowingly, waiting for me to speak about what I was comfortable with.

Isla's older brother, Stetson, entered the restaurant. I was friendly enough with him. He was big and had resting asshole face, but he broke into easy smiles and cracked jokes. He resembled his father, but I'd heard Bruce comment once that Stetson was the spitting image of his and Cameron's dad. Ink-black hair. Hard, dark eyes, and deeply bronzed skin. When he saw me, his brows lifted.

I gave him a little nod, afraid I had *I'm sleeping with Liam* tattooed on my forehead. The last thing I wanted while beginning to navigate my new life was to have the Barrons involve themselves in my relationship.

Stetson was closer to Evander's age than Derek's. Thirty-one. He'd been at all the combined Barron family functions. Liam had never been at those events, so I'd never seen the side of Stetson that was a dick to Liam. Mostly he pretended Liam didn't exist.

Stetson wove through the bar, nodding and waving at what seemed like every table. People in Coal Haven were wary of Cameron Barron, but they wanted to be on his good side. They genuinely liked Stetson.

He snuck up behind Lyric and ruffled her hair. "Hey, kiddo."

Lyric's face bloomed red, but she mock glared at Stetson. "I spent five whole minutes on this hairstyle, Stetson."

Stetson rested his hand on the back of her chair and propped his other on his hip. His gaze swept over us. "Ain't this a table waiting to start trouble."

Marion shook her head. She'd probably been his teacher when she first started working in Coal Haven. "If anyone knows anything about trouble, it's you."

Stetson hunched over like she'd punched him. "Mrs. Kasper, I'm hurt you'd think that of me." He winked, his grin packed with naughtiness.

Cameron and Bruce might pat themselves on the back about how well-behaved their boys were, but Derek, his brother, and Stetson had just been good at not getting caught.

He elbowed Lyric. "You stay out of trouble, kid."

Lyric's lips briefly pursed. "You mean when I'm helping save someone's life by running expensive analyzers to determine what's wrong with them." Her tone was flippant, but her gaze was full of yearning.

Oh. Oh, wow. The poor girl. She had it bad for Stetson, but in his older eyes, she was his little sister's best friend. Stetson might be good at reading people, but he was clueless about the way Lyric felt about him. I wasn't the only one with a secret crush. Only, my crush liked me back. And what was between us rose so far above a crush.

So what was it, then?

Nerves banded around my stomach. I was okay with saying I liked Liam. That I was his girlfriend. But what did I feel? Did I want to identify it?

Stetson's gaze caught on someone across the restaurant. "There's Holden. See you, ladies."

He slapped Lyric on the back like she was just another one of his buddies and walked away. Lyric glowered at her strawberry margarita. Aspen gave her head a small shake. I wasn't the only one who'd seen it.

An hour later, when each of us had an empty glass in front of us, Marion sighed and gathered her purse. "I'd better get going. Any longer, and this Cinderella is going to turn into a pumpkin. And Dermot waits up for me." Fondness filled her smile. She loved her husband waiting up for her. It made her feel cherished.

The closeness tugged at my heart.

Kelsey rose right after Marion. "Same here. Except no one waits up for me, and the dishes are probably still dirty. But Brinley has a tournament tomorrow. Long day in the sun."

The two women left. Aspen pushed her empty glass away. "We could always go sit with Stetson and Holden."

Lyric glanced across the bar to where Stetson and

Holden were. Her expression went blank, but storm clouds soared in her eyes. "I think he's busy."

A woman around our age was at the table, her chair close to Stetson's and his arm hanging around the back of the chair.

"Isn't she—"

"A nurse in town. Yup. I heard they were dating."

And Stetson came here all the time since another friend of his, Remington Gunn, owned the place. Was that why Lyric was dressed to kill, sex appeal her weapon? Only, Stetson was bulletproof.

Aspen tried to save the night with small talk about work, but Lyric had tuned out, and my brain was stuck on identifying what I felt for Liam.

It didn't matter. I didn't have to have the answers. But the sense that it was important loomed over me.

A new round of drinks arrived. I frowned at the server. I hadn't ordered anything but water since my wine cooler. It'd been so long since I'd had alcohol.

She cocked her head to a table on the other side of the bar. "It's on the guys over there."

Aspen and Lyric openly gawked at the table of three young men. Three of them. Three of us.

My stomach churned, threatening to upend the grilled chicken sandwich I'd had. I'd been brought another wine cooler. I could only handle one drink. I didn't know about handling guys hitting on me as I was silently panicking about whether I'd fallen in love with a man who wasn't my husband.

"We should go over there," Lyric announced. She eyed us. "You up for it?"

Aspen's gaze darted to me. I ran my thumb along my bare ring finger. The lack of metal amplified the tumble of my thoughts. A guy hits on me and the first thing I do is touch the place my wedding ring used to be, all while thinking about another man.

Aspen and Lyric were watching me. Lyric's eyes were wide, and she gnawed at her lower lip. I couldn't tell them about anything that was going through my mind. I couldn't talk to them about Liam. When I felt this way, Liam was there for me. He was in Williston, and I could call, but this wasn't exactly a subject I was ready to confess. Thinking about it had me near tears.

"You two go ahead. I might head out." Lyric and Aspen were going to do whatever it was single young women did these days. I'd never been in their shoes. I couldn't relate. I could relate to Marion, but that was part of my problem. I had no one at home. No other friends to talk to.

Pressure built behind my eyes. No way was I crying in public. Aspen and Lyric hadn't made a move.

"Seriously. You two go. I'm going to the restroom and then I'll probably leave." I would definitely leave.

I steadied myself on the way to the restroom, feeling eight hundred pounds heavier than I had sitting in my car wondering how I was going to walk inside. Relief eased the pressure in my chest. The restrooms were single stalls. I chose one and ducked inside. Gripping the sink, I sucked in hard breaths. I wasn't going to cry. My skin would get all red and blotchy, and everyone would figure it out. I'd have to walk out of the restaurant with people knowing I was crying, and they'd assume they knew why.

They had no idea. No one did.

I exhaled slowly, clenching my stomach muscles like I was doing a plank. Slow inhale. Long exhale.

A catty voice drifted through the door. "Good Lord, could you take longer? A girl's gotta piss, but three bathrooms and everyone's taking a shit?"

I pried my hands off the sink. This was my chance to

leave. Facing an irate woman with a bursting bladder would be a good distraction. She'd be upset with me for taking too long. She wouldn't consider that I'd been fighting off a breakdown. The kind of anonymity I needed right now.

I opened the door. Flashing blue eyes met mine, and recognition flared.

"Oh, it's you," Laney said flatly. "I should've known."

Fourteen

KENNEDY

The past slammed into me, overflowing the emotional well I'd been barely able to keep under control, while Laney looked at me like I'd ruined her night.

Tears sprang into my eyes, and I ducked back into the bathroom. I tried to slam the door, but Laney muscled her way in and kicked the door shut behind her.

"Good Lord, Kennedy." She grabbed a couple of tissues out of the container on the sink and stuffed them into my hands. "Of course I lose my patience waiting for an open bathroom and it's you." Her voice softened. "Have you been crying in here the whole time?"

I shook my head, but I couldn't answer. I leaned against the sink and sobbed, muffling the sound with my hands. Silent wailing. I'd perfected it in the first few months I'd gone back to work after the funeral before the final breakdown.

"Right." She didn't believe me. "Well, I've gotta pee. So hang on."

My tears stalled when she dropped her white shorts and sat on the toilet. I hiccuped and sniffled and tried not to look. Was this really happening?

Still on the toilet, she sighed. "So, I'm not the only one having a shitty night?"

The shock of group bathroom time had shifted my mind from active grief to confusion. Recent events had zoomed out as soon as Laney dropped her drawers. "Why does your night suck?"

"Lots of reasons. You?"

"Everyone knows my reason," I said bitterly, hoping it was enough of the truth that she wouldn't question it.

"Gotta love small-town life." She rose and pulled up her shorts. They showed off miles of tanned legs. Her teal top wasn't as tight and revealing as Lyric's, but it gave Laney a sophisticated, sexy vibe. "I could bawl too, and we could walk out together; really confuse everyone."

This time her tone wasn't catty. Laney cried? That was like picturing a marble statue having a meltdown. But when I looked into her ice-blue eyes, I didn't see the frigidness that had been there when we were younger. She was guarded. She was protecting herself. I recognized the look.

Really confuse everyone. It would. That she would cry—in public—and that she would do it around me. And if I looked like I'd been crying? The stares alone would almost make it fun. I couldn't believe that thought had even entered my mind. I moved in front of the door so she could wash her hands.

"Finally, a place that still kills a few trees." She whipped out a couple of paper towels and dried off. "Those hand dryers do a number on my nerves. Like having a jet engine blow my entire body instead of drying my fingers." She tossed her used paper towels. They landed perfectly in the basket. "Seriously, though. What's going on? Normal grief, or did someone say something?"

"Normal grief," I mumbled. Laney should be the last one I wanted to talk to about this. She was mean. But she'd also never let me hide away. She'd called out others when they'd done my work for me. Like how Derek had taken my car in for oil changes. How he had carried my backpack and helped me get my coat on after school. How Liam and Derek would stand up for me when she was being a bitch. *Your girlfriend should speak for herself.*

She hadn't been wrong.

"Some guys ordered me, Aspen, and Lyric some drinks." I tensed, waiting for Laney to snort and claim I was whining about men buying me drinks. For her to sarcastically say *how awful*.

"Not ready to date again?"

Liam was right. Laney wasn't the same. But then, neither was I.

I stared at my tissues. I couldn't shake my head. I'd done more than date with Liam. "Not ready to admit deeper feelings for another man."

She peered at me. I met her intense blue gaze and looked away.

"You and Liam, huh?" She switched her attention to the mirror and adjusted her long ponytail. Not one strand of her glossy blonde hair was out of place. She'd probably been working in the dirt all day, but she shone like a diamond. I'd always been a little envious of her easy beauty. I used to take solace in thinking she was ugly on the inside. Was that true anymore?

Her question sank in. My awkward giggle amplified my nervousness until that was all I heard in the sound. "Why would you think me and Liam?"

She shot me a *duh* look. "You had each of those boys wrapped around your dainty little finger. Bet the town's going batshit."

"No one knows. I mean *no one*." I pressed my lips together. I hadn't meant to admit it, but Laney had never faked cluelessness. She'd only call out the lying. But she could tell everyone. Liam was up against so much, and I was tired of my emotional roller coaster.

"Just me?" She faced me, her gaze direct. I used to dread having her focus on me. Tonight, it was refreshing. It was as easy as being around Liam. There was no sympathy, just blunt acceptance. Was that why I'd spilled everything? I needed a friend, and someone who reminded me of Liam would be a good fit.

"I care for him a lot, but being a widow makes it complicated." Some other force must have been operating my mouth right then. I couldn't stop. "Which sucks because he's usually the one who makes it all crystal clear. He just lets me decide and stays with me for the ride."

She lifted a pale brow as if she didn't believe that Liam didn't do everything for me like Derek had.

"He helps me, but he lets me do it myself. He's there for me." I tossed my tissues at the trash. One toppled out. Figured. I stooped to pick it up, threw it away, and rose to my full height. Laney was taller than me by only an inch, and she no longer loomed over me.

We were adults, and, for some weird reason, I trusted her. She'd loved to point out what she'd perceived to be my flaws, but she'd never fueled the gossip mill. "I can't have people chiming in with their two cents. Not when I'm trying to get a job so I don't have to move and leave the only town that feels like home."

If I didn't get full-time work, I might have to sell the house. I might have to move. Away from Liam. Away from his kids. As he was making his way back to town, I didn't want to be leaving.

"He shouldn't be your dirty little secret though." Plainly stated. No accusation, no sense of menace.

I recoiled. "He's not. It's just no one's business."

"Would it surprise you that I agree?"

The corner of my mouth lifted. "Yes. It would actually surprise me a lot that you wouldn't disagree on principle."

We shared a quick smile. "This town and how it talks and how we listen. I've always hated it."

Her words went deeper than gossip about me and Liam. "I'm sorry about what happened to your brother."

"You and me both." She didn't speak for a few moments, then she reached out and squeezed my hand. "I really am sorry about Derek. I know I didn't make it to the funeral, but it had nothing to do with us." She leaned her head back and blew out a breath. "Ugh, men. Fucking us up left and right."

My gaze dropped to her bare ring finger before I could stop it. She noticed and pointedly dipped her gaze to mine.

I flexed my hand. "I'm still getting used to not wearing it."

"I'm trying to get as much sun as possible before anyone else notices the tan line." She crossed her arms. "I swear, Kennedy, if anyone finds out I used to wear a wedding ring, I'm going to tell everyone about you and Liam."

"O-okay." A spear of panic hit my chest before I realized how secret she wanted to keep her marriage. A soft chuckle left me. We possessed each other's most significant secret. "Who'd have thought... You and me?"

Her smile wavered, and she glanced at her left hand again. "I tried to be like you."

"What?"

"You had this wounded-little-fawn aura about you. You

were the teachers' favorite. You commanded Derek and even Liam. The good boy and the rebel, falling at your feet, hanging on your every word. Meanwhile, I got called a bitch. The mean girl." She rolled her eyes. "I get that I was kind of both."

"Kind of?" It was my turn to lift a brow.

"I wasn't a saint, but if I had been a guy, would anyone have thought twice?" She had a point. "Anyway, sorry about dumping my Coke on you. It was mostly an accident, but it only made them rally around you harder. So when I met my...well, he was everything I'd thought I wanted."

Her gaze flickered, those blue depths hiding hurtful memories. "I tried to be you. Then Kane hurt himself, and I had to leave. I told my husband I had to go home and that I was doing it no matter what he said or what his mom had to say. He argued. Thought I should put his and his parents' wishes first. So I left him. And he let me go. Because it turns out, if I wasn't meek, he didn't want to be with me, and I'd been lying to myself."

When I'd first met Laney, I was struck by how strong she was, inside and out. I was weak, trying to project strength instead of spending a lifetime seeming weak. But I saw her clearer at the moment. We weren't that much different.

Her fingers stretched out, and she clenched her fist. "I should've known better."

She'd had the guts to act differently and had people treat her the same as before. I knew all about that. "I've been trying to be more like you. Confident. Strong. Say what I'm thinking." Like telling Bruce I absolutely did not want his help. Laney would've said it months ago. I seemed to always have reasons not to.

"Good luck with that. People resent it when you tell them what they don't want to hear."

"I'm not very good at it. I'm not brave enough." Some

days, I was the gopher, peering out of the hole, afraid of the dangers of the world around me. What would happen if Liam and I went public?

Laney put her hand on the doorknob. "Keep hanging around me, and I might rub off on you. Want a drink?"

* * *

Liam

Most men my age didn't spend as much time on the phone as I did. Sprawled out on my bed, phone pressed to my ear, like I was some kid in a '90s sitcom rerun Grandma Gin used to leave on when she was making supper. Only I was a grown man on a twin bed in a rented bedroom.

Calling was necessary when I was gone this long. Eli and Owen couldn't read more than their names. They could do that thanks to Kenny, but messages weren't the same as seeing my face on the screen telling them good night, to brush their teeth, and hug their grandma for me.

I talked to them on my second break, and after work I often called Kenny. Reading her words wasn't as good as hearing them. Her laughter carried over the line, and I could picture her smile. Mostly we talked about our days. She would get a four-day weekend over the Fourth of July. I'd be home by then, and we'd do something fun with the kids. She was painting the second bedroom that she used as an office and would tackle her bedroom next. I'd talked to Hattie; she'd wanted pictures of my other projects. Grandma Gin and the kids had done a photo shoot for me and had sent me all the pictures to choose the best to send.

Kenny and I kept in touch every day, yet found new

stuff to talk about. But tonight's conversation was more than routine.

"She did what?" Had I heard right?

"Stayed over. Slept on my couch. Laney Granger. After we bonded in the bathroom, we had a few drinks. Mine were water, but she drank too much to drive home. So I invited her here."

"And?"

"It was...fun." Kenny giggled, a delightful sound that I owed Laney for. An honest, innocent giggle, with no shadows of grief. Only my kids had been able to get that reaction from her. "She apologized. Can you believe it? Laney Granger. Apologized."

"How did she do it though?" I could see Laney say something like, *I'm sorry you were too dense to figure it out yourself*. In fact, she'd actually said that to one of the football players our sophomore year. She'd aced the algebra test, but the guy claimed she'd cheated when he'd failed and had to sit out a game until he raised his grade.

"Sincerely, except for what was the truth." Another giggle. "We're going out again this weekend."

"Rattler's?"

"Maybe, then a movie at my house."

I snorted. "You're dating Laney."

"I kind of am. *Weird*, right? I think living at home is a hard adjustment for her. Anyway, have you heard back from Hattie?"

"I did today. She wants to work with me. She'd carry the item, include it in her catalog, and then she'd keep a percentage of the sale. I'd need to provide her with a steady supply." Once I gave myself permission to brainstorm, I'd had a lot of ideas. Firepits, furniture, home decor.

"Will that be hard to do in the time you're home?"

"About that." My excitement rose as I thought back to

my call. I was as giddy as the boys Christmas morning. "Hattie said her friend is a manager at the mine in Washburn. She offered to put in a good word for me, so I applied."

"Liam." My name was a whisper on a cloud of excitement. "That would be awesome!"

I broke into a grin. No one could see, but it didn't matter. My life was finally turning around. "It would be a commute, but the drive isn't more than forty-five minutes on a decent highway. I wouldn't be far from Coal Haven. I'd still need Grandma Gin's help with the kids, but it wouldn't be twenty days in a row."

"I'll be here too. Oh, Liam. That would be so nice."

"Mm." My gaze bored into the off-white ceiling. "Not just nice for me, Grandma Gin, and the kids?"

"No," she said softly. "Not just for them."

My grin returned. "Good to hear. Because I took a gamble and put in my notice. I'll be home for my ten days next week, go back for my last twenty, and then I'm done. I want to make sure I'm around when the kids start school."

"You have your house and land. A local-ish job, and a second job as an artist."

"Artist?" She'd said that before, but that was when I'd been playing around as a hobby.

"Your work is beautiful, Liam. That firepit you did would make it hard for me to light a fire inside of it."

"I've been thinking of other designs. Firepits never go out of style." A lot of good things were happening, but I didn't want to dwell on them. I'd get excited when I was home for good and I had worked a few shifts at the mine. Good things like this didn't happen to me. It seemed too easy.

She might've tried to smother her yawn, but I heard it.

"I should let you go."

"I don't have to get up tomorrow. But you do."

"Nah, it's nothing." It was something. I wasn't used to pulling a ten- or twelve-hour shift and drinking all night anymore. Staying up late to talk to Kenny wasn't on the same level as those days so long ago.

I pictured her tucked into bed, only the bed I imagined was mine. Her rich brown hair spread over my gunmetal-gray sheets. Seconds later, blood redirected to the dick that wouldn't stay down whenever I thought of her. "Whatcha wearing?"

"It probably sounds sexier than it is, but bootie shorts and a tank top."

"There's no way that isn't as sexy as it sounds." Her laugh was breathy, a little flirty. Encouraging. "You lying down?"

Bedsheets rustled. "Now I am."

I sensed the hesitancy. She was in her home. In her bed. Getting kinky over the phone in the bed she used to share with her husband would be a new level of intimacy and a new hurdle for her. "Want me to tell you how I picture you, or do you want me to tell you good night and that I'll dream of you?" After a cold shower and a quick jack off.

During the silence on the other end, I prepped how I would tell her good night so she didn't feel one ounce of guilt.

"How...how do you picture me?"

My grin was easy. I flicked open the fly of my jeans. "Your hair's spread out..."

Fifteen

KENNEDY

"Any plans for the Fourth, Kennedy?" Anita Zachmeier breezed into the classroom. She stuffed her hands in the pockets of her wide linen shorts and wandered through tables and chairs, her eagle-eye gaze missing nothing.

It was her classroom, but it'd been tasked for summer school. I'd been teaching in it for weeks, cognizant of her *who moved my cheese* mentality. At the end of the day, I returned every toy, book, and learning aid to its original spot.

I tapped out of the grading reports I was updating. Mrs. Z had stopped in before, and she was so nosy I couldn't work. I might take the laptop home and update the reports I would send home to parents when summer school wrapped up in a few weeks.

"I don't have much planned for the holiday." I had plans, but she was the last person I would tell. Maybe second-to-last after Derek's parents. Third-from-last after my mother.

Liam and I were going to take the boys to the big Fourth of July parade in Mandan. The thing lasted almost an hour and a half, and we had to get there almost two hours early to nab a decent spot on the road. Then we were going to take them out to eat and soak up some restaurant's AC. Whether we hit up a lake for some swimming or came home to relax and grill would be determined by how all of us were holding up.

I couldn't wait. Yet, when anyone asked, I made it sound like I wasn't straying far from home. Bruce and Willow had invited me over, but I was still stinging from Bruce wanting to take over my expenses. Willow had invited me over for supper once since that night, but I'd had plans with Laney. I didn't tell them about my burgeoning friendship with her either. Then they might think I was blowing money I couldn't afford.

Being around Laney was better than therapy. I had monthly therapy sessions, but one night on my couch with Laney and a couple of White Claws, and I'd come to the conclusion that I wasn't ready to define what I felt for Liam and that was fine. He was important to me. Critical. And that was enough for now.

Mrs. Z watched me pack my things.

"You have holiday plans?" I asked to fill the empty silence.

"Nothing. It's a noisy holiday. I go to the home and see my mom, then stay inside and avoid all the drunks."

Okay. I packed my teaching laptop and gathered the spelling tests I had yet to grade. When I had worked at the school before, I'd brushed off Mrs. Z's attitude. She was from a different time; she was set in her ways. Since I'd come back, she irritated the shit out of me.

My irritation rose higher and faster today. Maybe because the other day, as I was returning from a walk, Bruce had stopped by, and when I hadn't answered, he'd let himself in. Worried something was wrong since my car was home.

His face had been flushed and his movements jerky. If he hadn't been so fraught that I worried he was going to stroke, I'd have asked for my key back. I'd give it a week or two, then talk to him, as much as I was dreading it. But I had to start setting limits.

So, yeah, I was a little cranky. Mrs. Z and her constant disdain could frown in someone else's face. Maybe she'd been a good kindergarten teacher thirty-five years ago, but she needed to find another job. One where she wasn't responsible for the self-esteem of malleable children.

"Classroom assignments have come out. Have you heard?"

Ah. That was why she'd been coming in. During breaks, Mrs. Z was on her phone. At lunch, she was on her phone. But when it came to doing extra work—even checking emails—outside of her teaching hours, she claimed she didn't have the capabilities at home. I respected her hard stance on not working for free outside the hours she was paid. I'd respect it more if it weren't out of sheer laziness. That she came in so often during the summer had surprised me. Until Aspen had said Mrs. Z would make sure her time was unofficially comped.

That made sense.

"That's always an exciting time." I used to love seeing who I'd get in my classroom the next school year. I'd start working on ways to reach usually difficult students and keep them engaged. One of my favorite challenges was finding out what approach worked with a student whom other teachers struggled with.

Mrs. Z sniffed. "It's going to be a tough year."

"Oh?" She said that every year.

"It's going to be hard." Her breath gusted out of her. "Did you hear Liam Barron enrolled his kids? He planned on moving them, but decided he liked his grandma raising them, I guess." She sniffed again. "Not a surprise. And I have not one of his boys but both. You'd have thought they'd have separated them."

Pressure built at my temples. So much was wrong with what Mrs. Z had said. She knew nothing about Liam other than having had him in kindergarten over twenty years ago. I willed myself to speak calmly. One of us had to be professional. "The boys have been together every day of their lives. Perhaps the committee thought it best to ease them into school first, together, and then separate them at a later date."

"Those two are too much for one teacher."

I rose and hefted my bag to my shoulder. "You know them?"

"Everyone knows Liam's boys."

It was Coal Haven. Yes, they did. But that wasn't what I meant, and she knew it. "You've met them?"

"I had Liam in class," she said flatly, as if that should be explanation enough.

"They're good kids." How would Mrs. Z handle Eli's speech? She was painfully blunt. I might appreciate that characteristic in my new world, but it had a place there. With five-year-old kids and an issue that could either be easily overcome without long-lasting effects or used to degrade his sense of self, tact was required.

Mrs. Z was notoriously tactless.

"That will remain to be seen. Obviously, I'll have to start the school year by seating them as far from each other as possible."

"Or you could see how they handle a big change in

their lives like kindergarten." My long-lost temper pounded against my skull. My voice came out hard as steel. "Or you could make their learning environment so difficult from the beginning that they start acting out and fulfill your low expectations. But it sounds like that's what you want."

Mrs. Z blinked at me, but I didn't want to waste one more minute with her. I breezed out as airily as she'd come in. I stormed down the hall, spun like a soldier on parade, and marched down the shorter hallway to the exit.

I was about to push out the door when the principal peeked out of his office. "Kennedy. Everything okay?"

I whirled on him, and he reared back. I couldn't see my reflection, but it must have been fierce. Gone was the slightly lost widow or the placating young teacher. "No, actually, it's not, Mr. Gilding. I'm tired of the way Mrs. Z treats kids she doesn't think are worth her full effort. I'm tired of her laziness, and I'm sick of her attitude. Most of all, I hate how we all accept that's the way she is and ignore it. Then the rest of us have to undo all the damage she does to those young minds, thinking they read too slowly or can't do math, so they might as well not try. And God forbid, a five-year-old kid acts like they're five and have a meltdown. That must be shitty parenting, and why bother trying to do her damn job?"

Ohmigod.

Oh my God. Had I just said all that? Had I just berated my boss for something he was as guilty of as the rest of us? Ignoring Mrs. Z was a job skill we'd developed after our first months here.

I pressed my lips together. "Have a happy Fourth." Pushing out into the sun, letting the heat fold around me, I dragged in a deep breath.

I didn't think I'd get fired, but I hadn't wanted to create

a work environment full of tension. Still. Mrs. Z had messed with my kids.

* * *

I angrily painted the office until I'd finished it. I probably looked a lot like Bruce had feared when he'd let himself into my house thinking I'd collapsed or something.

Deano from the bank had called yesterday. He'd said Bruce had asked that the mortgage payment come out of his account instead of mine. Deano couldn't, since Bruce wasn't on my mortgage.

Because it was my goddamn house.

I put my hand on my chest. Breathe in, two, three. Out, two, three, four. I'd have to ask for my key back sooner than later. And I had told Deano that in no way, shape, or form was anyone else responsible for my accounts.

I'd been unleashing hell on the old paint job ever since. And if I didn't get that key back, Bruce might see that I was working on a new project and step in.

This had gone on too long, and it was all my fault.

I glanced around the room, inspecting it for spots I'd missed. Looked good. My bedroom was next, but I had to rip off the blue hummingbird wallpaper behind my bed.

I pushed a hand through my hair and redid my bun. Someday, I'd get it to stay in place while I worked. Today was not that day.

My doorbell rang. I jumped and yelped, putting a hand to my chest. My heart raced. I shouldn't have been surprised, but I'd been stuck in my head.

I went to the door. Liam wasn't going to be home for two more days. If it was Bruce, I was upset enough to have words. I just didn't want to say something I would regret.

He was only looking out for me, but he obviously wasn't going to learn where to butt out if I didn't tell him.

I peered out. Laney leaned against the railing, sunglasses on, staring down the street. I opened the door. "You look like you're modeling that beer you're holding."

I could snap a picture and sell it. Her hair was in a classy bun, nothing like mine. Casual, but cool, and I doubted it slipped one millimeter from where she'd secured it. She had on short pink shorts and a sheer white blouse that showed off her pink bra.

"It's all in the attitude," she said and pushed off the railing. "You free?"

"If you don't count my date with wallpaper from the seventies, yes."

She pulled off her sunglasses, her blue eyes sparkling. "Is it demolition time?"

"Only of the wallpaper."

She vibrated like she was ready to destroy something. "Good enough. Want help?"

I eyed her outfit. "I can lend you something to wear so you don't get those dirty."

"I'm not worried about it."

"I am. At least borrow one of my shirts."

Laney grinned and beelined for the fridge. She stuffed the beer inside but grabbed a Bud Light with clamato juice and offered me one.

"No White Claw?" I asked.

"After your text about Bruce, I figured we needed something stronger."

Good thing she hadn't brought hard liquor. I accepted the drink and led her to the bedroom. I stopped at the foot of the bed.

Laney's gaze swept the room. "Cool lamp."

Residual guilt faded, both for placing Liam's gift in the

bedroom I had shared with Derek, but also for the round of phone sex. Having her in here made it feel more like a room. A place I could mold and change. This bedroom wasn't a mausoleum for my marriage. "Liam made it."

She sent me a measured glance, like she realized its placement hadn't been an easy decision. When he'd given it to me, I'd wanted to keep it close. It was like I put it next to my bed as a signal to my mind that this was no longer a room I shared with my husband.

She put her hands on her hips and studied the wall. "That's some atrocious wallpaper."

The paper curled at the top of a few seams. The birds were a sun-faded blue, the flowers they suckled out of paled to a baby pink. "I'm sure it was cute forty years ago."

Her expression said *doubtful* as she set her beer on the top of my dresser. "Those birds have seen some things."

"That's why they need to die."

Laney barked out a laugh and bent to pull the bed away from the wall. I set my can next to hers and helped. For the next few hours, we fought the wallpaper, and, at times, the wallpaper won. We drank through the six-pack.

"Damn," Laney announced from the kitchen. "We're in a paradox."

I followed her voice. She stood in front of the open fridge. The old college shirt she'd borrowed from me clung to her curves. I definitely did not sex up that shirt like her.

"What's wrong?"

"We drank all the beer and need more, but because we drank all the beer, we can't go get more."

"I shouldn't keep drinking anyway." The birds were getting blurry. I'd been fighting for control for so long it was freeing to have a little of it willingly given away.

"No one should keep drinking; that's why it's fun." She pulled a face. "My husband refused to drink beer." She never said his name. "The kicker was, I think he really liked it, but it wasn't an approved drink according to his rich friends."

"Your ex was rich?"

"Mm." She tossed a knowing look over her shoulder. "Money was almost as important as image, and I was like beer: I didn't fit the image."

"Dick."

"Grade-A asshole." Her voice was tinged with longing. Asshole or not, her feelings for him had been real.

My phone buzzed. Liam would call in the next hour or two, but he was still working. I had a message from Aspen. **OMG, I just ran into Z. What'd you do?!?!** Another message came in. **You know I'm kidding, right? I know whatever happened, it was Z.**

"What the hell?" I could only imagine what Mrs. Z was saying about me.

Laney let the fridge door close. "Who do I need to kill?"

I smirked. My first two years in Coal Haven, I'd heard several comments about her. People had wondered how Derek could stand Laney. Why had he dated her for so long? They'd been inseparable. Laney might've been in love. Derek, maybe a little, but he'd been dedicated to her until he met me. He'd never said, and maybe later in our relationship when so many years passed it wouldn't have mattered, he might've confessed that he'd missed her friendship. I'd seen the signs and, at times, worried that maybe he'd go back to her. That the uniqueness of the new girl would wear off. But I saw it now. Liam was like a brother to him, but she'd also been Derek's close friend.

"It's my friend from work. She's the one that got hired after I left."

"You haven't said no. I have a shovel and a lot of land. But you're doing the digging."

I rolled my eyes, but the image of us out in the dark with

shovels made me giggle. "No. She's great. But she must've heard that I kind of lost my temper at work. I didn't think anything came of it. Guess it did?"

"God heard our dilemma and sent us your drama. Tell your friend to bring a case over and tell us about it."

I stared at Laney. My in-laws and mother didn't know about Liam—or Laney. My actions were questioned enough. But no, I wasn't hiding Laney too. Dammit. I was an adult.

"What? Have I met her already? Does she hate me?" Laney stated it like a forgone conclusion.

"Aspen Whitfield. Know her?"

"Nope, haven't pissed her off yet."

"I think she'd like you." Before I invited Aspen over, I realized that I hadn't really done that. Ever. Mom had leapfrogged through town after town until we'd landed in Coal Haven. I hadn't had a chance to get to know anyone well enough, and then I'd been too sick to play or visit. School had taken everything out of me for so many years. "You're the first friend I've had over."

"I'm honored." Laney jutted her chin toward my phone. "Invite another one, and we'll increase our friend circle by thirty percent." She wrinkled her nose. "Is that math right? Wait, I don't care."

I might've chickened out on my own, but I did as Laney commanded. **I have a friend over and we ran dry. Want to bring a case here and I'll tell you what happened?** If she turned me down, would it be like getting rejected for a date? I didn't know what that was like either, and I didn't want to.

Aspen's reply was immediate. **You saved me from death by curiosity. Be right there!**

"She's coming." Aspen hadn't asked for my address, but it was Coal Haven. She'd figure it out if she didn't know.

"Let's put our stuff away. I need my full attention to hear about how Kennedy Barron lost her shit."

"It wasn't that bad," I mumbled.

Glee filled her eyes. "It doesn't have to be when they're used to sweet little innocent you. I hope Aspen brings something yummy. This calls for a celebration!"

She didn't even know that I'd been in the right. I had been. The twins deserved teachers who hadn't already decided how their year was going to go.

Aspen arrived right after we'd hauled out a trash bag of wallpaper and vacuumed my room. The bed was still pressed against the dresser, but I left it. The new position worked for me.

One round of phone sex in that bed had reignited the guilt I'd experienced that first time with Liam. That bed had been bought when Derek and I had moved into the house. One of those assumptions I'd forgotten I'd had. That the bed would be the place I would've slept with only my husband for years. Then it'd become the place where I'd thought only about Derek. A little intimate sanctuary. Until Liam. I had to realize that I was giving that bed a lot of power. A queen-size mattress wasn't going to dictate how I remembered my time with my husband.

But having the bed in a different spot helped.

I let Aspen in. Laney pressed a wad of cash into her hand. "For your service. We were out."

Aspen grinned and pushed her hair off one shoulder. "You're Laney, right?"

Laney smiled, but tension snapped over her features. "Damn. You've heard of me."

"I'm friends with Lyric. She said you're pretty badass. That you can tell off any Barron in town and get away with it."

Laney's expression rippled with surprise, like she hadn't

expected talk about her to be positive. "That is indeed true. Barrons have a hard time hearing the truth."

Aspen snickered and dug a can out from the case. "I hope you don't mind hard seltzer. I think it tastes like fruity piss, but I only have one swimsuit, and it looks amazing on me, so I've gotta fit into it all season." She cracked open the can. "I'm dying, Kennedy. Z said you yelled at her."

Both women stared at me, eyes wide. "I didn't...yell," I sighed. "She found out she has Liam's twins in her class."

"Liam? Oh, Lyric pointed him out one night when he came into Rattler's to grab pizzas. You two friends?"

I nodded and concentrated on the cold can in my hand to keep my expression from giving away that Liam and I were more. "We are, and I've been helping him and his grandma with the kids."

"But they're rambunctious little boys and Z is prepared to smoosh their little vibrant personalities." Aspen shook her head. "She makes me a little ragey. I want to say something, but I'm afraid I'll make it worse. I'm just the new girl."

"I bit her head off, but when I was leaving, Mr. Gilding stopped me, and I unloaded." I didn't regret it. Mrs. Z could make those kids' school life hell.

"*Nice*," Laney hissed. "Go right to the top."

"He talked to her," Aspen said excitedly. "She said she threatened to quit. Ooooh, if only. You'd be my new hero, Kennedy. Not many parents or teachers stand up to Z."

I lifted a shoulder. I didn't feel like a hero, and I didn't need drama at work. "I'm not the type of person that does that though."

Laney cocked her head. "But you are. Who cares what anyone thinks?"

Laney took a slow sip of her drink, eyeing me. I could see the subtle challenge in her eyes. I was the type who told

Mrs. Z off because I'd done it, and then I'd basically reported her to the principal. So why wouldn't I stand by what I did? What about when the rest of town found out? Liam had had issues with her as a teacher, and he likely wasn't the only one. But Mrs. Z had taught hundreds of children. She was well liked and respected in the community.

The Mrs. Z issue wasn't the only subject in Laney's knowing look. If I couldn't embrace the conflict between me and a fellow teacher and weather the fallout, how would I handle not just the town learning I was seeing Liam, but the rest of the Barrons?

Sixteen

LIAM

I arrived in Coal Haven earlier than planned. I turned off the highway and wound through town until I stopped in front of Kenny's house. She was going with me to meet with Hattie, not because I was nervous or because I needed a wingman, but because she was as excited as I was. It was nice to have someone to share this with.

I trotted to the door and knocked.

She opened it, her smile radiant and her hair thrown up in the loose bun that had its own personality. What would it be like to come home to this every day? Longing plugged my chest, threatening the strength of the return smile I was flashing her.

I was getting ahead of myself. We were a new couple with a lot of baggage. Only one other person knew about us. I hadn't told Grandma Gin, but I wanted Kenny to get comfortable with others knowing. I wasn't in a rush. That she had told Laney meant a lot.

She stood back to let me in. I stepped in, and when she shut the door behind me, I pulled her to me. Her eyes heated, and fuck, I wanted her to look at me like that forever.

That longing came back. I dropped my head and captured her mouth. She twined her arms around my neck. We made out until it was uncomfortable for me to bend. A perfect impression of my zipper was now in my dick. I straightened but kept her in my arms.

"I missed you," she murmured.

"What a coincidence. I missed you." I went to war with my zipper again as I bent and rubbed my palms over the globes of her ass. That didn't help the pressure in my jeans. "Phone sex is nothing like holding you for real. And I don't have to worry that a roommate will hear me ask you to cup a boob when you rub your clit."

Desire flared in her eyes, but she giggled. "I love how you make me laugh."

And I love you. I swallowed the words back. It was the first time I'd allowed myself to think about our relationship like that, but it had to be too soon for her. "I'm good for that."

She tipped her head back. "You're good for a lot of things, Liam, in a lot of ways."

Those expressive brown eyes stripped away all the identities other people layered over me. I wasn't illegitimate with her. I wasn't just a single dad. I wasn't some wild teenage kid that had been written off as an adult before I'd been old enough to drink. I was just Liam. A guy who fell hard for this special girl.

The emotion was overwhelming, and if I didn't do something, I'd say something stupid. "We don't have to meet Hattie for a half an hour."

The drive would take three minutes. I could do a lot in twenty-seven minutes.

She kissed the side of my neck. A shiver traced down my spine, and she kept at it. Licking my skin, she rimmed her hands along my waistband and untucked my shirt.

We stood in the middle of the kitchen floor; I was helpless to move. Her lips and her hands rooted me in place.

Then she kneeled.

I swallowed roughly, my mind reeling, stunned at what she was doing.

I knew what she was doing. But I couldn't believe it. "Kenny?"

"Can I do this? For you?" Stark vulnerability darkened her brown eyes.

I nodded, numb, except for the thick desire making my skin tight. I was a guy. I liked blow jobs. I never expected them. Never sought them out. If they happened, they happened. It was the last thing I'd expected today or anywhere in the near future.

I couldn't hold her while she was kneeling, but I had to touch her. I unhooked the band from the tangle of hair on top of her head and stuffed my hands through the silky strands. She gazed up at me as she unzipped my pants and pulled me out, her hand cool on my searing hot erection.

Just her touch was enough to threaten my balance. She gave me a firm pump.

I braced my legs and dug for my wallet. "Do you want me to put a condom on?"

Those puffy lips turned down. "I haven't..." Right. She'd never given head over latex. I was about to assure her that she could abort mission. I had no issues getting her off instead, but her hold on me tightened and obliterated coherent thought. "You're clean, right?"

"I got tested after I realized what a liar Payton was. I've

always used protection since." Even if the girl hadn't minded, I had insisted; it didn't matter what we were doing.

"Then you don't mind?"

My breath whooshed out. "Fuck, no. Kenny, you could just stare at it for a few minutes and I'd probably explode."

My balls were tight, and my cock strained for the woman in front of it. Like sheer will and perseverance would help it grow an extra few inches to get to her mouth.

She didn't put her lips on me right away. She explored. She ran her thumbs along the veins of the shaft. Cradled my balls, gave them a squeeze. I stood like a redwood. Tall, erect, and not to be moved until my time was up.

When her lips brushed the tip, I groaned. "Woman, you're killing me."

"Sorry."

I cupped her chin and ignored my obnoxious cock in her face. "There's nothing to be sorry for. You're killing me in the best way. I'm at your mercy."

"I've been thinking about this."

She'd been having wicked thoughts? Of me? I'd been daydreaming of holding her, kissing her, someday having people know that this magnificent woman had given me a chance.

"Show me what you've been thinking about." It came out as a growl, but I was ready to beg.

Her eyelids drifted shut, and she sucked me in. A small hum traveled along every inch of my erection and sparked up my spine.

Her hot tongue was hesitant but grew bolder, and her fingers dug into my thighs as she pulled back and then pushed forward. I died a small death every time she took me into the sweltering depths of her mouth. The tug of her suction. The way her cheeks hollowed. Dark lashes sweeping down with her eyes closed.

It was just the two of us. Fully dressed except for my dick in her mouth. But it was the most erotic thing I'd ever seen. This would keep me up at night. This would make every night I spent alone in my tiny rented bedroom on a borrowed twin mattress feel like eternity had come and gone and left me behind.

I didn't want to be by myself anymore. I wanted to come home to my kids and Kenny. I wanted to come home to this. Not blow jobs specifically. I wanted to come home and talk, tell each other our problems, and then help each other demolish the stress of everyday life.

I clenched my glutes to keep myself from swaying. She pumped my base as she laved the tip.

"Fuck, Kenny." It was getting harder not to move.

I clenched my fingers over her scalp but didn't dig in. I held myself still. The last thing I wanted to do was stab her throat and choke her.

She worked me until I was shaking. My hands were rock steady in her hair and my feet planted firmly in one spot. The rest of me was a quaking mess. Because one woman had my cock in her mouth.

"I can't—I've gotta—" I tried to warn her, but she hummed. *Hummed* dammit.

I couldn't withstand the onslaught of ecstasy. I came, long and hard. And she took me. Humming. Holding me. I was putty, molded perfectly into her grip.

I sagged, and she released me. Cool air wafted over my damp skin. I wouldn't be surprised if steam rose from where she'd had her mouth. She was about to get up.

"Stay down there. It's your turn."

Desire flared in her eyes, but she sat back. "You don't have to."

"We have time." I'd make sure of it.

I stuffed myself into my pants, to hell with the zipper,

and kneeled. I crawled over her, forcing her back. I kept going until her back hit the floor and I covered her.

I caught her lips with mine. She was hesitant to open, as if she worried the taste of me would be revolting. It turned on the caveman in my brain. That was me, and she was mine.

Mine.

And someday, maybe I would be hers.

* * *

Kennedy

Hattie took us on a tour around the showroom. I'd never been to Haven Furnishings. Derek would cross his parents when it came to people in his life, but he'd balanced it by staying on their good side when it came to business. Barrons were forbidden from doing business with Hattie Garcia, thanks to Cameron. No one wanted Thanksgiving with a pissy Cameron. I'd been through one and could understand why.

Hattie ran her hand over elegant sitting room chairs. "These pieces are from a supplier in Glendive. She hand-crafts the wood she uses for the frame and partners with a woman from Ethiopia for the fabric and designs. Her stuff is considered high end. I'm lucky to get pieces from her." Hattie paused, shooting each of us a grin. "I can mark them up like no one's business. It's a good profit margin—for all of us."

She paused at each section she'd created in the floor plan and told us about the designer, the builder, and how she'd met them. Her chin-length salt-and-pepper hair swung, and when she smiled, the right side of her face lifted higher, that eye squinting more. She also tilted her head, as if trying to even out the sides. A tic from childhood, perhaps, when a brash adult or unthinking kid had made a comment on the asymmetry of her features.

Bracelets on her wrist clattered together as she swept her arm out to tell us about a couch and loveseat set. The bracelets probably had a story too, and if Hattie were telling it, I wanted to hear it.

"These are factory built but are still quality construction with a simple design. I supply across the board. If someone in Coal Haven needs to outfit their bedroom, they can come here for a nice, boring headboard and dresser set. Or they can choose a handcrafted headboard." She waved for us to follow her. "Like this one here."

We reached a bed with a gorgeously simple headboard. Planks of wood were stacked on each other, much like shiplap, and each plank was a different shade of wood grain. From light gray to a rich cherrywood.

"That's beautiful." I ran my hand along the headboard. It looked rough, like I should pick up no less than five slivers, like someone had found these planks in the trees and hammered them together. Only smooth, cool wood ran under my hand.

"I get these from a man in Fort Berthold. He and his grandson do this as a side gig; it makes the pieces seem rare to the buyers. The guys have no interest in dealing with packing and shipping and sales. So I do that—arrange pickup and delivery—and we've gotten buyers all over the nation." She bobbed her head. "I think that's what your work can do, Liam. I think you're good enough to attract people from all over the country. I'd say internationally too, but I haven't wanted to deal with the increased cost and time." She let out a contented sigh. "I have enough work to keep me busy."

Despite Cameron and Naomi Barron. My hopes continued to soar. This would be so good for Liam.

He squatted down to get a closer look at an end table that matched the headboard. "This place is really something, Hattie."

She nodded like it was a simple fact, but she beamed. "Come here." She took us through the living room section to a corner that had an eclectic home decor vibe. Less staged and more displayed. "This is where I'd put your pieces." She spread out her hands to encompass most of the corner. "Locals can come in and shop, but I have a room in the back where I can keep props for photo shoots. I'll still put your work online."

I pictured the firepit and the chain-link cross that Liam had made on display. It wouldn't take much to add to their appeal. A few cute chairs. A couple of skewers for marshmallows and hot dogs. I'd want a firepit after I'd seen that display too.

They chatted about a few pieces that Liam had on hand and his ideas for the rest of the tractor seats that I'd found in my garage. She wanted a firepit, two preferably, with different designs than what he'd made for Charlotte.

Liam pushed a hand through his hair. "My grandpa had a lot of collections. Old bikes. Record players. I still have them. I've got some ideas."

Warmth spread through me. He hadn't wanted to touch his grandpa's junk, but then he hadn't thought any of it was junk. He couldn't throw it out, but changing it and selling it to take care of Grandma Gin was exactly something Liam would do. He was one of a kind.

And he was mine.

Hattie's gaze lit up. "Anything for the gardens or outside sells better in the spring and summer, so get me those first."

I wandered around while Liam and Hattie talked shop

and contracts. The information was interesting, but the store was full of eye candy. A treasure in our small town.

When they were done, Liam wore the same smile his kids did when we told them we were going fishing or to the lake. My body warmed, and I was tempted to throw myself at him for a big hug. He was happy with himself, and I didn't get to see that expression on him nearly enough.

I'd congratulate him later. We could lie in bed and talk about his projects and the store until he had to get home.

Or tomorrow, after we wore the kids out at the parade and the lake, then lit fireworks. It didn't get dark enough for fireworks until after ten. Closer to eleven was better. So, we'd concluded it was better for me to sleep over. A legitimate excuse to tell the boys.

I couldn't wait for tomorrow—or tomorrow night.

"Ready?" Liam held a few papers. The contracts. He was a contracted artist.

Never mind stealing him for myself. This was too momentous to keep to ourselves. "We need to celebrate. How about I treat for pizza this time? Tell Grandma Gin she's welcome too."

His grin widened, and he held the door open for me. I stepped out and blinked in the sun, wishing I had my sunglasses.

"Kennedy?"

I stiffened and spun. The man I faced was an older version of Liam, his expression nowhere near as friendly. Cameron Barron, in his standard black suit with cowboy boots. It was his schtick. A big oil guy who was still a small-town rancher. His graying hair was combed to the side, and the lines on his face only added to the aura of power he carried.

Bruce came to a stop next to Cameron. The perfect damper to my jubilant mood.

Liam stepped out. "I'll message—" He ground to a stop next to me.

I kept my smile as sunny as the sky. I was an adult, and I was out with a friend. I was not some kid busted with a forbidden boyfriend. "Hi, Bruce. Cameron. How are you?"

Bruce's scowl etched into his face until he looked twenty years older. Seeing me with Liam wasn't as much of a shock to him. "Good. Say, did Deano get a hold of you?"

"Yes." I wasn't getting into my finances around Cameron. Or had Bruce already talked to him? I was tempted to cower, but I cleared my throat and forced the words out of my mouth. "I told him that everything was fine as it was. Thank you for the offer, though."

Bruce frowned, his brow furrowing so deeply I could hide in the creases, but he didn't say anything. Damn, that shouldn't have been so hard. I'd wait to ask for the keys back when Cameron wasn't around.

A spear of fear shot down my spine. I'd have to do that soon. I couldn't risk Bruce walking in on what I'd been doing on my kitchen floor this afternoon.

Cameron's shrewd, glittering gaze danced between Liam, me, and the store. We were in front of the large picture windows emblazoned with "Haven Furnishings." His mouth twisted like Liam had shoved a lemon wedge between the man's lips. "William."

Liam's jolt was subtle. He'd probably rather be ignored. The men hopefully didn't notice. "Cameron," he replied flatly.

"Is it true you're staying in town?"

"Yes."

Bruce tugged his gaze off me. "You're not letting Ginny sell the place and get the money she's owed from it?"

"Yes, Bruce. That's exactly what I'm doing." Liam's reply dripped sarcasm. "If you'd like to keep leasing the land,

I'll be in touch with a new contract that'll address who's responsible for the property and how it'll affect the rent."

Bruce sucked in a breath, and Cameron's gaze glinted. I could practically see the plotting begin. If we stuck around, it'd be these two ganging up on Liam and using me as a tool to get to him.

I wasn't giving them that power. I peeked at my phone. "Oh, look at the time. We need to get going. Tell Willow and Naomi I said hi."

I edged around them. Liam gave them a nod, his eyes hooded. If he'd worn his ball cap, his expression would've been shadowed. Without the cap, the simmering resentment was harder to hide. And the resemblance to his father was clearer than ever.

We couldn't just cross the street or hop in a vehicle and close the doors between us and them. The lunch crowd for the diner had extended to this block, and we hadn't been able to park right in front of the store. Liam's pickup was parked several spots down. We hadn't thought twice about it. Until now.

Bruce pivoted like a sunflower following the sun as I walked around him. "Kennedy."

"Hmm?" I kept my expression casual despite the tension vibrating among the four of us.

"You need anything, you call."

I waved him off. "I'm doing good, but I'll keep it in mind."

Finally, Liam and I had created enough distance that the knot between my shoulders loosened. When I was closed in the pickup with Liam, surrounded by his soap and cedar scent, I rolled my head to stretch my neck.

Liam's jaw was clenched, the little muscles on the side flexing. How badly had that brief interaction rattled him? I hadn't talked to him about Mrs. Z yet; right now, that felt like dumping salt on a gaping wound.

I had my own worries. Would Cameron ignore me or encourage Bruce to be pushier? I had to be saved from Liam's bad influence and all that. I didn't want to do something drastic, but at the same time, I didn't want my privacy invaded more than it had been.

What I was going to ask Liam felt more drastic than it was, but it was a small change that would make us both feel better. "It's not hard to change locks, is it?"

Seventeen

LIAM

William. Never Liam. Always William.

The way he'd pissed me off hadn't faded overnight.

Fuck my dad. I'd offered the suggestions of the names Eli and Owen to Payton because they couldn't be shortened. She'd agreed. Her warped way of thinking that would encourage me to stay with her.

The irony was that my mom had named me William Barron to coax Cameron away from his wife, to prove that I was his, but growing up the spitting image of the man had done that.

Fucking William. That was Cameron's middle name.

No one called me William. Kenny occasionally used my full name, but the times she did were the only moments I didn't mind being William Robert Barron.

I wasn't going to let the run-in from yesterday sour my holiday. I was with Kennedy and the kids at a small lake outside Mandan. My kids splashed in the water. Each wore a little life vest that puffed behind their heads and around their little arms. Kenny had come armed with plastic pails and small plastic shovels. They were piled at the edge of the water. The boys alternated between digging to the middle of the earth and playing in the water.

Kenny reclined next to me on a blanket. I was out of my jeans and in blue trunks and desperately trying to ignore how short Kenny's black boy-cut swim shorts were. It was as impossible as keeping my gaze off her swim top. It was like a tight-fitting tank top, but the point was that it was tight fitting. And lower cut than anything Kenny normally wore.

She scanned the beach. "It's getting really full."

The stark blue man-made lake was tucked into rolling hills. The sandy beach wasn't large and was flanked by a boating dock on one side and a reedy fishing area on the other. We'd gotten here before the after-lunch crowd had arrived. The beach had been half full, but now it was filling back to the grassy slope that led up to the parking lot. Boats idled quietly on the no-wake lake, and kayaks crisscrossed in the distance.

"Wanna go into the water before it gets packed with people?" I'd already been in the water, but Kenny'd stayed behind to set up our little picnic area.

"Well, I don't know... Race you!" She jumped up and sprinted to the water, her laughter trailing behind.

I grinned and chased her down. She let out a squeal, and the boys cheered as I swooped her into my arms and carried her into the water. I didn't dump her in, though. She gasped as I sank until we were in up to our waists. I let her go.

There was a chance someone we knew was here, but Kenny hadn't stiffened in my arms. Encouraging.

"It's cold, but it's not." She didn't float far, but held her arms out to Eli.

He paddled to her, and Owen paddled to me.

Playing in the water with my family was the most care-free I'd been for years. Since ever. This was perfect. Having Kenny be a part of us was perfect.

A floating station popped up not far from where we were. An inflatable yellow monstrosity with anchors to keep it in place, a puffy slide, and at least two ladders.

I didn't see any kids playing around it and ignored it until I heard my name.

Holden was half rolled on his side. "Hey, I thought that was you." He pointed to Owen, who was clinging to my back. "Owen, right?" His brows shot up when he spotted Eli on Kenny's back. "Hey, Kennedy."

"Hi, Holden." Kenny smiled, but her shoulders were tense. After our run-in with Bruce and Cameron, we were both edgy. I would call the school when the holiday was over and deal with Mrs. Z. Kenny said I could ask for the boys to be transferred to the other kindergarten teacher.

Did Kenny hold her breath like me waiting for Holden's reaction? This could be written off as just friends, but no one could deny that a day at the lake out of town was more than a quick lunch in Coal Haven.

Holden blinked, but he recovered quickly. "And there's little Eli. Hey, big guy."

"Can we play?" Eli asked.

Holden cocked his head. He either couldn't hear or didn't understand Eli. Speech therapy was working, but Eli's new verbal skills hadn't crossed into everyday speech yet.

"No, hon," Kenny said, sensing the impending awkwardness. "They have their own group."

Holden must've heard that. "Nah, we got plenty of room. Get on over here."

I hesitated, but Holden beckoned us over. "It's just going to be me and Nora and some of her friends from college." His smile turned wry. "They needed me to haul and set up everything."

I chuckled but wanted to give him another chance to get out of hanging with us. "Sounds about right. You sure? It's not like I'm party boat material anymore."

"This isn't a party boat. It's a cranky older brother making sure his little sister doesn't get herself into trouble."

Nora and two of her friends from college waded into the water, each in a bikini that showed more skin than Kennedy ever had in her life, but I didn't have the urge to look. As for Nora, my gangly cousin had turned into a mermaid. She'd been a sullen thing whenever I'd seen her around town, but she'd blossomed in college.

Nora gave me a light hug. "I'm so glad we ran into you. Ohmigosh, Kennedy, it's so nice to see you too."

That made Nora the only Barron who liked Kenny being with me.

Nora patted me on the arm. "Don't worry. We'll deal with Mom if she finds out. Besides, she likes pissing off Uncle Cameron more than anyone."

Both Nora and Holden were okay with me? Suddenly, anything my father might plan on doing to prevent me from getting a job around Coal Haven didn't bother me. If two people close to him didn't agree with how he acted, then there had to be more.

There had to be.

The afternoon flew by, and we stayed hours later than we'd planned. When we'd eaten through our stockpile of sandwiches, chips, Gatorade, water, and cookies, I helped Kenny and the boys off the raft.

"I'd better get these guys home." I'd caught Owen digging through Nora's cooler, and she'd already shared the snacks she brought. The boys needed a solid meal and a good night's sleep.

Nora hung over the edge of the raft, waving at us. "We need to plan this again. When are you back?"

"I'll be back the beginning of August. For good."

"Hey, good to hear, man." Holden slapped me on the back as we waded out of the lake. "Let me know if there's anything I can do. I mean it."

Nora was helping Kenny herd the boys to our spot on the beach. Her college friends stayed on the raft.

I took the moment to tell Holden, "I appreciate it. I really do."

He did a double take when he noticed my solemn expression. "No problem, as long as it's not too little too late. The more my friends left town after graduation and never wanted to come back made me take a hard look at my family. Maybe the younger Barron generation can keep from driving everyone away." He glanced at the raft that was floating away, and his eyes widened. "Oh, shit. Those girls are going to drive me to drink."

I walked toward Kenny and shamelessly eyed her ass as she bent and gathered up our items. Nora had run to help Holden rescue the raft and her friends.

She glanced over her shoulder and saw my gaze on her round ass. She mouthed "later," and I groaned. I'd been thinking about *later* all day. She was sleeping over and would be all mine.

Once we drove out of the parking lot, AC blowing on us until Owen complained he was cold, Kenny dug out her phone.

"Oh. Holy crap."

I couldn't look as I turned onto the highway. "What?"

"Sh—crap. Mom's been trying to reach me." She tsked. "I have a missed call from Cassidy too. Crap. Mom must be really worried. I hope nothing's wrong."

Her phone buzzed. She answered. "Hey— No. I'm fine.

Fine. What? Why would he—" Kenny turned her luminous gaze on me. Her lips pressed flat. "No. You didn't have to; I have plans." A pause, then her tone pitched higher. "You're at the house?" Another pause. "Because I changed them."

Aw, hell. Her mom had been so worried she couldn't get a hold of Kenny that she'd driven from Fargo to Coal Haven on the Fourth of July. And learned that Kenny had changed her damn locks. I hadn't even helped her. We'd gotten our pizza, and she'd watched a few videos, asked me a couple of questions about tools and deadbolts, then gone home and changed both the front and back door locks.

She'd given me a spare key.

"I'll be home in an hour." She huffed and hung up. "Guess my plans have changed. Just like last time, my car was home and I didn't answer the door. Bruce tried my phone, and when I didn't answer, he called Mom. She and Benji are sitting in their car outside my house."

That whole scenario sucked, but eventually they'd realize that Kenny wasn't answering the door because she had a life. "They can come over and light fireworks too."

She propped her elbow on the armrest, her head in her hand. "No. They'll just fret and ruin the night."

"They'll do that anyway. Let them come see you have fun."

Her lower lip disappeared between her teeth. "I really wanted to light fireworks with you."

"We'll still do that. Really, Kenny. I have plenty of burgers and buns. Tell them what you're doing and that they're invited."

An adorable crease formed between her brows. "Okay, but I'm going to message her. Then I'll have time to prepare for her arguments."

Several minutes and even more miles went by before she slipped her phone into the console. "They're coming."

Good. Kenny had to realize that the more they witnessed her living the life she wanted to live, the sooner they'd come to accept it. This was one more step closer to being open about us. To everyone.

She peeked at her phone screen. "I think she wants to be nosy."

"She can nose away. We've got nothing to hide. Well"—I stroked my gaze down her tanned bare legs—"maybe a little."

"Liam." She pushed at my arm, but I only winked and made her blush deepen. "Thank you."

"Anything for you, Kenny." And I meant it.

* * *

Kennedy

"Bruce is really worried." Mom sat in a lawn chair. She looked like she was ready to go to a wedding instead of sitting on a folding chair in a gravel driveway and watching fireworks. She hadn't mentioned what she and Benji had been doing when Bruce sent out the SOS, but she was dressed in tan linen pants and a wraparound blouse. Benji wore similar pants and a solid navy-blue shirt. Instead of whatever they'd planned to do in Fargo, they were out in the country, surrounded by bugs and eating s'mores.

Liam was helping Eli light his smoke bomb. It was an hour until sunset, but he was allowing them to light the smoke bombs and the snakes that looked like turds. Benji stood close by, ready to lend Liam a hand. Benji had latched on to Liam, hanging out by the grill and holding the lit punk for Liam when he needed both hands to help one of the boys unwrap their smoke bombs. Benji laughed and would exclaim about the color of the smoke with the boys. He was really enjoying himself; it helped defuse the tension from earlier. It was nice to see another person in my life treat Liam well.

I'd known this moment was coming, I just hadn't known when. Knowing Liam and I were friends was different from seeing us hang out. Did Mom suspect there was more between us? I wasn't ready to get into that yet. Not after Bruce had interfered in our afternoon.

When Mom and Benji had arrived, Owen had latched on to her, showing off his truck collection, moving to his action figures, and then outside to his favorite places to play. Eli was next to her the entire time, demonstrating the techniques he'd learned to say the letter S and S-clusters. He gave Mom words to coach him through practicing.

She'd been stunned by the way the kids had dominated her visit from the start but had rolled with it, even smiled like she was having fun. I wanted more of her like this.

Liam had been right. She'd needed to be here, to play a role that was more than caretaker. And I was having fun tonight, despite the reason behind their visit, and despite the fact that they were staying at the motel and my overnight with Liam had to be canceled.

"He was nearly frantic on the phone." Apparently, she wasn't going to drop the Bruce subject.

"Bruce saw me at my worst. It's hard for him to realize that I'm not in that place anymore." I pushed my sunglasses to the top of my head. "He asked to take over my finances, Mom."

I monitored her reaction. She nodded at first, like it made all the sense in the world. Until she frowned. "Why would he do that?"

"He heard me listening to a self-help book on personal finances."

"Oh." She cocked her head. "Do you need help?"

I went with honesty. Telling them I was fine wasn't working. Just like she was seeing me celebrate the Fourth, maybe she needed to know I was working through issues. "Not like that. Derek didn't have much life insurance and I burned most of it during the year I didn't work. The rest will get me through to the start of the school year, but still. It's only one wage."

"And you bought that house on two," Mom murmured, nodding. "Well, if Bruce wants to—"

"I don't want him to, Mom. That's the thing. He helped me a lot last year, and I appreciate it, but you know what? I've been living on my own for nearly two years."

Sadness fluttered through her eyes. "Yes, you have," she said quietly.

"So, if, you know, if I have to get a teaching job where I commute, or I have to sell the house and get an apartment, or I have to move—I'll do it. I don't need to be saved."

I put my sunglasses back over my eyes. Mom didn't respond. She watched Benji and Liam work with the kids on lighting more snakes.

Finally, she said, "When you had Lyme, no one would believe something was wrong. And you were getting sicker and weaker. You needed saving then."

I nodded. I had needed saving twice if I counted the basement debacle.

"And I guess..." she sighed. "It's just hard. As a parent. We're not far away, but when your kid is in trouble, each minute of that drive feels like an hour. And now you're alone. I can't just shut the worry off."

"But you can give me space." I met her gaze, a lighter brown than my own.

She dipped her head. "I'll try. No promises."

"At least call or text first before you stop in." I gave her a small smile to let her know she was still welcome.

She chuckled. "I can do that." An easy silence fell between us until she said, "You've been spending a lot of time with Liam?" She didn't fool me with her innocent tone.

This was it. We were having an open conversation, our first ever. I could tell her. How would she react? Would she tell Bruce? Would it be too much too soon?

"When he's in town, I hang out with him and the kids sometimes."

Her eyes narrowed slightly, and she uttered a noncommittal, "Mm."

I swallowed hard and ignored the slight sting of betrayal. I wasn't ashamed of Liam. We were having such a nice night; I didn't want it ruined by unnecessary conflict.

I was protective of him, and I was protective of us. It might be a little selfish, but I hated the thought that people could intrude on our peace. I loved this place. I loved the kids. And I loved Liam.

I fiddled with the string in my shorts. I'd loved Liam before Derek died. As a friend.

That was no longer the case. I could finally admit it. Now I had to sit with it and think about how it made me feel.

I loved another man. So damn much. Panic like I'd experienced my first time with Liam roared back. My throat burned. The familiar pangs at the backs of my eyes spurred me out of my chair. "I need to run to the bathroom."

I charged into the house and went straight to the bathroom. I peered at myself in the mirror. My face glowed from the sun, my skin no longer pasty and drawn. My cheeks had filled out, thanks to eating real meals. And the dead-behind-the-eyes look was gone.

I thought I would love one man in my life. Not only did I love Liam, I was crazy about him. I couldn't wait for him to walk through the door. I wanted nothing more than to wake up with him in the morning. And when he touched me, I wanted to drown myself in the way he made me feel.

The final walls had crumbled. Overwhelming emotion poured through.

What would Sexy, Young, and Widowed say?

They'd tell me it was normal. All my feelings were normal. Falling in love again was normal. Dreaming about my husband being alive while planning for a future where I married another man and had the family I never got with Derek was normal too.

Too much too soon. My brain was moving faster than reality.

I drew in a steady breath. This was normal. I didn't know how he felt. I had to process my emotions first.

I heard movement inside the house. Had Mom come looking for me? I'd practically sprinted away after she'd asked about Liam. I might've upended my world, but I didn't need to overturn the night for everyone else.

I hadn't cried, so I washed my hands like I'd used the bathroom and breezed out. Right into that broad chest I had planned to lick tonight.

Liam backed me into the bathroom. The light was still off, and we left the door open.

"I saw you talking to your mom and then you left," he murmured against my ear like he couldn't resist touching me one moment longer. His hands were around my waist, desperate to touch me in a more-than-friendly way like I had been today.

I melted into him, soaking up his strength and heat even though he was the cause of my emotional tornado. I needed to hold him now more than ever, and I needed to be held.

"Everything all right?"

I was a mess, but I also had a deep sense that everything was all right. "Yes. I had a good talk with Mom. Hopefully no more speed-of-light trips from Fargo thinking the worst has happened to me."

He nibbled at my ear, and his warm lips brushed down my neck. "Good. I knew fireworks and grilling would bring her around."

"I almost told her. About us."

He paused with his lips against my skin. "Why didn't you?"

"It seemed like I was already pushing it." He didn't nod, didn't continue kissing me, but he also didn't pull away. Was he disappointed? Was he impatient? "Is that all right?"

"I'm ready when you're ready." He pressed a soft kiss against my skin, then another. My eyes drifted closed.

I enjoyed what he was doing too much. A full day that included an afternoon of him with no shirt was hell on my hormones. "We should get back out there."

"Yeah. We should." He didn't let me go. "Seeing you in that swimsuit drove me crazy."

He traced a finger over my breasts, his touch branding me through my shirt.

"It was just a plain swimsuit." I was breathless. I arched into him, my tight nipples grazing his chest through my top.

He groaned. "And I know exactly what you look like under it." His teeth grazed my neck.

I dipped to catch his mouth in a kiss that he instantly deepened. His tongue probed inside, and I sucked on him. He tasted like lemonade and sunshine.

The kiss was way too short before he yanked his head away. "Damn, Kenny. You need to go out there first. I'm gonna need a minute."

I palmed the front of his shorts. "I'll call you tonight, when they go to the motel."

His breathing was ragged, but he gave me a sweet kiss on the forehead. "Can't wait."

The words *I love you* crowded on my tongue. I used to say it with such ease. I'd get there again. If Liam felt the same way, we'd get there. But this wasn't the time.

KENNEDY

My classroom was quiet. All the kids had gone home and I would too, after I finished entering scores from their tests. With the Fourth of July holiday past, I had one more week of summer school.

Then what?

I had several projects I could do to the house, but limited funds to purchase supplies. School didn't start again until the end of August, and it was looking like there was a full crew of teachers. No full-time openings.

I guessed I'd be job hunting along with Liam. I didn't want to leave this school. Aspen was here. Kelsey and Marion. And I was looking forward to chatting with the other teachers and paras that I'd gotten to know on recess and lunchroom duty. Would I still be invited to their girls' nights out, or would I have to start over at another school?

I'd tapped in the last score when Mr. Gilding called over the intercom. "Kennedy, can you come down to my office?"

The principal hadn't said much to me since I'd lost my temper. If anything, he'd steered clear. Same with Mrs. Z. No more impromptu drop-ins while I was still in her classroom. Did she cruise by the school to make sure my car wasn't there before she came inside? Didn't matter. It had been nice to have a break from her negativity.

I packed up my schoolbag full of papers and my teaching laptop. Mr. Gilding was sitting behind his desk.

"Ah, Kennedy. Have a seat. Shut the door too, please."

Being called to the principal's office had lost its fear factor as an adult, but the ominous "shut the door, please" made it come crashing back. The last time he'd told me to shut the door was when he'd asked whether I could keep teaching in the same capacity I had been before Derek died. The day I had quit.

"Liam Barron called me today." Mr. Gilding tapped the tip of his pen against his desktop. "He wants to switch his kids to Miss Perez."

"Good." I wasn't backtracking on what I had said to Mr. Gilding the day Mrs. Z had pissed me off, yet my heart rate accelerated and my palms grew clammy. His expression didn't make me think he wholeheartedly agreed. "I think that's a reasonable request."

"After the way you spoke to Mrs. Zachmeier, I can't help but wonder where Liam got the idea she wouldn't be a good teacher for his kids."

After the way I spoke to Mrs. Z? Calling her on her bullshit without yelling or throwing a fit was now a bad thing? "Uh, maybe it's from the way she spoke about his kids?"

Mr. Gilding straightened. Okay, my tone might've been too flippant, but come on. He needed to support the kids as much as his staff.

His stern expression solidified, and he tapped the pen to

his desk again. "And how exactly did she speak about them?"

"She said it'd be a tough year and she'd have to separate them." Yeah, when I said it like that it sounded harmless enough. Mr. Gilding knew her tone and her attitude. He had to understand.

"That's it?"

"She insinuated it'd be a tough year because of them and because of what Liam had been like—*twenty-two years ago*."

Mr. Gilding tipped his chin down while keeping his gaze on me, as if I needed to elaborate. Did he not see the problem? "Kennedy, I realize you've been through a lot, but Mrs. Z confided in you as a colleague."

I scoffed and caught myself too late. His gaze sharpened, and I smoothed over my expression. Professional as hell. I still wanted a job here. As a full-fledged teacher with a flawless record, I would've had more footing in this disagreement. "She was complaining. About children. Those boys are important to me, and I want them to have the best start to their school year as possible."

"Right." Tap, tap, tap. "I realize that you're more qualified than many of our paras, and that's why I'm concerned about what you're telling other parents about the teachers here."

"It wasn't other parents. It was a friend, and I gave him a recommendation that would benefit his children."

Mr. Gilding laid the pen down like it was a fuse ready to detonate. "Mrs. Zachmeier has been a teacher here for thirty-five years. Eli and Owen Barron are in good hands, and I've reassured Liam of that."

I recoiled. How could he pretend this wasn't an issue? The set of his shoulders and the hard lines around his eyes told me he wasn't going to change his mind. I could still hold him accountable. "Then I can be assured that should there be problems, you'll use your best judgment to rectify them in a way that helps them, regardless of how Mrs. Z feels or how defensive she gets?"

Mr. Gilding blinked. "Of-of course."

My anger continued coalescing until it oozed out of every pore in my body. It was as if my silence in other areas of my life spurred my vocal cords to flap away. "Good, good. And the other parents were understanding when you refused their requests for a preferred teacher?"

He cocked his head. "Excuse me?"

"You rejected Liam's request, but all the teachers here are good, right?" I didn't wait for him to answer. "So, I'm assuming that you've turned down all other requests and will continue to do so even after school starts. You'll just assure them their children are in good hands."

"We have very few requests—"

I looked at him like I just *couldn't possibly* understand. "You don't reject them all?"

He paused and stared at his pen, like he wanted to tap-tap away but didn't want to show me that I'd unbalanced him. "There are outstanding cases, and you understand that I can't discuss them with you." He straightened as if a steel rod traveled up his spine. "As I'm sure you understand that I won't be discussing Eli and Owen with you any further. I believe it's only Liam and his grandma, Ginny Pewter, on their records."

If we'd been having a face-off, he'd be considered a winner. To him, and to the rest of the town, I wasn't anything more to Liam and his kids than a family friend. I wasn't their teacher or a teacher at all in the school. Another reminder I wasn't full-time staff.

The most I could do was watch and listen. And if I had to get a job outside the Coal Haven district—after this meeting it looked like I'd have to—I'd let Liam know everything he could do to check on his kids. It was all I could do. As just a friend.

I was keeping our relationship quiet to protect us, but for the first time, it felt like it might be hurting us.

* * *

Liam

The sound of a vehicle pulling up tore the boys' attention away from the task of painting a spare piece of plywood. They'd wanted to help, but there wasn't much they could do while I was welding. I had no use for the plywood other than to keep them occupied.

Was Kenny coming over early? I had to leave in a few days, and we'd decided to work in an overnight before I left. Her idea. One I gladly went along with after missing our planned sleepover on the Fourth.

I put my torch down and took my gloves off. The apron was next. I only had a couple of new singe holes in my shirt. The sweat-soaked garment stuck to my torso. I needed a shower but would have to greet the new arrival how I was.

I slapped my ball cap on. At the overhead doors of the shed, I noticed the boys standing on the edge of the drive-way. They were eyeing a large pickup.

"Who's that, Daddy?" Owen asked.

The pickup was as big as mine, but several years newer. Fully loaded luxury edition. There were people that drove nice pickups like this through town. They all had the last name Barron.

Cameron slid out. His mirrored sunglasses reflected my property; the finish of the lenses didn't help it look better. Decent shop. Beat-up house. Lawn that needed mowing. I'd get to that tomorrow. The house was waiting until I was home for good. I had to deal with Cameron now.

"William."

Eli scrunched his face up. "Who's William?"

Cameron's brow scrunched. "Excuse me?"

I put myself between Cameron and Eli. I wouldn't let this man's bullshit affect more than one generation. "It's me, kiddo. My full name."

"What's mine?" Eli asked.

"You don't have a nickname."

"Can mine be Tony Stark?" Owen asked.

I kept my tone neutral. "Why don't you two go inside and watch a show?"

"Yeah!" Owen raced ahead of Eli.

Cameron watched them pass, his gaze less stern than when he looked at me.

"What do you want?" I held back my hostility, but my father wasn't here for a congenial visit. He wasn't going to say he was sorry for ignoring me my entire life. He wasn't going to apologize for driving my mom away until she was gone for good. He wasn't going to embrace my kids as his grandkids.

He took his shades off and held them loosely in his hands like he was pondering what to say. He knew what he was going to tell me. A guy like Cameron was always prepared—especially when it came to me. "Bruce is worried about Kennedy."

I didn't say anything, just folded my arms and waited for the inevitable *stay away from someone you really care about* lecture. Bruce had sicced Cameron on me after Derek and I had gotten the four-wheelers stuck in the watering holes the spring we were in seventh grade.

"Bruce told me that he appreciated how you were there for Kennedy. He said that she really needed the extra support." The bands of the sunglasses flipped up, then folded. "The thing is, she's doing fine now."

"Then why is he worried? And why are you here speaking for him?"

"She's still hurting."

"Of course she is. Her fucking husband died, Cameron."

The permafrown he wore around me deepened. "Don't cuss at me, William."

"And don't talk to me like you're my dad."

His cheeks pinched. Not quite a wince, but more reaction than I expected from a guy who'd spent his life denying my existence. "You should give her some room." I stared him down. He gave a disgusted grunt. "What are you doing, William? You're almost twenty-eight. Single. Kids. Look what happened with their mom."

"You know nothing about that. Or are you afraid what went on between me and their mom resembles what you did? Like father, like son?"

His eyes filled with warning. "Don't."

"Don't what? Don't talk to you about shit I know nothing about like you're doing? Don't spend time with Kenny, who can make her own damn decisions without consulting you or Bruce? It's a tired argument. Kenny's an adult, and instead of questioning her, maybe you and Bruce should ask yourselves something. Why do you think Derek and Kenny would both equally conclude that I'm a decent guy and that they want to be around me?"

"Derek was—" Cameron's voice hitched. "He was a good kid, but Bruce spoiled him. He didn't think through his actions."

That part had been true—when he'd been a teenager and we'd done stupid shit like with the four-wheelers. As an adult, Derek had been the best there was. "Bullshit. No one was as balanced as him. Same with Kennedy."

"And what do you think he would say about you spending so much time with his wife?"

I sucked in a breath. Cameron was aiming low today, but he wasn't the only one prepared for conversations like this. "I don't know. But that's the thing, isn't it? He can't tell us, and it gives you and Bruce free rein to write the script about what you would want him to say. You're going to have fun telling everyone what an awful friend I am now?"

Cameron shook his head. "You always were hardheaded. What's with you and Hattie Garcia?"

"Gonna tell me to stay away from her too? Want me to get so upset that I drive off, hysterical, and poof—you don't have to deal with me anymore?"

Cameron charged forward, shoving a finger into my shoulder. "You have no idea, William." He backed up and glanced at the house. His gaze swept the rest of the yard like he was worried someone had witnessed a rare loss of temper. "You have no idea what your mother put my family through. I made a mistake, and she wouldn't let it go and..." He waited until his breathing slowed. "I was young and stupid. You might think I expect the worst out of you, but I don't want you to make the same mistakes as me. It's obvious you care about Kennedy. You want what's best for her. The thing you don't seem to get is that you're not always what's best."

I reared back. "Get out of here."

"Think about Kennedy."

"Fuck you, Cameron."

He shook his head, his lips smacking against his teeth. His boots ground into the gravel as he sauntered to his pickup, like he didn't have a care in the world. Like he hadn't suggested that I was no good for anyone. Like the insinuation wasn't there that my mother hadn't been good for anyone either.

Before he climbed behind the wheel, he turned to face me, his calm, frowning mask in place. "Good luck trying to get a job around here, Liam."

The issue of seeing Derek's widow hadn't been the only subject I was prepared for. I'd had time to think about this move. I wasn't an impulsive teen anymore. "Good luck trying to convince your golf buddies that I'm not good at what I do. In case you forgot, I work for King Oil, and my manager promised a glowing recommendation. Should look good, considering you just lost your vice president to King Oil."

Cameron's nostrils flared, and I smirked. For the first time I wasn't drowning in rage or helplessness around my father. Relief that I hadn't been raised by this man seeped through my anger.

He got in his ride and slammed the door. I didn't move from the middle of the driveway. He had to pull around me, leaving tire tracks in the overgrown lawn.

Think about Kennedy.

I thought about her every waking moment. No one knew how important she was to me. But someday soon, I hoped they would.

* * *

Kennedy

The boys had asked for me to tuck them in tonight. They'd given Liam hugs and run upstairs to pick a book for me to read. While I read what ended up to be ten stories, Liam went out to the shed to finish some work for Hattie.

I finished the last story, and Owen asked, "What's your real name, Kenny?"

"Kennedy, but only you two and your daddy call me Kenny." I leaned down to his little face sticking out of the blankets. "I think it's really special."

Eli's nose scrunched. "So, is that guy that calls Daddy 'William' special too?"

A chill swept down my back. Only one guy called Liam by his full name. "No, he's... When did you hear him say William?"

"Earlier. Daddy talked to him outside."

Liam hadn't mentioned a thing since I'd arrived. Had it gone that bad?

"William is your daddy's full name, but we all like to call him Liam. That guy doesn't know Liam well enough to call him that."

I stayed until they fell asleep. I wanted to talk to Liam, and I wanted to do it without worrying about being overheard. But by the time I got downstairs, he still wasn't inside.

I found him in the shop, on a stool, painting one of the end tables we'd picked up when we'd last been in Bismarck for Eli's speech therapy.

He didn't look at me, but my steps echoed through the shop. He was toward the back, on the opposite side of where he welded. Farthest away from the dust. The main color was slate gray, but he was painting the handles and trim a sky blue.

"I told Hattie about these, and she said I should give them a try. People love colorful furniture for kids' rooms."

I stopped next to him. "What happened with Cameron?"

The brush stopped. "History repeated itself."

There was so much history between him and Cameron, yet so little variation. "Meaning?"

"Instead of telling me to stay away from Derek, it was you he warned me away from."

Cameron had driven out here and warned Liam away, but he didn't even know we were dating. What would he do if he learned otherwise? I repressed a shudder.

I put my hand on Liam's shoulder. "I'm sorry."

He set the brush on the tarp he'd laid down to protect the floor and put the metal lid on the paint can. "It was Cameron being Cameron. Doesn't want a damn thing to do with me, but swoops in and thinks I'll listen to him."

"I'm still sorry."

"It's not your fault, Kenny. None of this stuff is."

"It's not yours either."

He rose and grabbed a blue-paint-speckled rag from his back pocket. "It is. Because I can't seem to stay away from you. And I don't want to."

After hearing him say that, I was grateful to spend the night with him. I followed him to the sink, where he rinsed the paint off the brush. His forearms flexed as he washed his hands.

I leaned against the counter next to the sink. This part of the shop was newer. It'd been a bare wall in high school. Liam had built it into a nice workstation.

He was a talented guy. Multifaceted. I couldn't wait to see what he did with this place once he was here for good. And I didn't want to be the one getting a job where I'd need to commute. But he'd done it for so long. With kids. While supporting Grandma Gin and me. I could suck it up.

I let my gaze linger on his broad chest. "I don't want you to stay away from me either. In fact, I want you to stick pretty close."

He shut the water off. Dried his hands on a clean towel next to me, then tossed it down.

He stepped in front of me, caging me against the counter with his arms. "What else do you want me to do?"

I pretended to think. "You already fed me."

"I did." His head hung lower, our lips closer.

I tugged his shirt out of his pants. "You already filled my low tire." He had talked me through it, but he had a compressor—and he'd given me a tire gauge to keep in my glove compartment.

"I did." Our mouths were closer. "Anything else?"

My fingertips grazed his hot skin. His abs clenched. "I don't know, but I suppose we should go inside and think of more?"

"Nah. You can be noisier out here."

My lips parted. *Yes*. I wanted to be noisy with him. It was the opening he must've wanted. His mouth was on me, his tongue inside me, and my ass was being lifted.

In his bed, in my house, there was always a sense that we could get caught. The big shop doors were open, but we were tucked in the back and surrounded by shadows. This was the privacy I craved.

He trailed kisses away from my mouth as he loosened the ties of my shorts with a finger. They dropped down my thighs to my feet. My underwear followed. As he worked, I tangled my hands through his, got his jeans open, and freed his granite-hard erection. I hadn't worked out the logistics of how we were going to do this, but like always, Liam was ready for me.

He dropped to his knees, his erection pointing up. He steadied me as I stepped out of my shorts. I thought he'd rise, but he lifted my leg, opening me right in front of his face.

The exposure left me vulnerable, like it had that day on my kitchen floor. But I'd been on my back, staring at my kitchen ceiling while clinging to a table leg with one hand, the other buried in his hair.

There was no pretending to hide like this. He met my gaze as he kissed the top of my mound as if to prove that I had nothing to be self-conscious about, then kissed lower. When he licked out, the leg I was standing on trembled and I was aware of only where he touched me. To hell with what my stomach and thighs looked like. I gripped the counter as he licked through my seam and tackled my clit.

He toyed with me. The other times we'd been together, he'd been sensitive, like he'd measured my response and used his best judgment. This moment was for him, his joy, and I wanted him to have it.

So I clung to the counter, my legs vibrating when he increased the pressure, my body sagging when he backed off. A few cycles of that and there was no sagging. I was strung tight, the pressure mounting.

He put my other leg over his shoulder, his head buried between my thighs, supporting me completely. I was going to die from the erotic sight. Die of embarrassment. Die of need. Die of sheer ecstasy that flooded my veins and threatened to rupture my heart.

"Oh, God, Liam. I don't think I can do this much longer." I had to gasp out a few words at a time. He was relentless.

I hung my head back but couldn't resist seeing the dirty picture we made. I wasn't just drawn to the way he devoured me, but how he was doing it like he knew exactly what I could take and he was showing me. He was proving to me that I could do it. Like he always had, only with his body. With soul-destroying pleasure.

I'd never think I was strong enough to crack the counter, but it creaked when I hit my peak with a bang. Rapturous sensations burst from me, and I rode his face while my hands yanked at the edge of the workbench. Last week, I couldn't open a jar of pickles, but right now all my muscles were clenched like I could tow a semi down the highway.

I hollered his name, my voice echoing off the walls. It probably carried out of the shop, but not far. I couldn't tug his hair; I couldn't roll away. I was at his mercy. Completely.

He pulled away, kissed my thigh, and helped me anchor my feet on the floor as I panted and attempted to catch my breath.

He rose, jerking his wallet out, and jamming a condom on in record time.

"How are we—"

He lifted me. His face was savage beauty, carved from harsh rock into something that almost hurt to look at. His hair hung over his forehead, shadowing his eyes. Primal.

Grabbing my hips, he lifted. I wrapped my legs around him, and his blunt head pushed into me. It felt so good but wasn't nearly enough. I flexed and relaxed my thighs until I was seated completely on his erection and so full I wasn't sure I could take all of him even though we'd done this before.

Again, he took what he needed. I tried to start a rhythm, but he was in control. He stood with his feet planted wide, and he supported me. It was the two of us in the middle of the floor, an island of ecstasy. His strength, his confidence that I could keep my legs secured around him. My strength and my confidence that this would work because he would make it so.

"Liam?" My breasts rubbed against his chest as he lifted and lowered me.

"Yeah," he breathed against my mouth.

"This feels really good." I should feel stupid for saying that, but I wanted him to know. I wanted him to know a lot more, but I wasn't ready to go there yet.

"Fuck yeah, baby." He grunted and ground me into him until my jaw dropped. "This is only the beginning. I have you to myself all damn night."

All. Damn. Night. We had to make this happen more often. His breath puffed against my face. I meant to kiss him, but euphoria made me sloppy. I ended up licking along his lips onto his cheek.

He seemed to like how I lost control when he had all the power.

"Grab on to the counter. Keep your legs around me." He tipped me back. I flailed, but my palms smacked smooth laminate and my fingers curled around it. I wasn't worried about falling. Around Liam, I never had to worry.

Our new position gave him more room to swing his hips. He pounded into me; it was up to me how much I wanted the edge of the counter to jab me in the ass. He adjusted his hold until he secured me with one hand. With his other, he thumbed my clit.

I barked out a cry. Sensitive bordering on painful, it was exactly what I needed for a second orgasm.

"Liam, I'm—" A long moan left me as I escalated to the tip of my peak and catapulted over.

Our moans and grunts mingled as he continued to drive into me. I caught glimpses of his harsh expression, his sheer focus on coming, and it was fucking hot.

Heat flooded into me, around me, as he climaxed.

My arms were shaking. I pressed my back along the edge of the counter and leaned back, using my elbows to take hold.

Liam was barely done orgasming, but he helped set my feet on the ground. Considerate Liam was back, but I'd gotten to see him at his most raw. Vulnerable. When he wasn't trying to be the best at whatever he did—the best grandson, the best father, the best lover. He got to be Liam with me, and I'd treasure that trust forever.

Nineteen

❧

LIAM

I was driving to Williston soon. My last long stretch there. It was the end of the twenty days that I was really looking forward to. After the epic sex in the shop, Kenny and I had made our way to my bed and we'd talked. And I'd invited her out for my last few days.

I reviewed the non-Kenny parts of my plan with Grandma Gin as I put chicken strips in the oven for supper and steamed a bag of vegetables. Minimal prep, minimal cleanup for her. I'd even talked to Eli and Owen about wiping their plates off and putting dishes in the dishwasher.

"So, I was supposed to work until the thirtieth, but uh..."

Grandma Gin paused in her prep of the tomatoes and cucumbers she'd bought at the farmers market. She didn't go to the one I was banned from, but drove to Hazen and visited theirs, and she'd do that until I was issued a formal apology. So, forever, but Grandma Gin had my back. "Yes?"

"I have some days of leave, and I'd like to spend them..." Fucking Kenny's brains out while we spent some kid-free days together. We wouldn't be asking Grandma Gin for more than she'd planned already.

All Kenny had asked was that I be discreet. I hadn't talked to Grandma Gin yet about Kenny, and I hadn't asked Kenny if she minded. I kept meaning to, but then I wasn't sure how I'd take it if Kenny said she didn't want Grandma Gin to know.

"Anyone special you're going to spend those days with?" She sliced neatly through a tomato, cutting even slices, waiting for me to answer.

"Yeah." *Please don't ask for more details.* I didn't want to lie to Grandma Gin. She'd done so much for me.

"Owen said you'd had an overnight guest." Slice. Slice.

"Kenny stayed to tuck them in and then helped out in the shop." We hadn't gotten a damn thing done other than epic sex.

It didn't feel right to play it off, not to Grandma Gin. Kenny had told Laney about us. I needed someone on my side, and Grandma Gin had been there from the beginning. She might have reservations based on my history and Kenny's, but she'd be happy for me.

"We're seeing each other, but we're keeping it quiet."

"Mm." That wasn't exactly the reaction I expected. I couldn't tell whether she approved or she was disappointed in me. She switched to a cucumber. "I also heard Cameron was here."

The boys were shit at keeping secrets. And I was shit for expecting them to. "When I went to Hattie's to discuss how I'd work with her, Kenny came along. Bruce and Cameron saw us. He had to warn me off. You know how he is."

Grandma Gin snorted at the last statement. "Sounds

like him." She dumped the cucumbers into the bowl. "The thing with Kenny... I don't know, Liam."

Grandma Gin's tone wasn't resigned. It wasn't full of warning. She said she didn't know, and she meant it. She'd had my back since before I was born. If she wasn't ecstatic, then I couldn't ignore it.

"She's really important to me."

Her tone was gentle. "Are you important to her? Or is this a hurdle she has to get over? Part of moving on?"

I wasn't a hurdle. I had to be more than that with Kenny. Why couldn't I be the stopping point? My boys were thriving. I had my own place. I'd find a good job.

I had a lot to offer. For once in my life, I realized that. "She's moving on, but I don't think she plans to leapfrog over me. Why would she?"

Less drama. A chance to find someone who didn't put her at odds with Bruce and Willow or make her defensive with her mom. Someone she could proudly be with around town.

Thoughts I hadn't allowed to exist crowded into my brain. She wanted time. She wanted privacy. But what if, in the end, she didn't want me?

Grandma Gin diligently worked on the salad, her lack of an answer increasing my anxiety.

No. I knew Kenny. She wasn't a user. I was having a moment of panic that told me that maybe I should tell her how I felt. Tell her that I was in love with her. Then what? What if she didn't love me? I'd just wait like I had been doing?

Grandma Gin started making homemade ranch dressing to add to the salad. Homemade so she could add buttermilk and sour cream—better than store bought. Only, her forehead wasn't normally creased when she stirred her ranch.

"Then how long are you two keeping things quiet?" she

finally asked. "If she's already doing overnights, how long? Are the boys going to say something in town and be the ones to face the backlash?"

I scowled. "No." I hadn't wanted the kids to be confused, but I didn't think about what they'd say in school, the teachers who would overhear.

"Then when, Liam?" She held up a callused, wrinkled hand. "It's not my business; I get that. But when you're using more energy to hide what you're doing instead of talking about how to deal with people and their many opinions, that energy's going to be wasted. You understand?"

"We aren't hiding." We'd gone to the lake. Her mom and Benji had come over. And we'd pretended to be platonic. No hand-holding. No public kisses. We didn't even hug. We might not be hiding, but we were acting like something we weren't, which wasn't how I lived my life.

"It's complicated," I finally said.

"Never claimed it wasn't." She finished one last stir and pushed the bowl away. "I want you happy, Liam. You've worked really hard these last few years. You're providing for two kids, for me—don't think I don't know what you're doing there—and you've built a second business based on word of mouth about your talent. A partner would see that. A real partner, who cares about you, wouldn't want to hide you. She'd want to show you off. You shouldn't be a secret."

My mouth went dry. My mom had been a secret, and what happened to her was directly related to that. Grandma Gin was scared for me. Worried. "This isn't like Mom and Cameron."

"No," Grandma Gin huffed. "I'd have a lot more opinions about that. I know Kenny's on a journey not many of us have weathered, and she's doing it so young. But, Liam, this isn't like you and Derek either. That kid didn't care what anyone said. You were family. He didn't care who knew it. I respected him for it. But he also let you take the blame when the stupid shit you both did was his idea. When you being Liam Barron was convenient, he was okay with it. I don't want that for you again."

Defensiveness for my friend rose. "It wouldn't have done any good to tell anyone any different."

"You can let others do what's best for them, but when it comes at the cost of hurting you? Just remember, it's okay to do what's best for you too. All right?"

"All right." I wasn't going to argue with her. She'd said what she needed to say, and maybe she could feel better. Lighter.

As for me, I thought about myself all the time, and it was hard not to see how much it cost the ones I loved to be associated with me.

* * *

Kennedy

After two and a half agonizingly long weeks of painting and job searching, I had finally gotten my week away. Laney had given me a ride to Dickinson. Liam had picked me up from there and driven back to Williston. Dickinson was too close to Coal Haven for us to be comfortable. We'd gotten a hotel with a restaurant attached in Williston and spent our time there. He'd even coaxed me into the hot tub.

The next two days had flown by. He'd taken me out to the site where he'd worked. The countryside was dotted with wells, but other than getting a tour of town and where he worked and going out to eat, we'd stayed at the hotel. Stayed lost in each other's bodies.

And we'd celebrated.

Last week, Hattie's friend from the mine near Washburn had called Liam. They'd talked for almost an hour, and by the time the call was over, the job had been offered to Liam. It'd be a commute, but regular shifts and steady pay.

Now we were driving back to reality. We'd lingered until checkout, had a quick lunch, and hit the road. He had an arm casually draped over the wheel and the lock of hair that fell over his brow gave him a devil-may-care appeal.

Everything was falling into place for him, and it made me beam brighter than the sun to witness it. Being with him for three full days only cemented how I felt about him. I hadn't brought myself to tell him. Doing it in Williston hadn't been personal enough since it was a place where we were getting away from it all.

I'd do it. Soon. At his place. Telling him how I felt at his house had a sense of rightness I couldn't shake. My nerves liked the delay. I couldn't lie to myself about that. I hadn't been an instigator in my last relationship, but things were different with Liam. I was different with Liam, and I liked myself this way.

I watched the scenery scroll by. Softly rolling hills inter-rupted by random buttes so much taller. Some were flatter on top than others. I could imagine Eli and Owen scaling the sides, determined to get to the highest spot. We passed fields. If the crop wasn't corn or sunflowers, I had to ask Liam. He'd name canola or soybeans or barley. Pastures interspersed the fields. Cattle grazed.

So peaceful.

I'd been lulled into thinking that since there wasn't much going on in my life, I didn't deserve time to myself. Three days, and I felt like I knew who this Kennedy Barron was. I'd been with Liam the whole time, but that'd always been the lure of him. I could be myself around him.

My phone buzzed and kept going. "Must be Mom." I

glanced at the screen and froze. It was Bruce. It buzzed as I stared.

Liam glanced over. His brow lifted when he saw who it was, but he turned his gaze to the road.

The ringing stopped. "Shit. I should've answered."

My phone vibrated again, and I hit answer before I froze again. "Hey, Bruce. Sorry I didn't answer in time earlier."

"Kennedy, where are you? Are you okay?"

A sense of déjà vu hit me, and Liam gave me the same look he'd given me when my mom had called in a panic while I was at the lake. "Everything's fine. Why?"

"You're not answering, and I talked to your neighbor. She said your car's been parked in the same spot for days. I didn't want to worry your mom again. Where are you? Are you at home?"

I stared out the windshield in front of me. "I went out of town."

"Without your car?"

"I'm with a friend."

"Who?"

I bristled and chewed the inside of my cheek. Where was the steel I'd had when speaking to Mr. Gilding? But the principal wasn't like a father to me, and he hadn't been terrified like Bruce. "Laney took me to Dickinson."

Liam cut a look at me. I couldn't bring myself to face him. I hated lying, but I wasn't telling Bruce about the weekend over the phone.

"Laney?"

"Yes. Laney Granger. We're friends." I chanced a peek at Liam. His jaw was rigid as stone.

"Oh." There was a moment of tense silence. I willed myself not to babble and dig myself further into the lie. "When are you getting home?"

"Actually, we're on our way back."

"Good. Yes, that's good. Drive safe."

I hung up and let out a long sigh. "Sorry. I felt like my sister when she told Mom she was at a friend's house when she was at a concert. I didn't want to tell him over the phone."

"I understand." There was a heaviness in his tone that hadn't been there before when we talked about keeping us a secret from Bruce.

"Thanks for having my back on this."

"It's what I do." His profile remained the same, but his tone carried a ring of resignation. I'd hurt his feelings. He'd been so careful with me. Had he been hiding how he really felt about not telling anyone about us?

The cows in the pastures didn't deserve my glare, but they got it. Had I upset Liam? He understood. I knew he did. But the thought of hurting him, of letting him down, bothered me more than the idea of worrying Bruce.

Twenty

LIAM

The trees surrounding town came into view. Then the houses on the edge of town. The golf course and the country club. I turned down the street that would take us to Kenny's house.

I tried not to let Bruce's call bother me. I tried, and I failed.

Bruce wasn't an idiot. If she had told him she'd been with me for three days, he'd have read between the lines. And no, the phone wasn't the right time to tell him.

But it was hard to get Grandma Gin's words out of my head. We'd spent three sex-filled days together where I'd had to hold back the words *I love you* a hundred times. I wasn't telling her when she had no escape. Telling her right after she'd lied about being in Dickinson with Laney didn't exactly settle right in my heart either.

As I rounded the turn, she sat up. Another pickup was parked in front of her house.

Kenny shot forward so fast her seat belt snapped tight. "What's Bruce doing here?"

The lawn mower sitting in the middle of the front yard answered the question. He might not have a key to the house, but he could still get into an unlocked garage.

"Maybe we should—"

Bruce crossed the lawn to the mower and spotted us. His head cocked and his eyes narrowed.

Had she been about to tell me to keep driving? Acid burned its way up my throat. Maybe it was the talk with Grandma Gin. Maybe it was spending the weekend days together. *Three days.* But I could no longer do this. There was the point where it was about Kenny's healing, and then there was crossing the line into being a shameful secret. We might be on opposite sides of that line.

I parked behind Bruce's pickup.

"I'll handle him," she murmured. "You don't need to deal with it."

I wasn't dumping Kenny and running, leaving her with the mess to explain. Nor did I feel like hearing about how she'd spun a story about how I met Laney and gave her a ride the rest of the way or some shit.

"I ain't going nowhere, Kenny." I got out and lifted her bag out of the back.

She slid out of the pickup. I didn't miss the tremble in her voice when she said, "Bruce."

She didn't move toward her house. I set her bag behind her and stood next to her.

Bruce's gaze jumped between us. "I thought you were with Laney."

"She took me to Dickinson, yes. But I was with Liam in Williston," she finished quietly.

Not exactly a grand announcement, but it was further than I thought she'd get. Now, we just had to endure the storm of Bruce's emotions. Then he'd tell Cameron, and I could probably expect another visit about staying away from Kenny.

Red infused Bruce's face. His confusion and upset bloomed into rage as his face flushed deeper. He shook his head, like he was hearing incorrectly, but then his gaze landed on her luggage. He shifted his glare to me.

"You don't think about anyone else, do you?" He shoved his hands on his hips, his mouth an angry slash. "I had to deal with you when it came to Derek, and he's gone. Why the hell am I still dealing with you?"

"What are you talking about?" I knew what he meant, but the sheer fury directed at me didn't make sense.

He shoved a finger in my direction, very much like my father had, only Bruce wasn't close enough to touch me. "When it came to my son, you were behind all the trouble. Now you want to do that to her?" He stepped closer. "Every time I see you, every time I hear your voice, and every time I worry about Kennedy and what she's doing, and you're behind it, it's like I'm reminded..." Grief rippled over his face. His jaw clenched, and he looked away.

Dread ghosted across my shoulders. "It's like being reminded of what, Bruce?" I asked quietly. I didn't want the answer, but I had to hear it. I had to have him say it. I had to have it laid out there. What I'd felt my entire life.

"Say it, Bruce. What do you think when you talk to me? That I shouldn't have been born?"

His hard hazel gaze swirled back to me, and his upper lip twitched. He was a man destroyed. A man holding on to his pain. It had nowhere to go.

Until me. Until I pushed him.

He took another step forward, his voice shaking, loss and pain pouring from his gaze. "I'm reminded that you're here and my son isn't and that it doesn't make a damn lick of sense. It's unfair on so many levels, I can't stand it. Just like I can't stand you."

A soft gasp broke the stunned silence. Kenny. "Bruce…"

He whipped his head toward her, his gaze pleading with her, like he wanted her to confirm that she thought the same thing.

Her eyes filled with tears, and she pressed her fingers to her lips.

I couldn't move. This guy had just said he wished I had died in place of his son. After a lifetime of making it clear he thought I shouldn't have been born in the first place.

Tears streaked down Kenny's cheeks. "You can't mean that."

Bruce shook his head, then he bent and crumpled the rest of the way to the ground, sobs racking his body. Kenny rushed to his side. "Bruce, are you okay?"

I took a step back. And another. Spinning, I walked numbly around the pickup to the driver's side.

"Liam." Kenny ran up behind me. I didn't think she'd abandon Bruce. "He didn't mean that."

"Yeah. He did."

"No, he just needs to calm down. I need to make sure he's okay and then I'll talk to him."

I'd be an ass if I told her that I needed her now too. That after hearing a man who had made me feel like shit my entire life tell me that he wished I were dead, I might need a little support too. But I wasn't collapsed on her front lawn.

What was it Grandma Gin had said? It's okay to do what's best for me too.

Leaving was best. And if she wasn't coming with me, so be it. "Take your time. Don't worry about me."

"Liam?" Hurt and confusion scrawled over her features. She glanced back at Bruce. He was sitting with his elbows on his knees and his head in his hands.

"Look, I don't mean to add more pressure. Just take some time. Think about what you really want. Because Bruce isn't going to take this well, and I can't have another person who's supposed to be important to me flake on me. I just wanna go be with Eli and Owen. Grandma Gin. Their love is unconditional. They accept me, and I just really need to be surrounded by that right now."

A divot formed between her brows. She gave her head a slight shake, like she didn't understand something that was so clear to me.

Right.

I got in my pickup and drove off, and I didn't bother to look in my rearview mirror.

* * *

Kennedy

Liam drove away. He didn't spin out. He didn't speed off and roar around the corner and out of sight. He didn't hesitate to go, but he hadn't made a scene.

Unconditional love.

I hadn't even told him I loved him, yet my love had come with so many conditions.

Shit.

The last few minutes replayed in my head. What must that have been like for Liam to hear?

And I'd gone to Bruce first. What he'd said had shocked me, and then he'd collapsed. Liam had stood there, being strong and enduring the abuse like he'd always done. How much less severe would Bruce's reaction have been if I had told him the truth earlier, sat down and talked to him, and then held Liam's hand as the fallout happened?

I had messed up.

I went to Bruce and squatted in front of him. "Bruce, are you okay?"

"I can't believe I said that to him. I can't believe…" He hung his head. "I just really miss my son."

"I know. So do I. But I think it's past time we had an honest discussion." I put my hand on his shoulder. "You and Willow have cared for me so much, and you have my undying appreciation. But you need to realize that I'm going to have a life that's different from what I had with Derek, and who I choose to do that with is my business and mine alone. I want you to be in my life, but not at the cost of keeping others out."

"I can't… I just don't know what to think right now." He scrubbed his face. "I can't believe I said that to him."

"Quit listening to Cameron when it comes to Liam and decide for yourself. Maybe trust that your son wasn't wrong when it came to him. And neither am I."

He nodded but kept his face buried in his hands.

I pushed my hair off my face and let out a weary sigh as I rose. "I'm going to go talk to Liam now. I'll call Willow. Just wait here for her, okay?"

He nodded without looking at me. I grabbed my luggage, tossed it into the house, and snagged my keys. I sped through town and hit the gravel. The minutes ticked by so damn slow as I flew to his place.

I didn't bother to park, just stopped right by the porch. Grandma Gin met me at the door. "Is everything okay?"

I refrained from barging in. "I need to talk to Liam."

She cocked her head, her frown deepening. "He's not here. He messaged, saying he was grabbing pizza before he came home. Is something wrong?"

"Only because of me." I hadn't even noticed his pickup wasn't parked by the shop. I spun and raced down the stairs.

I gave a confused Grandma Gin a wave and traced my route back to town, straight to Rattler's.

This time I looked for Liam's pickup. It was parked on the edge of the lot, like he had needed the extra walking time to gather himself before he faced people. I didn't blame him for not wanting to drag himself home and then cook and clean up and go about life like it'd been a normal day.

I parked next to him and power walked across the lot. I banged through the doors. Several pairs of eyes landed on me, but I ignored them all.

Liam's back was to me as he slumped on a stool at the bar, waiting for his pizza to be ready. I wound through the tables until I was behind him.

"William Robert Barron, I have something to tell you."

His head popped up, and he craned his neck to look over his shoulder. "Kenny? What are you doing here?"

I stepped forward, and he swiveled on his stool to face me. Perfect timing. I wedged myself right between his legs and fisted the front of his shirt. "I'm here to tell you that I love you. Unconditionally. And I'm going to prove it."

The people around us went quiet. The whole bar went quiet, the silence spreading to the rest of the restaurant. Liam looked like he thought I was either a hallucination or a mirage in the middle of the desert.

I planted my mouth on his. He jerked but didn't pull away. I kept the pressure up, willing him to kiss me back. Finally, his lips went pliant under mine, and his arms snaked around my waist. One second, I was in charge, and the next he was dominating the kiss. His hold tightened until I was plastered against him as he plundered my mouth.

The sheer force he used to pull away reverberated under my hands. His eyes were hooded as he regarded me. "I love you too, Kenny. But I've been waiting for you to say it first, just in case."

"I've been chicken. About so much and for the wrong reasons."

I was still between his legs and the place was quiet, but we were an oasis. He brushed a hand down my face. "How's Bruce?"

"He'll be okay. I didn't talk to him long. I ran to your house. Grandma Gin is going to want an explanation for why I charged to the door and then sped away."

His gaze searched mine, and I saw the moment he realized I hadn't even gone to Derek's grave first. And I wasn't running there now. I needed to be with Liam.

He glanced around at everyone minding our business. "Are you okay with this?"

"I've never been surer of anything." I loosened my hold on his shirt and brushed my thumb across his cheek. "Did you get Canadian bacon pizza?"

His grin was lopsided. "With pineapple."

"Oof, my love might have one condition—no pineapple near my pizza." I pressed another kiss to his lips as he chuckled. I had feared I'd lost him. I never wanted to feel that way again. "Mind if I invite myself over?"

"Never, baby. Let's go home."

Twenty-One

KENNEDY

I stood next to Liam on the porch and watched Bruce and Willow drive away.

"That sucked," Liam muttered.

"Yeah. But it's done."

It'd been three months since Liam and I had kissed at Rattler's and the town exploded with speculation and gossip. Some of the talk was hurtful. Had Liam and I been dabbling together while I was with Derek? Just plain ignorant. How could I move on so quickly? And encouraging. We both deserved to be happy, and if it's together, all the better.

I was happy. Liam was home every night. His new job was going well, and his pieces had been selling within a week of Hattie stocking them. I had sold my house and put the money toward renovating this one. Liam, the boys, and I had had a bonfire when I'd moved out. We'd burned the couch I had spent so much time on.

I'd even gotten a teaching position at the school in Center, a town a half hour away. But I'd had to turn it down. Mr. Gilding had learned about the offer and called to beg me back. After many of the staff had heard I was leaving, they'd approached Mr. Gilding. Headed by Aspen, they each outlined several instances when they felt Mrs. Z was doing more harm with the kids than good. They argued that a workplace that drove off good employees while nurturing problematic employees wasn't where they wanted to work. Then they cited the openings for teachers in Hazen, New Salem, Mandan, and Bismarck. Basically, there was a job opening for each teacher who'd complained. Mr. Gilding could listen, or he could try to replace five teachers immediately before the first day of school.

It was a helluva bluff. Aspen swore it wasn't, but either way, I was in their debt. When Mrs. Z had found out what had happened, she'd quit on the spot and moved with her mom to Arizona. A little bit of employee shifting before school started, and Aspen was the new kindergarten teacher while I got my fifth-grade classroom back.

Aspen said I'd earned it, but it was a gift from excellent coworkers who cared about the kids they taught.

Eli and Owen were going to love Aspen. They called her Miss Whitfield even when she came to the house. She and Laney had helped me move to Liam's. Laney sometimes rode her horse out for a chat, or Aspen brought Lyric over and Liam grilled.

After Bruce's pickup disappeared, Liam swooped me into his arms. I cuddled into him. Since we weren't hiding anymore, he never quit touching me.

"Think he'll live up to what he said?" Liam kicked the door open. Grandma Gin had taken the kids for ice cream while Bruce and Willow had been over. The heaviness of the conversation wasn't meant for interruptions.

After Bruce had apologized for what he had said, he and Liam had talked about the land lease and Derek and Liam's friendship. They'd traded stories about Derek that included the real story behind the four-wheelers in the river, in the water holes, and in every other place the guys had gotten stuck with something that had wheels. Bruce had asked about the barn and Liam told him the truth, but he asked that Bruce keep it to himself. Grandpa Bob was gone, and it didn't matter.

Bruce said he'd talk to Cameron about leaving Liam the hell alone, that it was the best way he could show Liam he hadn't meant what he'd said.

"He will." Cameron was already losing power over Liam's life. Liam's new boss had already had a phone call from Cameron he'd promptly ignored, muttering something about how *good welders don't grow on goddamn trees.*

I nuzzled his neck as he carried me straight through the house to our bedroom. "Isn't everyone going to be back soon?"

"Nope. Grandma offered to take them overnight." I popped my head up, and he smirked. "I packed their bags when you were making breakfast and put them by the garage."

I adopted a clueless expression. "Whatever are we going to do with our time together?"

He bent to set my feet on the floor. "How 'bout you turn on the lamp and I'll close the door."

Grinning, I turned to the lamp, the one I'd replaced with the piece he'd done when I moved in. "You know, we don't need to close the door if—"

A ring was hung around the switch under the lamp shade. A small gasp left me when I saw the golden band filled with diamonds. I picked it up, the metal cool on my fingertips. "Liam?"

By the time I turned, he was kneeling. Tears sprang up in my eyes.

His smile was gentle. "Kenny, will you marry me?"

My mouth still hung open, my eyes glued to the simple band full of small diamonds. It was different from what I'd worn before. So was the proposal. It was me and Liam. It was perfect.

This was the easiest decision I'd had to make in a long time. "Yes, Liam. I'll marry you."

He grinned and rose. I swung my arms around him. We didn't kiss or jump around. I hugged him, hard. And he grounded me as waves of feelings splashed through me: guilt, elation, anticipation.

Excitement won out, and I pulled back, holding the ring between us.

He touched the top with his finger. "There're a few things we can do. That's a wedding band. You can wear it by itself. Or you can wear your wedding ring and add this." I stared at him, eyes wide, and he lifted a shoulder. "Derek's always going to be a part of us, and I know you miss wearing your ring. But if you want to get a separate engagement ring for us, we can pick one out."

I glanced at the special jewelry box in which I kept my wedding ring on the shelf above the dresser. I hadn't worn it for six months, but I did miss it. "You don't mind?" It seemed...fitting. And like always, Liam had sensed what I needed the most.

"The thing about Derek being my best friend is that I knew where he got your set, so I found a matching band. They'll go together, just like the three of us did."

Could this man get any more perfect? "I love you, Liam."

"I love you too, Kenny." His grip tightened around me.

"Did you shower today? Because I want to shower with you."

"Did you shower today? Because I want to shower with you."

Epilogue

LANEY

The backyard wedding had been fucking adorable, like I thought it would be. I didn't consider myself a kid person, but Eli and Owen Barron were pretty cute ring bearers. It was early June, and the only music the happy couple included were the crickets and frogs. Liam had even sprayed his yard for mosquitos so the only bloodsuckers in attendance were family.

Not my family of course.

I avoided weddings. More like, I hadn't been invited to any. My own wedding had been—

Nope. Not going there.

It had been hard enough to keep memories of my own happy day from superimposing Kennedy's day. Just like the last nine months of watching her fall stupider into love. Old jealousy threatened to flare up, but I wasn't the same girl I'd been in high school. I wasn't jealous of Kennedy. My envy was that she'd found two decent guys in her life. I must repel good men like the mosquito control Liam had used.

The wedding was over, and I was at Rattler's with some of the other guests. The happy couple was on their honeymoon with two little boys in tow. Next year, they might have another little one to drag along. Ever the teacher, Kennedy was planning to "work on it" this summer so she limited her maternity leave next year during the school year.

There'd been a time I had considered removing my IUD since I'd been happily married. Good thing I hadn't, or my in-laws would have reason to interfere in my life more than they had.

I kicked back in my chair and almost put my cowboy boot on the table. I refrained. I was a fucking lady, like my husband had wanted. Besides, I didn't need to give the town any more reason to think I was a bitch than they already had.

I took a drink of my fruity piss water, as Aspen called it.

She was sitting next to me with Lyric. Nora was even here. That girl was so young and sweet, she probably farted rainbows that smelled like Skittles. Lyric's BFF, Isla, was not here. Big surprise. Cameron had probably taken his family to some resort to forget the fact that the son he ignored was getting married.

Bruce had attended. I saw him sneaking out after the wedding vows had been said. I would've said something snarky, but his head was dipped low. Not low enough for me to miss his red-rimmed eyes.

So, yeah.

I cleared away the tightening in my throat and took another drink. I wouldn't be making snarky comments. I missed Derek too. Couldn't believe he was gone. We had history. I hadn't been in love with him, same for him with me. But we'd grown up together. We'd spent a lot of time together before we broke up. And after we broke up, I'd felt like a limb had been severed. I'd had no one to talk to. My closest friend had moved on. Ironic that my best friend now was his widow.

Aspen scanned the bar, her amber gaze on the hunt. "I thought Liam would have more hot friends show up."

I chuckled. Aspen liked men. I could live vicariously through her since I wasn't exactly free to date. People could call me a lot of things, but I wasn't a cheater.

I took another drink of my fruity piss water. I wanted something stronger, which meant I shouldn't have something stronger. "Are you saying that Coal Haven lacks hot men?"

"Most of them are Barrons." Aspen's tone was wry. "No offense to Liam—he's cool—but I don't need a Barron of my own. That whole last name seems to come with, like, *a lot*."

Lyric grunted her agreement and pushed a hand through her purple hair. "I was hoping he'd have some of his buddies from Williston come out."

Kennedy had talked to me about that. "They wanted a small, intimate wedding. They kept it at family and local friends only. He just wanted everyone close to her to be there to support her. As long as they had their two witnesses, he didn't care who was invited."

"Damn, that's sweet," Aspen said.

"Isn't it?" Neither of us were bitter. I sensed Aspen and I had that in common. We'd been burned. There was no point dwelling on some other man's romantic gesture if it'd only bring up how we'd been let down in the past.

"Where's Holden?" Lyric asked Nora.

Nora's big cornflower-blue eyes swiveled to the left, then the right, as if she was afraid her mom would jump out and slap her hand over Nora's mouth. "He's um...distracting Stetson."

So Cameron had whisked only his wife away. "Keeping the Barrons from storming the wedding?"

Nora grimaced. "Uncle Bruce said he wanted what was best for Kennedy and told my uncle and Stetson to leave them alone."

I ran my tongue along my teeth. "Cameron ordered Liam to stay away from Kennedy and now they're married. He's going to be pissed for another twenty-seven years."

"Cameron scares me," Lyric muttered. We all stared at her. "I mean, not like physically. He's just so..." She swirled her hand around her head. "Negative. Terminally angry. I swear, when he walks by a garden, the flowers wilt."

I flicked the tab on my can. "Naomi steals the souls of children and sells them on the dark web." Nora coughed, her innocent gaze wide. "Sorry. I don't say things I wouldn't say to their face, but my mom already told her that so..."

Aspen snorted. "I think I'd like your mom. I missed a lot not growing up here. I kind of know Bruce. I hear a ton about Cameron." She tipped her head toward Nora. "And I see your mom around town. What's with the other Barron brother?"

A chill traced down my spine. "The other brother?" Did I manage to sound nonchalant?

Nora ran her fingers along the delicate chain at her neck. "He's, um, in Texas, I think."

"Does he have kids?" Aspen asked.

Lyric's gaze flicked to Nora. Smart girl. If the gossip spread, it was Nora spilling the deets. Lyric would be shunned by the family on Cameron and Naomi's decree if either one thought she was talking about them.

Nora chewed her bottom lip like she knew she wasn't supposed to say but couldn't talk herself out of answering.

"Two sons. I haven't met them. I-I don't know much about them."

"How old are they?" Aspen leaned forward, her curiosity spilling out like her cleavage. I would cut a bitch for tits like that. But I refused to get cut for tits like that, like some of my husband's friends suggested. Assholes. All of them.

"Um... I think the oldest is close to Stetson's age, maybe a little younger, more like Evander and Holden's age. Thirty-ish. The younger one is, I don't know, maybe your age. That's all I know really." Nora's leg bobbed so hard under the table, her entire body shook.

"Ohmigosh, more Barron men? And with a Texas drawl? Can you imagine?" Aspen held her hands up. "Sorry. It's none of my business."

Nora's grin brimmed with relief, but she played it off. "It's not a wedding if we aren't talking about everyone and their relatives."

Lyric snickered. "Right? Only with Nora here, we're safe. She's a Barron."

I bit the inside of my cheek and fiddled with the tab of my can. What would they think—what would they all think —if I told them that Nora wasn't the only Barron at the table? That I was terrified of getting pulled over anywhere in the county because I wasn't divorced like I had let Kennedy and Liam assume and my Texas driver's license had my legal name on it: Delaney Barron?

———

Thanks for reading!

What happens when Archer Barron leaves Texas to track Delaney down in Coal Haven in Make Me Shiver?

Get an extra epilogue with a peek into the life of Liam and Kennedy—and some characters from Oil Kings by signing up for my newsletter. You'll get extra scenes, the latest sales and release updates, and be able to participate in my giveaways.

Marie Johnston writes paranormal and contemporary romance and has collected several awards in both genres. Before she was a writer, she was a microbiologist. Depending on the situation, she can be oddly unconcerned about germs or weirdly phobic. She's also a licensed medical technician and has worked as a public health microbiologist and as a lab tech in hospital and clinic labs. Marie's been a volunteer EMT, a college instructor, a security guard, a phlebotomist, a hotel clerk, and a coffee pourer in a bingo hall. All fodder for a writer!! She has four kids, cats, and a half blind Corgie.

mariejohnstonwriter.com

Follow me:

Also by Marie Johnston

Return to Coal Haven

Violet Promises

Daisy Whispers

Poppy Kisses

Crocus Valley

A Reckless Memory

A Temporary Memory

An Unfinished Memory

A Fearless Memory

An Endless Memory

Coal Haven

Make Me Whole

Make Me Shiver

Make Me Blush

Make Me Dream

Make Me Exhale

King's Creek

King's Crown

King's Ransom

King's Treasure

King's Country

King's Queen

www.ingramcontent.com/pod-product-compliance
Lightning Source LLC
Chambersburg PA
CBHW050829190726
48286CB00007B/2017